THE FULL CIRCLE SERIES BOOK 1

IN DUE
Time

A Novel

Annette G. Anders

Copyright IN DUE TIME © 2021 by Annette G. Anders.

Email: Author@AnnetteGAnders.com

First Edition

ISBN: 978-1-7350261-3-8 (e-Book)
ISBN: 978-1-7350261-4-5 (paperback)

To those who don't give up on their dreams.

The timeless in you is aware of life's timelessness. And knows that yesterday is but today's memory and tomorrow is today's dream.

(Kahlil Gibran)

CHAPTER 1

Revan —Christmas Eve 2018

S oft holiday music mixed with the laughter and lively banter among his closest friends, all lounging comfortably on the grouping of couches and chairs in front of a crackling fire. Hundreds of warm white lights wound through the decorated branches of the Christmas tree and reflected tenfold in the darkened windows. His friend and roommate, Stella, had done a nice job.

"You're the perfect man for me." Naomi's purring voice reached his ear.

Excuse me?

Revan sat up too fast, sloshing his red wine dangerously close to the rim of the glass. Man, those six words had crudely—and effectively—jolted him out of his semi-festive mood.

Just as he wanted to ask if she was delirious, her boyfriend said suggestively, "We'll pick up right there later, baby doll," before locking lips with her.

Revan walked to the French doors and switched on the outside light. Thick snowflakes drifted down in silence, accumulating quickly in the small backyard.

The last time they had a white Christmas in Philadelphia was almost ten years ago, and he vividly remembered it. It was the first winter after he and Luca bought this townhouse and renovated it top to bottom. Home improvement was now on the top of his list of things he never wanted to do again.

As a photojournalist, the tools of his trade were his cameras and accessories, and he'd gladly leave miter saws, drills and hammers to someone who knew what they were doing. Revan sipped more wine and perused the room, his attention moving from friend to friend.

Luca, his best friend since middle school. Their old motto—friends for life—came to mind. *My buddy.*

Stella—Luca's sister, always kind and caring—and her boyfriend, David. *Nice guy. Was in the doghouse for a year but found his way out a few months ago.*

Naomi—his friend and the biggest thorn in his side lately—and her current boyfriend, Frank. *Yeah...well, I'm not going there.*

Josephine, Naomi's cousin, and close friend of Stella's. *Good-natured, sometimes a bit spacey...but, so what?*

Everybody who was important to him was here except his family, and he'd see his parents and sister tomorrow. Revan cringed, remembering his mother's not-so-subtle inquiry earlier, "Can I add an extra place setting for a lady friend?" Which he answered as usual with, "No, Mom, that won't be necessary."

Revan heard the girls laughing. Of course he knew they were all women of thirty now, but in his mind they were forever thirteen.

As Stella's BFF, Naomi was usually around when he visited Luca. Stella had always been quiet, but Naomi was a tomboy if he'd ever seen one. She popped up when he and Luca least expected her, wanting to know, "What are you doing? Can we hang out with you?"—which of course was out of question. There had been an insurmountable five-year age difference between them and the girls.

Through adolescence into adulthood they all developed a special connection—the kind of friendship where they were always there for each other, and he'd never do anything to break their bond.

He noticed Stella watching him intently, but before he could ask why, David's voice interrupted his musings. "There is one more thing I want to do."

All three women responded with a well-choreographed, "Ohhhh..."

Revan mumbled, "Are we in a Hallmark movie?", which earned him a smack over his head from Naomi, followed by a snarky, "Stop being such a Grinch. Where's your holiday cheer?"

He didn't think she expected a reply and gave her a crooked smile instead.

David reached behind Stella and pulled something out from behind the cushions. "Sorry, my love, but you're kind of sitting on it."

"Neat hiding spot, man," Luca laughed and rested his arm along the back of the sofa.

Revan almost choked on his wine when Jo immediately snuggled her head on Luca's shoulder.

Thankfully, his buddy completely ignored her move. Yeah, Revan knew he could count on his friend to keep a cool head. They had made a pact after college to enjoy life and not get sucked into diamond-shopping and diaper duty for a long time—and nothing had changed.

At thirty-five, Revan planned to continue filling his life with challenging work and thrilling trips on his motorcycle. Throw in casual hookups with stimulating women, and he had everything he wanted.

But when he noticed Frank's hand slide under Naomi's shirt, his gut churned. He needed something stronger than wine and went to his well-stocked bar to find his favorite whiskey.

After pouring himself a generous amount, Revan rested his elbow on the fireplace mantel and studied the shades of amber in the lowball glass. He welcomed the fiery bite of the first sip sliding down his throat.

"Man, you're quiet tonight." Luca joined him. "Are you okay?"

"Just shit going through my mind. Don't worry about me." He held up the bottle and asked, "Want some?"

"Sure, hit me." Luca grabbed a glass and held it out after adding an ice cube. "Things were getting a little too cozy over there on the sofa."

"Yeah, I saw that. What's going on with the girls?" Rev asked. "I get why Stella doesn't let David out of her sight, but Naomi and Jo? Do they have a family bet going about who's getting hitched first?"

"No idea," Luca laughed and clinked his glass to Revan's. "To independence, man!"

"And to freedom and happiness," Revan replied.

When he looked up again, his and Naomi's eyes met across the room. Something in the way she studied him made his knees go weak.

Forrester, a man's knees don't go weak. Maybe they're being knocked out from under you, but they don't go weak.

CHAPTER 2

NAOMI - JANUARY 2019

D odging piles of dirty snow and puddles of icy water, Naomi muttered a few unflattering expletives, cursing the weather, the city of Philadelphia, but mostly the asshole she'd been on the phone with earlier.

"Telling me to chill and check with my mother," she groused, startling an older woman close by. "I'm a full partner in our travel agency, and if I tell someone our business relationship is in jeopardy, they better believe it."

She glanced at the low-hanging clouds. *Great...more snow on the way.* Even her Colorado-tested winter jacket couldn't hold its own against the bitter wind.

After slipping on a patch of half-frozen slush, she forced herself to pay attention to the seasonal hazards on the uneven sidewalks. She didn't even notice her favorite pub-style restaurant until she almost collided with another pedestrian and looked up.

Inside the tavern, she saw Revan sitting at the bar, his eyes glued to the beer bottle in his hands as if it held the secret to the Holy Grail. The woman next to him flashed her pearly whites—and a few other goodies—at him. *Too bad he's not even looking at you, Blondie.*

For a moment she watched Blondie's lips going a million miles an hour while Rev continued to gaze trancelike at the beer bottle.

He was not only one of her oldest and best friends, but—unfortunately—the guy she'd been crushing on since when her mother still braided her hair and he sported unflattering braces and a face full of acne.

Her infatuation with him was no secret, either. Everyone in their group of friends knew it.

All except—him.

Who told her last year that he loved her like a sister! Just thinking about it made her blood boil.

Hah! Wasn't it her sisterly duty to say hello, especially since she hadn't seen him since Christmas Eve?

On impulse, she entered the tavern and marched straight toward the bar, not paying attention to the wet spots on the floor until she lost her footing. Arms flailing, she barely managed to grab the back of Revan's chair.

"Nugget, what are you doing here?" He jumped up and circled his arm around her. His eyes traveled to her boots and he grumbled, "What are you wearing?"

She turned her foot left and right and said, "My new ankle boots, aren't they cute?" Who cared about the two-inch heels—they'd look fabulous in the spring.

Then she patted his cheek, "But enough about me. I didn't expect to see you out and about. Don't you have to polish your lenses or something? Stella said you're flying to the Middle East soon."

"You and your BFF spend too much time talking about other people's business. But yeah, I'm leaving the day after tomorrow. Where are you off to?" He dropped his arm but remained standing close to her. Close enough so she could smell his aftershave, and she was tempted to take a deep sniff.

"I'm meeting Stella at the deli. But when I walked by and spotted you, I felt the urge to wish you a safe trip." She smiled angelically at him. "Please come back in one piece! I don't want to have to fly around the world to collect your bones—again."

"What does she mean?" Blondie asked while puffing out her chest.

"Nothing, Barb, it's an old story," Revan said over his shoulder, then looked back at Naomi. "How was Colorado? Did that boyfriend of yours behave?"

"Let's just say it reminded me why I'm more a summer than a winter person. And aren't you the sweetest to ask about Frank? I'll tell him you said hi, but now I've got to run and let you get back to your company," she smiled widely at the woman. What she got back was a squint and another chest lift.

She kissed his cheek and said quietly, "Bye, Shutterbug, be careful. It's a wild world out there."

Back on the street, Naomi glanced once more through the windows. Revan had already resumed his silent conversation with the beer bottle.

What would it take for him to notice her?

And why did it still matter? She was thirty years old, had a boyfriend who was fun to be with, and she should be happy about it.

Should...

CHAPTER 3

Naomi—January 2019

"I can't believe I haven't seen you in almost three weeks. Tell me all about your trip to Colorado," Stella said after they were settled in a booth in the back of the deli and ordered their food. Being regular patrons, they didn't need to look at the menu to know what they wanted. Out of habit they checked the huge blackboard covering half a wall for daily specials, but the yucky weather called for grilled cheese sandwiches and tomato soup.

"It was so cold," Naomi reached for one of the complimentary pickles the waitstaff served as soon as customers were seated. "I mean, the scenery was gorgeous, with the snowcapped mountains and blue skies every day, but overall it wasn't the vacation I expected. Frank wanted to get out on the slopes as early as possible in the mornings, and he met some guys from Connecticut and they went skiing or snowboarding together every day."

"And what did you do?"

"I had one spa day and otherwise went for walks and explored the little shops in Beaver Creek. It's supposed to resemble a village in the Bavarian Alps and was pretty. But pricey. Holy cow, they have no qualms about milking their guests."

"What did you do in the evenings? How were the restaurants?"

"They were good, lots of German food. Sauerbraten with dumplings and red cabbage were my favorite. We usually ran into Frank's new buddies—so often that I wouldn't be surprised if they planned it ahead of time. But we still had plenty of alone time afterward," she grinned and wiggled her eyebrows.

Stella covered her ears and laughed, "TMI! But seriously, how did you feel about being left alone most of the day?"

"Not great, to be honest. But the thing I noticed more was his competitiveness."

"Competitive how?"

"Frank and those guys always tried to outdo each other. They constantly compared who went down which slope the fastest, the riskiest, the best, who could drink the most beer, who'd come up with the best pickup line, all the stupid guy stuff."

"Did you never notice it before?"

Naomi studied her half-eaten pickle. "I guess it simply didn't bother me. You know Frank and I take things as they come. When we started dating last fall, he told me he wants to use his advanced degree in Sport and Exercise Science to get a position in the athletic medical service of a major sports team. There aren't many open positions, so he'll take the first one coming his way and be out of here."

"Too bad. It seems like you and Frank have something good going," Stella reached for Naomi's hand. "I think he's your longest relationship so far."

"I enjoy spending time with him, but I don't think I'll be falling into a bottomless pit when the time comes to part ways."

"At least you know it's coming and can be prepared."

Naomi shrugged it off. "How are things going for you and David? No second thoughts for him about leaving the world of performing arts?"

"You know why he's giving up his opera career. But I don't even want to think about the year when we were separated." Stella shuddered. "Last week he accepted a job at the Peabody Conservatory in Baltimore. And he'll be teaching Master classes at the Hippodrome Theater. He's not totally stepping away from music."

"Baltimore, really? I assume you'll go with him. You okay with leaving Philly?" Naomi scraped her spoon around the soup bowl. "You were always so deeply rooted here."

"Yes, I know. But I need to be where David is. Being apart for long periods of time broke us once, I'll not let anything come between us again. And I'll be only two hours away."

"When are you moving?"

"We'll start house-hunting when he's done in France. His closing night is March twenty-ninth," Stella squeezed

Naomi's hand, "and I'm so thrilled you and I will be there together."

"It was very generous of him to invite me too."

"Maybe he thinks he owes you. If you hadn't dragged me to Paris last summer, he and I wouldn't have reconnected."

"If you wanna put it that way, I think you're right," Naomi said with a self-congratulatory smirk. "End of March means it won't be as hot as it was in July. Let's hope it's not raining nonstop, though. I don't care what people say, but no place is romantic or beautiful in the rain."

"If we can arrive in Paris maybe two days before the show, we'll have time to do some sightseeing again," Stella said. "You're the expert, I'll let you come up with ideas."

As soon as they finished eating, Stella asked, "Wanna come over for a glass of wine?"

"Sure, one glass, then I'll head home," Naomi agreed. "I didn't have a chance to tell you, but on my way here I saw Revan with some chick at the Red Owl."

"Oh yeah—aanndd?" Stella stretched out the word while putting money on the table to pay for their dinner.

"Heaven knows where he finds his women." Naomi wrapped her warm scarf around her head, then noticed Stella watching her. "What? Why are you looking at me like that?"

"Nothing." Stella shrugged, but didn't elaborate.

Back at Stella's place, they hunkered down in front of the fireplace. Naomi stretched her legs toward the crackling fire. "It's nice of David to start a fire. He's a keeper!"

"I agree one hundred percent," David called from the kitchen, where he made himself a cup of tea and arranged a few cookies on a small plate. "Stella, can you buy more of this Sweet Orange Tea?"

"No problem, I'll get it tomorrow. The store's on my way to work."

"Great, thanks. Can I get you ladies something before I go upstairs and leave you two alone?"

Stella said, "We'd like a glass of wine if you don't mind."

While he opened the bottle, he said, "Naomi, as soon as you know the dates you'll be in Paris, let me know and I'll arrange a room for you where we're staying."

"Thanks, I'll get back to you about it. Tell me, Troubadour, how do you feel about saying goodbye to life on the big stages? No more crooning in front of thousands of people?"

"It's a strange thought, but I can always sing for my favorite audience." He winked at Stella.

One glass turned into two. From upstairs, they could hear muffled snippets of music. The fire was keeping them toasty warm, and Naomi sighed. She pulled a burgundy throw blanket closer and let her hand slide over it, drawing patterns on the soft material with her fingertip while letting her eyes sweep the living room.

"You know, when Luca and Revan pooled every dollar after college and bought these two fixer-uppers, I thought they were nuts. Who in their right mind spends everything they have on a house when they're in their twenties? But as soon as they partially removed the first-floor walls and opened it up into this large living area, I changed my mind. They did a great job. I love this place."

"Luca's invitation to stay here when I returned from Boston after grad school was perfect," Stella said. "As much as I love my parents, living with them didn't tempt me at all. And since he relocated to New York, I'm getting away with paying him minimal rent and enjoying his half of the house. Most of the house, actually, because Rev travels so much."

"Have you told Revan he's losing his quasi-housekeeper?" Naomi asked.

"No, I'll wait until after Paris." Stella chewed on her bottom lip. "But I think he'll figure it out himself once he hears about David moving to Baltimore."

Across the room, the front door opened, letting in a blast of cold air, and Revan walked in, followed by Blondie. Naomi smacked the throw blanket. Of all evenings, he had to bring someone home when she was visiting Stella?

Earth to Naomi—it's his house!

"Here's my cue to go home." She pushed the blanket away.

"Nugget! It must be my lucky day since I've seen you twice," Revan called and grinned from ear to ear. "But don't leave. Barb and I are only grabbing a cup of coffee to end the evening."

"I'm afraid David used the last pod," Naomi replied and jumped up, watching while Rev helped Blondie out of her coat. With a side-look at Naomi, he said, "David drinks tea."

Naomi hugged Stella and whispered, "I'll call you tomorrow. Tell me how long she stays."

Next to the front door, she stood on one foot to zip her boots. Losing her balance, she reached for the doorknob, but Revan's hands shot out and steadied her. She straightened to her full 5'9" and looked up at him, his face only inches away.

His eyes reminded her of the dark storm clouds covering the sky this afternoon. And they pulled her directly into the center of a wild turbulence, almost making her dizzy.

Only he was able to create this sensation in her.

And it was getting worse than ever.

"I told you earlier those heels aren't safe in the winter, Nugget," he said in a low voice. His hands were still on her waist, his fingertips touching the skin where her shirt rode up.

She slipped her arms into her jacket and could barely whisper, "Thank you," before she opened the door and fled into the night.

When would she be able to stop longing for him?

CHAPTER 4

REVAN—FEBRUARY 2019

Damn, it's cold this morning.

Revan reached for the bed covers as the alarm clock radio in his hotel room began to play an old Cat Stevens song. Soon the sun would rise over the city of Hama in west-central Syria.

He didn't need the music to wake him up. For the past three weeks the muezzin had done a fine job when he called his flock to the first prayer before dawn. Usually Revan was able to snooze for another hour until he had to get up, but it wasn't enough to make up for the hours he spent tossing and turning.

"What time is it?" a soft, sleepy voice asked while an arm snaked around his waist.

"Six," he mumbled.

"How much time do we have?" Fingers trailed lower.

Revan stopped the hand on its southward journey and turned around to look at Jane. "Not enough." He wasn't in the mood for a quickie—he wasn't in the mood for anything.

Because the brown eyes looking at him right now weren't the bright blue ones that visited him every night. And Jane's short brown hair was the opposite of the longer blonde hair trailing through his fingers in his dreams.

"Okeydokey," Jane kissed his cheek and sat up. "Whoever she is, she's a lucky girl."

"Jane, listen…"

She put a finger over his lips. "We've had fun, Rev, and we'll always be friends. But I knew this day would come."

"I don't know what to tell you; but it's not you," he said. "I'm sorry, Jane."

"There's nothing to be sorry for, and I have no reason to complain. You've been attentive as always while we've been together the past few weeks. But in your sleep you've been talking to someone you call Nugget. It doesn't bother me, but it's not fair to her."

"She's a friend, nothing more." He winced when he realized how lame he sounded.

"I'm not so sure." She kissed him on the cheek, then jumped out of bed and dressed quickly. "Be safe out there. See you later."

After the door quietly clicked shut behind her, he shoved the box of condoms into the drawer of the nightstand. There would be no need for them for the rest of his stay.

He and Jane had known each other for years and frequently reconnected on assignments. Early on they both concurred that having sex didn't require a lifelong declaration of love. Revan once wondered whether they should give a committed relationship a try. But she lived in Melbourne, and neither one had the intention of leaving their home country to live on the other side of the world for good.

Abandoning hope for another thirty minutes of sleep, he got up and grabbed clothes from his suitcase, since he seldom unpacked when he stayed at a hotel. Before he ran out of clean clothes, he sent everything to the hotel laundry, and once they came back, he dropped the folded stacks in his suitcase, just to snag whatever was on top the next morning.

He opened the blackout curtains. The cloudless sky still had an early-morning pink hue which would soon give way to blue before it turned orange in the evening. A neighboring high-rise blocked most of his view, but he knew how the damaged city around him looked.

Whenever he and the team drove through Hama, Revan caught glimpses of the beautiful city it must've once been, full of history and brimming with culture. He had already taken numerous photos of the last seventeen remaining *Norias*, the enormous twelfth-century wooden waterwheels on the banks of the Orontes River, and the eighteenth-century Azm Palace, which was said to have been one of the loveliest Ottoman residences in Syria.

In less than two hours he'd be out there again, documenting the damage and unpreventable decay, trying to preserve the past through photos.

For more than ten years he'd traveled around the world to cover war zones, areas under the iron fists of drug cartels, and pretty much everything in between. And he loved it. Not the despair, brutality, and poverty he witnessed, but being able to bring the darkness and the cruelty out in the open. Besides putting together documentaries, he also visited challenging places in his free time and took photos which he sold to major magazines and publishing houses worldwide.

But every now and then Revan asked himself whether it was truly all he wanted out of life.

Several hours later, after he washed off the ever-present sand and dust, Revan sat in the small, sheltered outdoor restaurant of his hotel. Somewhere a muezzin called for the sunset prayer, but Revan tuned it out together with the rest of the background noise in the big middle eastern city. Turning his phone in his hands, he let his mind wander.

Working with his camera, coaxing brilliant photos out of her, was almost like making love to a beautiful woman. His fingers tingled when he zoomed in on an object he saw through the viewfinder.

He thought back to when his fingers tingled the last time, and he hadn't been holding a camera. It was when he touched an inch of Naomi's skin. If he hadn't caught her when she put on her boots, she'd have ended up with a nasty bruise and probably a bump on her forehead. When his fingertips accidentally touched her bare skin, he felt a jolt like he'd never experienced before. It went through his fingers, up his arms, through his chest—and much lower.

Something had changed since Paris.

When he replayed the events from last July, he remembered her leaning over him in his hospital bed, recalled the worry for him in her eyes, and his brain cells started to act up and sent him very confusing messages. Messages and images inappropriate between friends.

She was off limits. First, because she was in a relationship. And, just as important, because she was one of his closest friends. It shouldn't be too difficult to steer clear of her for a while. It wasn't as if they were hanging out all the time.

Revan nodded to himself. Staying away from her was a good plan and should be easy enough to stick to.

"Care for some company?"

Revan looked up to see a colleague approaching his table. "Hey, Christopher, have a seat."

When a waiter came to take their orders, Revan asked for a bottle of local beer and silently thanked whoever allowed alcohol to be served in restaurants in this part of the world. He preferred a neat whiskey or a nice glass of wine, but the Al-Shark beer was at least better than strong, sugary tea.

Christopher asked, "Have you heard anything new about Ahmad?"

Two days ago a group of journalists were ambushed while having dinner at a local restaurant. Luckily nobody died, but Ahmad, a colleague who worked for a London-based news agency, was hit by shrapnel and had to be taken to a hospital several hours away.

"They're flying him home in the next few days," Revan replied.

"I'm beginning to question whether the price we pay for what we're doing is worth it," Christopher said, "Ahmad has a wife and two young kids."

Revan accepted the cold beer from the waiter and used the bottle opener on his Swiss Army knife to take off the metal cap, thoroughly wiping the bottle's neck with his napkin before taking a long swig. "Shit like that always makes me wonder why we pull partners into our lives." He held up his hand and said with a half-smile, "I know, I don't have a significant other, but it can't be easy on the families." Thoughts of his parents and sister briefly crossed Revan's mind.

Christopher nodded, "I agree. They must live in a constant state of worry and fear. 'Thank you for your service' sounds so great, but it doesn't help them when the person they love doesn't make it home alive."

It wasn't the first time members of the press had been attacked. And, as usual, the typically involved groups and foreign governments denied the responsibility. Revan knew of two other recent incidents where their jackets labeled PRESS might as well have been invisible. Or, maybe worse, marked them like sitting ducks, pulling the wrong attention to them. They were expected to wear protective vests covering their chest and abdomen, but those were useless if someone stepped on a mine or got hit directly in the face.

"Have you ever thought of doing something else?" Revan asked while he peeled the label off his bottle.

"Yeah, more than I'd like to admit lately. My first marriage was a casualty of always being away, and I missed a lot of my kids' milestones. There must be something for us to do where we don't always have to look over our shoulders or take cover."

"I'm beginning to hear ya, man."

After another beer and some chicken with couscous, Rev called it a night and went to his room. Where he was alone with his thoughts about Naomi.

But he needed to push them away, because he couldn't afford to let them distract him from to the war around him.

The Cat Stevens song from this morning played in his mind again. A while ago he read that "Morning Has Broken" was originally written in the 1930s as a funeral hymn.

He hoped it wasn't a bad omen.

"Maybe it's time to do something else," he muttered to himself. "But first I have to make it out of this shithole alive."

CHAPTER 5

Naomi—April 2019

"Naomi, can you come over this afternoon? I've got so much to tell you!" Stella's voice came over the speaker while Naomi was in her bathroom, where she applied eyeliner, then added diamond stud earrings to her earlobes.

After tucking her hair behind her ears, she turned her head to check both sides. The only thing missing was a dab of the perfume Frank gave her for Christmas, and then she'd be good to go.

"Please say yes." Stella sounded impatient, as if she was up to something.

"Okay, let's see. I'm on my way to meet Frank for brunch. How about I swing by around four?" Naomi touched the glass stopper to her wrist, then put the perfume bottle back on the shelf.

"Perfect. I'll fix something to munch on."

"Sounds good. Just make sure you have enough, it'll be my dinner."

"Don't worry, I will. David's going to want something to eat, too. There'll be plenty," Stella promised.

"Gotta run now! See you later."

Naomi rang Stella's doorbell shortly after four in the afternoon, eager to find out what Stella wanted to share with her. It couldn't be the still-fresh news of her engagement because Naomi had been in Paris, too, when David proposed after his final performance. And she gave him bonus credits for finding the perfect setting.

Stella met him when he sang the lead role of *The Phantom of the Opera* on a Broadway tour. After two years of dating, he unexpectedly broke off with Stella, only to reunite with her last summer when fate brought them both to the Paris Opera House. And a few weeks ago he popped the question of all questions.

"Wow, something smells amazing." Naomi took off her coat and hung it in the closet. She kicked off her red boots, placed them by the door, and skipped over to the kitchen island, where Stella had put out several platters with finger food, crackers and dips, but also a bucket filled with ice, two glasses, and a bottle of champagne waiting to be opened.

"Ooh, what are we celebrating? We already toasted your engagement." She reached for Stella's hand and said, "I have to admit the Troubadour has good taste. Look at this bling! He clearly didn't skimp. And you deserve it, my friend. How does it feel to be a bride?"

"Awesome! I still can't believe how he pulled it off. Someone must've lit the hundreds of candles in the cave under the opera house and put the champagne in the bucket right before we arrived. But I didn't see a soul. Maybe he'll tell me one day, when we're old and gray." Stella popped the cork and filled their glasses. "Cheers!"

Naomi sipped, then screamed and put her glass down. "What does this say?" She squinted at something written on her glass.

Stella said, "Will you be my maid of honor, please?"

"Yes, of course, silly! Someone has to make sure everything goes according to plan." They hugged and laughed.

"What plan?"

"See? You already need me for this! But tell me the four W's," Naomi sat down on one of the barstools and took another sip.

"The *what*?"

"The four W's," Naomi repeated. "What color is my dress going to be? When are you getting married? Where are you tying the knot? Who are your bridesmaids?"

"Leave it to you to ask the most important question first." Stella giggled, then held up her glass and clinked it to Naomi's. "I've brought a few French bridal magazines, but David stopped me after I bought the fifth one. I snuck one more into my carry-on while we waited for our flight at the airport, though."

"Uh-oh, already doing stuff behind his back...I don't know..." Naomi made a rolling motion with her hand. "Okay, keep going!"

"Let's see. Where should I start? I'd like each bridesmaid to pick her own color. It annoys me when everybody is wearing the same shade of pink, looking like the three little pigs. As for the date, we think in September. But first we want to talk to our parents and see if it works for them. Especially David's family, since they're coming from Chicago."

"I hate to interrupt you, but Chicago isn't too far away. Although it does depend on where you're getting married. Are you thinking about a destination wedding?"

"Oh, goodness, no," Stella said. "It's not going to be a big affair, only family and close friends. We're trying to keep it off the radar because David doesn't want a big media circus, and it's going to be here in Philly. As for bridesmaids, I'm definitely going to ask Jo, since the three of us have always done everything together. And I'll ask David's sister, Sabrina, and Rev's sister. Dinah will get a kick out of it."

At the mention of Revan's name, Naomi looked around. "Speaking of...where is he?"

"I'm not sure. I know he's back from Syria, but I haven't seen or spoken to him since we arrived last night. Luca said Revan's been taking out his motorcycle a lot and is disappearing for days. Why?"

"Just curious—" Naomi said and looked in her glass. "Oh, look, it's empty, let's change that."

"You have to do something, Nam. You can't go on forever pretending you don't have feelings for him. Why don't you tell him?"

She shrugged, "I want him to see me and to notice me on his own."

Stella nodded. "Okay, I get it… So, any questions I didn't answer to your satisfaction?"

"Let's see," Naomi held up a finger, "the ceremony is probably going to be in September, and I know who the other girls are. We covered, kind of, the color of the dresses."

She took a breath, then continued ticking off items on her fingers. "You said the wedding is going to be here, and I already have a great idea for the location. I've been to a bridal shower at this beautiful old inn, and I just know you'd love it."

She held up the five fingers. "But…who is David's best man? Is it his agent-slash-friend, Aaron? I hope it's not somebody who'd look terrible next to me in church."

"We won't get married in a church. We want a civil ceremony."

"Okay, even better. But back to the best man! Maybe David can show me pictures of his possible candidates and I can pick one for him? Does he know someone who looks like, let's say, George Clooney?"

Stella snorted, "I don't know. We didn't talk about it, to be honest. And George Clooney isn't much taller than you, so he wouldn't work if you want to wear heels."

"I didn't say I want George himself, I said someone who looks *like* him. If it's George, I could go barefoot, though," Naomi said. "Does David know George?"

Stella snickered, "I don't know. If he does, he never mentioned it."

Naomi walked around the kitchen island and snatched appetizers that looked like pinwheels off a platter. "Where are you going for your honeymoon?"

"To France, of course," Stella said. "It's a special place for David and me. Without Paris, we wouldn't be together again."

"If you were destined to be together, your paths would eventually have crossed again," Naomi said, even though she didn't really believe in destiny.

Stella pointed to a chair. "But sit down for what I have to tell you next."

"I'm very capable of listening while I'm standing here. Wait..." She glared at Stella, "Are you pregnant?"

Naomi eyed the assortment of appetizers and said, "Keep talking while I grab my phone. I need to start taking pictures of everything to use at your bridal shower."

"No, I'm not pregnant. But I can't wait to go off the pill as soon as we're married," Stella admitted.

"Please, have mercy! I can't organize a wedding and a baby shower both within a year. Oh, and we need to have an official engagement party for you lovebirds, for the families to meet and check each other out. Okay, I really have to start taking notes! Where's my purse?" Surveying the room, she spotted it on the floor next to her shoes.

She squatted and skimmed over her messages. Nothing from Frank. *Fine.*

Their brunch date had ended with an argument about something silly instead of a little action between the sheets. *Oh, well.*

Holding on to the doorknob, Naomi pulled herself up just as the door was pushed open. Hanging on to it, she wrenched her arm and faceplanted against a solid chest. Two hands grabbed her hips.

"You need to work on your pick-up tricks, Nugget. This is getting old."

"What are *you* doing here?" She put her hands on her hips, jerking back when she touched Revan's hands.

"Last I checked, I paid half of the mortgage for this place." He looked at her with a slightly crooked smile. "But I like to see women swooning when I walk into a room."

"I'm not swooning because of you, Shutterbug. Don't be so full of yourself. You can let go of me now," she swatted him away. "I'm sure you have something to do in your darkroom, or wherever your man cave is."

"Oh no, my man David here and I are going to open the bottle of whiskey I bought on my last trip to Virginia. Our first president made surprisingly good stuff, and not too many people know about his distillery in Mount Vernon. Did you know it was one of the largest distilleries in the nation at its time? It produced eleven thousand gallons of whiskey annually, compared to six hundred fifty gallons produced by other distilleries in Virginia."

"Yeah, yeah. But what's your reason to celebrate? Latest bike tour went well? You didn't fall off and get a booboo?"

she teased him and reached for a small scar on his left temple. She didn't want to step away from him. If anything, she wanted to move closer and run her hands through his thick, ash-blond hair.

His hands were still on her hips and she could feel their heat through her two layers of clothing. Besides his signature Old Spice aftershave, there was a hint of whiskey on his breath.

She wrinkled her nose and sniffed around his face, "I think you've already had a sample, Shutterbug."

"You're neither my wife nor my mother, so it's none of your business. And don't...call me...that name."

She waved her hand and stepped away from him. "Too late, it's engraved in my brain. Can't teach an old dog new tricks."

She could've sworn she heard him say, "Not if you don't try," but ignored it.

In the kitchen, she refilled Stella and her glasses and said, "So how come you two walked through this door at the same time? I hope you're not dragging David to your shady hangouts, Shut..."

She didn't hear him coming. He put his finger over her lips. "Don't say it, Nugget."

Naomi sucked her lower lip in and turned around, her lips burning where he had touched her. She shouldn't enjoy the moment, but she did.

Somewhere far away, she heard David say, "Baby, I'd like you to meet my best man."

Revan still stood close and reached around her to grab a cube of cheese, then dropped it in his mouth.

"Where is he?" Naomi stretched her neck to see around Revan, tried to push him out of the way. "Move over. I don't see anybody. Did you leave him outside?"

He lifted her chin with one finger, with only inches between them. "You're looking at him."

Her eyes widened and she whispered, "You?"

"In all my glory." His green eyes had turned dark, almost black. "You have a problem with it?"

"No, Shutterbug," she said quietly.

Revan glared at her. "Stop. It."

Naomi couldn't believe it.

One of them had to step back from their newly-assigned wedding responsibility—and it wouldn't be her.

CHAPTER 6

NAOMI—APRIL 2019

Naomi held her phone to her ear and paced back and forth in her living room, looking out into the backyard, where the late afternoon sun cast long shadows. She didn't see the daffodils and hyacinths in the flower beds her mom was so proud of. She didn't notice the dogs happily digging holes under a large rhododendron bush until she heard her mother yelling, "Get out of there, you two monsters."

It had been ten days since Stella asked her to be her maid of honor.

Ten days of nightmares about receptions and dances.

"Jo, how can I tell Stella I'm not going to be her maid of honor?" she asked her cousin.

"You can't. Stella would be devastated if you changed your mind. And why would you?"

"Hello-o-oh?? Have you heard who David picked as his best man?" She held her phone away from her ear and stared at it.

"Yes, but so what?" Jo asked. "I was surprised he didn't ask Luca, though. He's the brother of the bride, after all. At least he asked him to be one of his groomsmen along with Aaron."

"David and Revan have this male-bonding thing going since Paris. You should hear them calling each other 'my man.' Urgh. And to answer your other question, it has *everything* to do with it." She stopped the pacing and leaned her forehead against the cool windowpane.

"You and Stella know how I feel about him. I can pretend I'm fine if we're hanging out as a group. But do you have any idea how much time I'll have to spend with Revan planning this wedding?"

"I don't think guys are getting as involved as women do. He'll probably sign off on everything you suggest just to be left alone. And even if you did drop out as maid of honor, you'd still be in the bridal party. Stella would never let you off the hook."

"Good point," Naomi agreed.

"I'm really excited to be a bridesmaid. I've never been in a wedding before," Jo said.

"I've been in a few, but some were more stress than fun. At least Stella doesn't want anything over-the-top. But you're right, I can't do that to her," Naomi paused before she said, "Well, then David needs to find a new best man."

"You know very well he'll never change his mind about Rev. You need to suck it up and be a big girl about it. It's over as soon as they're hitched. And you'll have Frank with you, so he'll help you get through it."

"Yeah, I'm not so sure about Frank being with me. He's dropped out of a few things lately. And it's starting to bug me more every time."

Naomi heard Jo putting something in the microwave and asked, "What are you doing while we're on the phone? This is important to me."

"Heating up leftovers. Someone gave me some vegan thingy to try."

Naomi scrunched up her face, even if Jo couldn't see it. "So, let's talk about the engagement party this weekend. When exactly are you getting here?"

"Luca and I are driving down on Friday. We should get there around 6:30 pm."

Interesting... "Oh, really? You and Luca? Driving together?"

"Leave it alone, Nam. Why would I pay for a train ticket if he's going to the same place?"

She couldn't wait to watch them interact...

"Want to grab a drink on Friday night? Meet at nine at the Red Owl?" Jo asked.

"Okay, sure. See you then. Bye." Naomi ended the call.

She knew something was brewing between Jo and Luca, even if *they* didn't know it yet. But she had eyes in her head, and they told her something was up. Well, she'd make sure they were sitting together at each and every event she, Naomi Winters, had a hand in. Phew, good thing she didn't drop out as maid of honor.

Before she could put the phone away, it rang again. She smiled when she saw the caller ID.

"Hey, I'm looking forward to dinner tonight. Just the two of us..."

"Baby doll, I have to cancel. An interview with the *Washington Nationals* came up kind of last minute and I've got to go. I'm leaving within the next half hour, and I have meetings with the athletic director and his team in the morning. I'll call you afterward, okay?"

"Yeah. Hmm... When are you coming back?"

"Probably not till Sunday. Depending on the signals they give me, I might stay an extra day and look around for nice neighborhoods where I can rent something affordable."

"So, you're not here for Stella's party on Saturday, then?"

"No, baby, I'm sorry. Can you tell them we'll catch up another time?"

"Sure, good luck with the interview. Keep me posted," Naomi said and ended the call. *Thanks, buddy. So much for having him by my side for those dinners. This is getting old.*

What was she going to do now? This sucked big time, and if she stayed home right now, she'd spend the evening brooding.

Maybe Stella would meet her somewhere for a glass of wine and a chat. Telling her that David needed to replace Revan would be easier to discuss in person. If Stella saw how distraught Naomi was over the situation, she'd have a hard time refusing her.

"Hi, you've reached Stella. Please leave a message!" Not what Naomi wanted to hear after she speed-dialed her friend.

"Hey, it's me. Are you able to meet me for a drink in a little bit? I was thinking of heading to the Red Owl in an hour. Let me know, or just meet me there. You know where I usually sit." She hung up.

An hour later she walked into the Red Owl. She liked the eclectic mix of styles and décor, the atmosphere of part tavern, part bar, and the huge pipes visible under the high ceiling, making it look like an old factory building. They served great appetizers and simple meals, a good selection of drinks, and she enjoyed sitting at one of the tables in the corner to watch the comings and goings. Even though it was a Wednesday evening, the place was busy.

Naomi's favorite table was occupied, so she went to sit at the bar and ordered a few hot wings and a glass of wine. She didn't mind sitting there since she'd be by herself. Stella had texted back saying David's parents had already arrived to meet her family and they had plans for dinner together.

In the background, low bass tones started playing, then percussions joined the rhythmic plucking of strings. Sting's iconic voice joined the instruments and Naomi tapped her foot to the rhythm of "Every Breath You Take."

She half-listened to the song, feeling the beat more than following words, and munched on the wings until her table became available and she made a beeline for it. Sitting down, she pulled out her phone and checked Facebook.

Ah, Revan had posted photos of his latest motorcycle trip to somewhere in Pennsylvania.

"Nothin' like a nice beer 'fter a long day." The chair next to her was pulled out and someone sat down heavily. Glancing over, she saw a guy with beady eyes smiling at her. No, it wasn't a smile, he was leering.

"Sorry, the chair's taken," she said.

"I ain't seen nobody otha' sittin' here," he said and took a noisy swig from his Budweiser bottle.

Naomi cringed. "You might as well get up right now, because you're not staying at my table," she told him and looked back at her phone.

"Why not?" he burped and took another swig.

"I'm busy." She didn't even look at him.

"Name's Ronnie. Ya look lonely, sweets." He reached inside his pants and adjusted his man parts.

But not THAT lonely, she thought, put her phone in her purse and got up. She wasn't in the mood to argue with this guy. Her first answer should've told him to leave her alone. Finishing the rest of her wine at the bar, she settled her bill and left the tavern without looking back.

Waiting at the intersection across from Independence Hall for a green light, she heard someone call, "C'mon, sugar. Let's have some fun. How 'bout a beer?"

He has the nerve to follow me outside!? Naomi looked around for police. Go figure—here she was, in an area usually swamped with police and park rangers. But right now? Not a single one.

"Leave me alone," she said.

"What's one drink? Be a nice gal," he said too close to her, his beer breath almost making her gag.

He wasn't just annoying but revolting too.

Naomi took a step to the side, but he blocked her way. Could she outrun him? He didn't look too fast on his feet.

She tucked her purse under her arm and was ready to sprint, when she heard, "What's going on over here?"

Revan jogged over the three-lane street and put his arm around her, leaning down to kiss the corner of her mouth. Then he glared at the other man and said, "I heard the lady asking you to leave her alone."

The guy muttered, "Can't blame a guy for tryin'. She's a hot chick, and me and my di..." He didn't get any farther, before Revan held up his free hand and said in a menacing voice, "Not one more word, or you'll eat soup for the next few weeks."

Bar guy seemed to get it and turned around, but not without muttering under his breath, "Stupid tease."

"Nugget, what are you doing here by yourself?" Revan asked as he dropped his arm once they were alone.

She shrugged. "Nobody had time to meet me for a drink, so I came to the Red Owl by myself. Thank you for getting rid of that idiot."

"My pleasure," he replied and slid his hands in the pockets of his jeans. "You didn't call me. Want to grab another drink?"

She shook her head. "I don't want to go back in there today."

"We can go to my place. You're safe there from unwanted attentions," Revan offered.

"Thanks, but I'll be heading home. Bye, Shutterbug, and thanks again for coming to my rescue. I'm sure I would've shaken him off myself soon." She gave him a quick hug, then started walking. Had to put a safe distance between herself and Revan, or she'd change her mind and go home with him for a drink.

And while she'd be safe from his attentions, she wouldn't be able to guarantee he'd be safe from hers.

CHAPTER 7

REVAN—APRIL 2019

Sitting alone in his living room, Revan sipped his whiskey while flipping through a few pages in the photo album on the coffee table. The corners of his mouth curled up when he saw a picture of Naomi and Stella in a restaurant, raising two glasses of champagne. The caption read, *Our first night in Paris. Life's good!*

Naomi was grinning into the camera.

He was glad he happened to show up while she was having trouble with the guy from the bar. He knew she was capable of getting rid of the creep by herself, but still...there was something... Revan's blood started boiling when the guy referred to her as a hot chick. Just because a beautiful woman sat alone in a bar didn't mean she was up for grabs and lewd comments.

And Naomi was a gorgeous woman. Even when she was dressed casually in slim jeans, heeled boots, and a warm jacket, she looked amazing.

The next question was, what had possessed him to invite her home for a drink? Granted, they'd spent time alone before. But today felt different. Had he subconsciously hoped she'd say yes? And then what?

It could've been the perfect time to have his little chat with her about Frank, etcetera. Speaking of... Where was her loser boyfriend tonight? She said nobody had time to meet her. If she was his girlfriend, he'd make it a point to have time for her. Plenty of time.

Stop it, Forrester, don't go there. Remember...she's off limits.

Revan turned a few more pages of the album and stopped at a group picture. They were at dinner, his arm resting loosely around Naomi's shoulders. The caption said, *We've got Revan back.*

He ran a hand over his hair. Something changed on that day, when he was freed after being held hostage for four days in the catacombs of Paris.

He was being taken to a hospital for exams and observation. When he heard Naomi fibbing to the desk nurse at the Emergency Department about being his fiancée, he at first thought he was hallucinating. Hadn't known she was in the city. But she managed to weasel her way through to him. Whether it was the effect of the cocktail of medications being pumped into his body, or exhaustion, or simply the relief at seeing a familiar face, he hadn't been able to stop himself from kissing her. And it wasn't a chaste one.

Interestingly, he hadn't felt compelled to kiss Stella the same way when she followed Naomi into his partitioned section.

He still hadn't forgotten how it felt to kiss Naomi—a real kiss...

And today, thanks to his own stupidity, he got a refresher. It was only a quick peck, but it was enough. Just like with the desk nurse, Naomi had weaseled her way past his protective shields and stirred up feelings that were new to him. And that went against everything he believed in.

But there were three good reasons to ignore those kisses—and they had become his mantra.

She's an old friend!

She's in a relationship!

She's off limits!

But every time he saw her it got more difficult to keep a cool head—and to keep his hands to himself.

At least as long as lover boy was with her, he had a visual reminder to keep his distance.

CHAPTER 8

REVAN—APRIL 2019

When Revan walked into the restaurant on Saturday evening for Stella and David's engagement party, a romantic 1980s ballad played in the background.

He searched the room, automatically scoping out the best place to put his camera equipment and scouting out first ideas for unique shots.

A long hot and cold buffet was set up against one wall, with waitstaff behind the table serving and refilling the dishes. A bartender mixed cocktails and poured drinks at the open bar across the room, and more servers carried trays of appetizers and champagne to the groupings of small tables scattered throughout the room.

Revan saw Stella's parents talking with a couple who had to be David's parents. David favored his father's athletic body and complexion, and the young woman who stood with them favored the mother, shared her slim body and long, straight brown hair. He thought she resembled an actress who recently married into European royalty, something even he had read about. She had to be Sabrina, David's younger sister.

Sabrina talked animatedly to Naomi's grandmother and laughed at something the old woman said. Revan loved Gram Annie, as she insisted on being be called by Naomi's close friends. For as long as he had known the woman, she'd been full of energy. But tonight she looked frail, and he made a mental note to sit with her later.

After putting his camera bag on a chair, he began to check the camera settings. He never assumed people expected him to take photos when he was only a guest, but David had specifically asked him for the favor.

Someone hugged him from the side. "There you are. Mom and Dad wanted to know why you weren't here before the guests arrived. Isn't it your job as the event photographer to document everybody's arrival?"

Revan kissed his sister on her head and said, "Hi, Peanut. I'm here now, so chill. I hope you're not pestering Stella. Remember...this is her party, not yours."

His sixteen-year-old sister was thrilled to be a bridesmaid and talked his ear off about hair styles and dresses every chance she got.

"Stella said I can ask her anything I want, and that I'm an important part of her girls. It's what she calls us, her girls. But I've gotta go. Sabrina wants to show me photos of dresses she's found. We're trying to coordinate what we're wearing. She gave me her cell phone number and said I could always text her. And have you seen her boyfriend? He's hot," Dinah said without taking a breath.

"You're too young to look at men. Don't get any ideas, Peanut. I told you you're not dating until you're at least thirty." Revan hung one camera around his neck and held another in his hand.

"Remember what Mom always says? Worry about yourself," Dinah smiled at him.

He loved his sister, but—like most teenagers—she could be a pain in the butt.

Where he'd been his parents' little *oops* when they were only twenty years old, Dinah was their second surprise when they were forty. And because of becoming a brother at an age when others started families, he felt the need to protect her. Whether she wanted it or not.

Revan began to walk around the room, taking pictures and chatting with people he knew. He didn't only focus on faces, he always looked for small details like entwined hands, fingers holding the stem of a crystal glass, and sometimes half-eaten food or lipstick on the rim of a glass turned out to be an interesting object. He let his camera tell him what she wanted to capture. Some of his best photos happened that way.

The folding doors to the foyer stood wide open, and a bright patch of color made him turn his head. And blink his eyes. And look again.

Naomi walked in wearing a royal blue dress with a slightly flared skirt which ended mid-thigh and showed off her long legs. A bodice with wide shoulder straps hugged her like a second skin and allowed just enough of her creamy décolletage to peek out—and make his fingers twitch. Her summer-blonde hair was held back with some sort of oversized hairclip he wanted to pull out on sight. Didn't she know her hair looked best if it hung loosely around her shoulders?

Revan swallowed hard. He had not been prepared for—this.

"Look at our little Naomi. She sure knows how to make an entrance," Luca said from beside him, while handing him a napkin. "You're drooling."

Stopping a passing waitress, Revan reached for a glass of champagne and emptied it in one gulp. Then reached for the next one. Holy shit! If he'd been hit with a two-by-four it wouldn't have knocked the breath out of him the way Naomi just did. He had a suspicion that, contrary to what Luca said, she had no clue what effect she had on people, especially men.

"Ooh, Rev, doesn't she look like a movie star?" His sisters' awed voice came from his other side. Just what he needed. He knew Dinah already thought Naomi could walk on water.

"Peanut, go find Stella and ask her to tell the manager to turn up the air conditioning. It's getting too warm in here." He dabbed his forehead with the napkin.

"I think it's comfortable. But you're really sweating. Maybe you should go outside and get some fresh air," Dinah said, pointing to a drop of sweat running down the side of his face. "Take Luca with you. Jo just got here and says she has stuff to bring in from the car and could use a hand. Actually, she asked specifically for Luca."

"Move on, talk to kids your own age," he grumbled. It was totally unacceptable how he treated her, but the last thing he needed was for her to notice the effect Naomi's appearance had on him—or worse, blurt it out. Dinah didn't always have a filter in place when it came to pointing out embarrassing things.

"I'm not a kid anymore, you moron. I'll tell Mom."

Besides sweating profusely, his body's reaction to Naomi was painful and difficult to hide. Maybe going outside wasn't a bad idea. He cleared his throat and looked for an escape route. "Since when do you tattle? I thought I taught you it's not a good character trait."

"Being mean isn't either. So leave me alone," she replied before hurrying off to hug Naomi.

He didn't hear what they said, but when Naomi looked at him with a wicked smile, pulled a tissue from her small purse and lightly dabbed her forehead, he wished he'd gone out to help Jo.

The two glasses of champagne didn't sit well with him. He needed a large glass of water and some food. And then he'd go talk to Gram Annie, which might not be the best idea either, because knowing her, she'd find a way to steer the conversation to Naomi, too.

He was so screwed.

The next day in his home office, Revan gazed at his photo of Naomi standing behind a flower arrangement and, with half-closed eyes, leaning forward to smell the roses while a tiny smile curved up the corners of her mouth.

He didn't remember taking the picture. But who else could've taken it? His cameras were absolutely off limits for everybody—no exceptions.

He mostly used digital cameras, but last night he brought along his most revered camera. To him, nothing came closer to the art of photography than old-fashioned roll film, and his Hasselblad XPan was a real gem. More than one of his award-winning photographs had been taken with her. But best of all, after developing the films in his darkroom in his basement, he often found hidden objects in the photos, tucked away in the background. Like Naomi's expression when she was unaware of the lens focusing on her.

It was like a treasure hunt.

The treasure in this image was the peaceful, contented look on her face. Exactly as he imagined her after a long night of gentle lovemaking—falling asleep in his arms.

Don't go there, Forrester. Not happening. Remember your mantra...

Which made him think of another development he didn't like. Frank never showed up last night. When he asked Stella about lover boy's whereabouts, she told him, "Oh, he's not coming. Naomi said he's in DC for an interview and house hunting. I don't know how much more we'll see of him."

He couldn't believe it. Not last night, and not now.

He had to get out of town. Running away wasn't the solution, but he couldn't come up with a better idea.

If what Stella had said was true, he needed a shoulder-to-shoulder row of solid linebackers to stand between him and Naomi.

And they needed to have their backs to her or they'd never see him coming.

CHAPTER 9

N<small>AOMI</small>—M<small>AY</small> 2019

N aomi shoved boxes into the rented van, then leaned against the rear bumper and put her hands in the back pockets of her jeans.

"This was the last one I'm lugging out of there. Let the men carry the rest," she said. "I can't believe you're really moving. Are you sure you don't want to store everything in the basement? Just in case..."

"Nam, stop it." Stella laughed. "I can't wait to start my life with David, and I'm excited about the townhouse we found in the neighborhood Andrew recommended."

"I'm happy for you, really, but I'll miss getting together on the spur of the moment." Naomi kicked a small rock from side to side. "By the way, did you look at the brochures I gave you about venues for the wedding?"

"Yes, and I called the inn from the 1780s, the one with the gorgeous private backyard. They can accommodate us in September. I was going to show you later what their event planner sent me."

After another hour of boxing up, labeling and cleaning, they sat down in the backyard with coffee and cookies.

Naomi said haltingly, "I have to tell you something. Well, two things, actually."

She looked at the chocolate-dipped cookie in her hand and put it back on the saucer, then picked up a sugar cube from the little covered glass bowl. A moment later she dropped it into her coffee.

"What are you doing? You already put two sugars in your coffee." Stella reached for her hand. "What's going on?"

Naomi didn't look at her friend when she said, "The easier thing first... Frank and I are over."

"Oh, Nam, I'm so sorry. Since when?"

"After he came back from Washington. He got an offer to work for the *Nationals*. I'm happy for him, of course, but then he told me he already rented an apartment, and it bugged me. He didn't even think about asking me for any input. It was just the last straw, I guess."

"I'm really sorry," Stella said again. "I know you liked him a lot."

"Yes, but to like someone isn't enough. The signs have been there for a while now, all saying our relationship was heading in this direction."

"Can I admit something? I thought it was rotten when he didn't come with you to our party. I know he was in DC, but if he'd wanted, he could've found the time to come home on Saturday evening instead of Sunday morning. Especially because it was important to you." Stella hesitated. "But...if that's the easier of the two, what else is going on?"

"Gram Annie's really sick. At your party, a few people asked me if she was okay, and I thought she was. She was tired, but she's almost ninety, so she can't party like a twenty-year-old anymore." She reached for the cookie again, and bit into it this time. Then put it back on the saucer.

"Mom was getting concerned and mentioned it when she took her to one of her doctor's appointments. They ran a few tests and the results came back yesterday. Long story short, she has pancreatic cancer, somewhere between stages three and four." Naomi's eyes filled with tears and spilled over, and through the watery veil she could see Stella's shock and concern mirror her own.

"Oh, no, how terrible. And pancreatic cancer of all things. It's almost impossible to cure."

"Yup... Mom wants to have Gram close and move her into my in-law apartment. But, as you know, it only has one bedroom and one bathroom. I'll have to find somewhere else to live until...you know...until Gram..." She couldn't say it past the lump in her throat and swallowed hard.

"Can you move back into your old room?"

"Mom is using it as her 'hobby and reading' room and has stashed lots of stuff in there. And I don't want to move back upstairs." Naomi sighed, and wiped her eyes again. "My apartment is perfect for Gram. She can walk out into the backyard without having to climb stairs, and she still has some privacy from Mom and Dad. And vice versa."

"What about your Aunt Mary's house?"

"Her house is a huge construction site. She's turning the den and powder room into a first-floor master suite, but the work is moving along at a snail's pace and she doesn't know when it'll be finished.

"And before you ask, I'm not moving into Gram's townhouse. I love her, but to me it feels like a mausoleum with her antique furniture and dark colors. And besides, it would feel weird to be trading places with her."

"Hmm, it was worth a thought. Are the doctors recommending any treatments?"

"No, they'll focus on keeping her comfortable. Which I get. The treatments would most likely be too harsh for her. And she said she isn't going to try a million things just to die in the end anyway. Gram has maybe six months to live."

They sat silently for a few minutes, watched the birds sipping water from the backyard fountain and the butterflies flitting from one flower to the next.

Suddenly, Stella grabbed Naomi's arm and said, "Oh my goodness, why didn't I think of it right away? You could move into my rooms here!"

Naomi's roaring laughter filled the backyard. "Me? Living in Revan's house, with him?"

Stella didn't laugh. She eyed her cautiously. "I think it's a fantastic idea. He's hardly around, you know. Sometimes I don't see or hear him for days, and I know he has another trip to some hellish country coming up soon. Then you'll have the house to yourself."

Naomi put the rest of the cookie in her mouth and chewed slowly. "Hmm, it would only be for a few months…"

"I can talk to him when he gets home," Stella offered. "And I don't think Luca would charge you more for rent than I paid him."

"Do you think Luca's ever going to move back here?" Naomi said. "And what are Rev and Luca going to do if one of them decides to marry and have a family? The house is big, but it's not built for two families."

"I wouldn't be surprised if they swore a blood oath to never get married," Stella laughed. "But seriously, I don't think Luca's coming back since he has so many more opportunities in New York. I can see Rev buying him out eventually. Which would be a heck of a bill. But that's between them. So, do you think you could live here?"

Naomi gave Stella a wicked smile. "Yeah, sure. As long as we talk to Revan together. I've gotta see his face when he hears about it!"

After finishing her coffee, Naomi got up and carried her cup to the kitchen. Just as she closed the dishwasher, the front door opened and Revan walked in with Barbie trailing behind him.

"Well, look what the cat dragged in. Having a yearning for coffee again?" Naomi smiled angelically. "But the machine is acting up. It made weird noises earlier," she mimicked sputtering sounds and accentuated it with wild hand gestures.

Revan folded his arms and leaned against the doorframe. "Nugget, I don't know what you're doing to my coffee maker. Barb and I had a business meeting and I forgot to bring something I promised her."

If Rev really believed they only had a business meeting, he was stupid. Did he not see the way Blondie acted around him? Men could be so blind. Or maybe he didn't mind having Barb's boobs almost shoved in his face.

He still leaned against the doorjamb, and Naomi gave him a hand signal, "Move over, Shutterbug. You're blocking my way." He didn't budge when she put her hand on his bicep and tried to push him aside.

"How about asking nicely, maybe saying, 'Please, Revan, can you move a little faster?'" he said, and grinned.

"I bet you'd love to hear me beg. Now, move." She stretched to give him a peck on his cheek. "Oh, and... I really need to talk to you about something. I'll call you. Bye."

CHAPTER 10

Revan—May 2019

On his way home after some early-season whitewater rafting in Lehighton, Revan ended up stuck in weekend traffic. He was hungry, tired, and had run out of patience a while ago. All he wanted was something to eat, a beer or two—and to be left alone.

By the time he parked his Harley in the garage where he rented two spots year-round, it was getting dark and his mood had gone from bad to menacing. And when he rounded his street corner, he swore.

What the heck? Stella was in Baltimore for the weekend, and he knew for a fact that he turned off the lights before he left this morning. But the whole first floor of his house was lit up.

Revan unlocked and opened the front door—and almost backed out. He rubbed his eyes and shook his head.

In the middle of his living room, wearing a black sleeveless maxi dress, Naomi danced slowly and sensually while Elvis Presley crooned.

Unable to look away, he closed the door and put his motorcycle helmet on the floor together with his backpack. She really had a gift for driving him crazy, and in more ways than one.

She swirled around, still swaying to "Love Me Tender."

Revan ran a hand over his eyes again. *What is she doing?*

"Nugget, why are you rubbing your face against that dirty thing?"

Startled, Naomi opened her eyes and clutched the object in question to her chest. "Oh, Shutterbug, you scared me. Why can't you make noise when you come in, like normal people do?" She went to the kitchen and put the broom in the closet.

"I did. The question is, what are *you* doing here?"

"Stella asked me to water your plants today. She knew you'd forget."

"I don't have plants," he grumbled and walked toward her, dropping his heavy leather jacket on a chair.

She reached behind her, "And what do you call *this*?" She held up a tiny succulent in a stone container.

"I'm not even gonna ask," he shook his head and took a beer out of the refrigerator. Before the door closed completely, he yanked it open again. "Where's my dinner? Stella put leftovers in there."

"I couldn't tell how old the chicken breast and potatoes were, so I tossed them. But there's a yogurt and an apple."

Revan slammed the fridge door closed and reached for his phone. "I'll order a pizza. Care to join me since you're already here?"

"I thought you'd never ask. Can I have mushrooms, olives, and broccoli on mine?"

"Whatever you want." After he ordered, he said, "They said twenty-five minutes. I'll go and change. And then I want to know how you got into my house and what you did with the broom." Beer in hand, he stormed off. So much for a quiet evening...

Naomi had already poured two glasses of red wine and was sitting on the sofa in front of the cold fireplace by the time Revan came back downstairs from his room. A bowl of marinated olives and some crackers were on the table.

"So," he said and sat down in the chair opposite from her. "Spill it. Start at the beginning. How did you get in here?"

"Shutterbug, think..." she tapped the side of her head with a finger, "with a key, of course."

"You have a key?"

"If I didn't have one, I couldn't use one. Stella gave me a spare. To water the plant. Remember?"

"Don't forget to take it with you when you leave."

"Oh, you ignorant man," she shook her head. "Succulents remove toxins. This plant is cleansing the air in here. I have a feeling you need it."

"If I need to, I open the windows," he reached for the wine she had poured for him and took a long sip. Cleansing the air. He'd never heard anything more absurd. But he had to give her credit for being inventive—which shouldn't be news to him either. She'd always been fast on her feet.

His stomach grumbled. "Do we have anything else to munch on while we're waiting for the pizza?"

Hell, why did I ask her what kind of food we have? She doesn't live here!

"What do you call the olives and crackers?" she pointed to them.

"Martini garnish. And those aren't crackers. In fact, they look like cornflakes."

"Then why don't you go check what's in the pantry?" she asked and folded her legs under her hips.

"So, tell me about Mr. Bristle," Revan prompted, ignoring her jab.

"Who?" Naomi giggled. "Oh...good one, Shutterbug. Well, I was practicing our first dance. And since you weren't here, I used the second-best thing. Did you notice his broad shoulders?"

She looked directly at him while she drank some wine. He held her stare.

"Our first dance?" He hated giving her the satisfaction of asking.

"You're really slow today. Yes, whether you know it or not, we will be expected to dance at Stella and David's wedding. Remember...maid of honor," she pointed at herself, "...best man," she pointed at him. "And I thought if I practice with—what did you call him, Mr. Bristle?—and snuggle with him, it'll help me get used to the scruff on your face."

"The scruff on my face?" He ran a hand over his two-day stubble.

"Well, come here and touch the skin on my face. It's so soft," she tipped her face toward him. "I can't have you scratching it up when we're dancing. I'd probably break out in a rash, and how would it look—my face covered in hives in the middle of Stella and David's wedding? So I'm slowly desensitizing my skin to be ready for you."

Revan couldn't believe his ears. And she sounded as if she believed all the bullshit she was trying to feed him with a silver spoon.

The question came out before he could stop himself. "What kind of dances did Mr. Bristle practice with you?" He watched her unfold her legs and put them on the ottoman between them. She wiggled her toes, and he saw her dark gray toenails. Perfect...they matched his mood.

"Oh, we only did a few slow ones. He's a little challenged when it comes to his moves, because he's not overly flexible in the hips, you know."

Naomi wiggled her hips to underline her point, and—*shit*—his body responded in a flash.

Not again. And where's the damn pizza guy? Revan vowed to double the tip if the kid arrived within the next two minutes. He took another sip of the red wine from his almost-empty glass.

"But then I had another great idea. Since you and I never have formally danced together, I signed us up for private dance lessons." She had the nerve to smile at him.

Revan spit out the rest of the wine. "Shit! Nugget, you are going to be the death of me. Dance lessons? Not happening."

"Why? Do you want to look like a clumsy fool in front of everybody? Not happening, not as long as I'm the one on your arm."

"I've gotten lots of praise for my moves so far."

"Yeah, yeah. But for the moves with me you need to be in an upright position. We're not doing the mattress mambo, Shutterbug. Listen...there are strict rules and protocols to follow for weddings. I've read a lot about it lately. But don't worry, I'll fill you in on everything you need to know between now and the wedding."

Naomi paused, then grinned at him, "On the other hand, if you think it's too much for you to handle, you could always drop out. Ask David to give you a pass or something."

Ah, now we're getting closer. He'd known there was a motive hiding in there somewhere...

"Not happening, I'm honored David asked me, and I'll fulfill my duties. Sorry, Nugget, you're stuck with me, and we'll somehow get one dance done. Now I'm going to go change into a clean shirt. We'll have to pause this enlightening conversation."

He watched her wave her hand almost dismissingly. "Just drop the shirt somewhere like you usually do. Stella's going to pick it up when she's back tomorrow night. But I'm glad you didn't hit me with the fountain of red wine you spewed. It would never have come out of my dress."

"Your dress is black." Revan stood and crossed the short distance between them. "When the pizza gets here, we'll eat and then I'm going to bed. I'm tired."

Naomi stood as well and replied, "I can't leave until I've talked to you about something important. We didn't get a chance the other day with Barbie trailing after you like a lost puppy." She started toward the kitchen and held up her empty glass. "Refill?"

Revan couldn't stop himself. Without thinking, he reached for her and pulled her close.

The loud knock on the front door was the best thing he heard so far this evening.

And not a second too soon, he thought. He released her and answered the door. Next he'd listen to whatever Naomi wanted to discuss with him, send her on her way, and take a shower.

He counted out enough bills to pay, including a hefty tip, while Naomi took out plates and utensils. By the time he put the pizza boxes on the kitchen island, she'd also refilled both wine glasses.

"Weren't you going to change your shirt?" Naomi looked him over.

"Not anymore. We're not going to be socializing much longer."

She helped herself to a slice of her pizza and reached over to pluck a few pepperoni slices off his. Revan asked, "Why didn't you order pepperoni for your own pizza?"

"They don't go well with my vegetables."

"Excuse me?"

"I'm trying to eat healthy, here. More veggies, less meat, you know? I can't gain weight before the wedding."

"Then keep your fingers away from my pepperoni."

"It was a little slip...a mini sin, so to speak." She licked her fingers and reached for her glass of wine. "I like this wine."

A mumbled, "Thanks," was all he could force out.

"So, here's what I have to discuss with you. Good thing you're already sitting down." She rested her chin on the backs of her fingers and looked at him. "Are you listening?"

"Do I have a choice?" It didn't bode well when she said he needed to sit to hear it.

"Okay... Gram Annie has pancreatic cancer, and Mom wants her to move into my apartment so she can help her. Which means I need another place to live. And Stella and I thought I could move in here." Naomi bit into her slice of pizza and grinned at him while she chewed.

He jumped up, his pizza plopping onto his plate. Both his hands were planted firmly on the counter. "Say. That. Again?"

"I. Am. Moving. In. Here."

He stared at her. She had the nerve to copy his tone—and to continue eating.

"And it's only for a few months." She sniffled and swallowed. "Gram Annie doesn't have more than six months or so to live."

What could he say? He was shocked and saddened to hear about Naomi's grandmother's illness, and knew he'd miss the old lady, but Naomi moving in with him? He'd have to ask Stella whose brain fart this was, although he assumed it was a team effort.

"I'm sorry to hear about Gram Annie, and I want you to let me help if she needs anything." Anything except her granddaughter moving in with him.

"Look, Rev, Stella is leaving town. Nobody else is staying in her rooms upstairs. And you've known me pretty much my whole life, so where's the harm?" She looked at him with big blue eyes. They were full of tears.

The idea of having Naomi constantly under the same roof terrified him. How would he be able to avoid her without being openly rude? Family and friends always came first for him, and he prided himself on helping them no matter what. Which meant he couldn't refuse Naomi's plea.

But wait...why didn't she move in with lover boy? Hmm... that idea didn't sit well either.

"Okay. I'm leaving soon anyway. But we'll have to set some ground rules."

"Thank you! Thank you! Thank you! You won't even notice me. I'll be as invisible to you as always," she said. He saw her fingers sneak over to his pizza again.

"Okay, what are the ground rules? Do you want me to do your laundry? I can iron and fold your boxer briefs if you want."

"No, we're each doing our own laundry," he managed to grind out. The thought of her hands anywhere near his underwear was enough to make him regret his decision to let her move in temporarily. He couldn't think straight, at least not using the gray matter he was supposed to use to reach a sound decision.

"Rule number one, you're to stay out of my rooms upstairs. Rule number two, I prefer no overnight visits from your boyfriend when I'm here." It was a petty thing to demand, but a man had his pride. He wasn't going to listen to them doing—whatever they were doing—in his own house. Especially since his own bedroom hadn't seen any action in a long time and probably wouldn't for even longer. Which was his own fault, but...

"No problem. Frank and I aren't together anymore." She licked her fingers. "Anything else?"

SHIT!

"We'll have so much fun, Shutterbug," she beamed at him. "Aren't you excited about having me come and keep you company?"

"You have no idea, Nugget," he growled.

By Saturday two weeks later, Stella had officially moved out, Naomi had moved in, and after the women assured the men their presence wasn't required anymore, Revan and Luca went straight to the pub.

"What do you think the girls are doing right now?" Revan stretched out his legs and crossed them at the ankles.

Luca mirrored him and said, "They claim they're helping Naomi unpack."

"I bet what they're really doing is plotting more ways to make my life a living hell. You know, a year ago none of this would've bothered me. And to be fair, Naomi isn't doing anything wrong. She's no different than usual. It's all me."

Luca raised his eyebrows. "Why didn't you tell her you'd rather she didn't move in?"

"Really?" Revan threw his arms in the air. "With what excuse?"

Before Luca could answer, David walked into the restaurant and plopped down on a chair at their table. "I don't want to see one more storage box. Between the stuff from my old place in Chicago, Stella's million boxes of books, and then bringing Naomi's clothes and whatnot from her apartment to your house, I'm done. What are we drinking?"

"Beer for now, but I see a bottle of whiskey smiling at me from across the room," Revan waved the waitress over. "Bring us three glasses of Hudson Manhattan Rye, please. Make 'em doubles."

David added, "We'd also like enough wings with dips to share. Thanks."

They sat quietly for a moment. Revan's focus was drawn back to the bar, where he noticed a man staring at him. The guy's attention lingered at their table before he turned it to two young women sitting next to him. Revan watched while they shook their heads and turned away.

Then it hit him. It was the creep who followed Naomi a few weeks ago. If he saw the guy do anything weird with those women, he'd go over and tip off the bartender.

The waitress arrived with their whiskeys. "Wings are coming out shortly."

Revan swirled the whiskey in his glass and inhaled deeply. "Wish me luck, guys. I'm gonna need it." He took a sip and let the whiskey sit on his tongue before swallowing it.

A song started playing, the bass guitar almost dark and sinister. *Quite fitting.* He felt Luca watching him from the side and turned toward him, saying, "What?"

"Wanna talk about it?" Luca tipped his own glass and watched the amber liquid running down the inside.

"There's nothing to say. I won't get to spend much time in my own house until she's able to move back into her apartment."

"You've never run away from anything before, Rev. Why now?"

"Because not even when I sat in those fucking bombed-out ruins in Syria or any trenches in Afghanistan did I feel as screwed as I do now." He closed his eyes and ran his fingers through his hair.

"I'm not following," David said. "What exactly is the problem?"

"His new roomie," Luca said, barely loud enough to be heard over U2's "With or Without You."

"I see." David nodded.

"No, you don't," Rev said with more intensity than he meant to, then downed his drink. He hissed, "Because I can't stop thinking about Naomi. I want to hold her in my arms and kiss her. And do a few more things, none of which are appropriate between best friends."

Revan put his glass on the low table in front of him. "I owe it to her, to me, and to all of us, to protect her from myself."

"Does she know about your feelings?" David asked.

"No, and don't any of you say anything to her—or Stella, or Jo—about this. Naomi is vulnerable right now. She and Frank broke up, her grandmother is dying, and her best friend is leaving town."

He took a deep breath, "I'll do my best to support her, but from as far away as possible. And hopefully she'll find someone who can give her what she deserves."

Revan noticed Luca and David exchanging looks. Before either one could open their mouths and make a smart comment, he raised a hand and added, "Guys, don't say it. Believe me, I see her, and she gets to me like no other woman ever has, but she's off limits. There are invisible lines I can't cross. End of discussion."

CHAPTER 11

NAOMI—JUNE 2019

Naomi didn't pay much attention to the lovely afternoon sunshine, or the people running errands, window-shopping, or just hanging out as she walked along Arch Street. Tourists streamed from Independence Mall past Reading Terminal Market toward City Hall, making this area a beehive of activity.

Her thoughts whirled around the same thing they always did when she had a free moment.

Revan "Thickhead" Forrester.

He was as sexy, funny, unreadable, and tear-your-hair-out annoying as always. And her feelings for him hadn't changed since she moved in with him a few weeks ago. *Humph...*why should they?

She should really make up her mind whether she wanted to pursue him or leave things the way they were. But one thing was clear...if she waited for him to notice her, she'd be a dried-out, shriveled prune before—no, *if*—it ever happened. So she was leaning toward taking matters into her own hands.

The tempting aroma of coffee made her stop in front of a coffee shop, then walk in. Why not pick up a café latte to go? Just as she pulled out her wallet to pay, she thought of something.

"Add a large Americano to the order, please." She almost snickered. He'd need the extra energy for what she planned for later. This Saturday afternoon would be so much fun...

Stepping aside to allow other customers to order, she waited for her name to be called when a sharp whistle made her look up. She didn't expect anyone she knew to get her attention in such an immature way, but it was an automatic reflex to react to it. When she didn't see anybody familiar, she went back to checking out the destination mugs in the shelf behind her.

"Order for Naomi," the acne-stricken teenager behind the coffee bar called, and pushed the steaming cups toward her.

"Thanks," she shoved a tip into the strategically placed jar and picked up the two cups. Turning to leave, she almost collided with the person behind her. Her first impulse was to demand, "Ever heard of personal space?" but decided to go with the friendlier, "Sorry."

"Nice name, sweets."

Her breath hitched. She couldn't recall his name, but she remembered his face. And she had no intention of starting a conversation with him. Without a word, she left the coffee shop. Where had he come from so suddenly?

When she reached her street, she looked over her shoulder one last time. She didn't see the jerk, but the fine hairs on the back of her neck tingled all the way home. She stacked the two cups and searched for her keys. *Darn, why do they always have to be at the bottom of my purse?* She opened the door and closed it with a swift push of her hip.

She found Revan at the kitchen island, leaning over a huge map with a red Sharpie in one hand. She set the coffee next to him and craned her neck to look over his shoulder. *Hmm, he used the new shower gel.* She sneaked into his bathroom a few days ago and put it in his shower.

"Going away, Shutterbug?" Only inches away, he glared at her. His index finger touched her lips and he shook his head.

For a split second she wondered what he would do if she sucked his fingertip into her mouth.

"Told you I was planning to leave town again. I'm heading south on Monday." He reached for the cup and took off the lid. "Thanks for the coffee."

"What are you circling on the map? And—come on—who on earth still uses actual paper maps?"

"Me, obviously. I like to look at the whole area at once and mark the places I want to visit."

"Have you heard of Google maps? Imagine—it tells you how long it takes to get from one place to the next. You

79

don't even need to use a ruler and your precious brain cells. So, where are you going, exactly?"

"I'm working on a photo series for *The New York Times Magazine* about old South Carolina and Georgia cemeteries and their histories."

"Oh, really? I'll be in Charleston for two days at the end of next week, too. Maybe I'll run into you there." She gave him a big smile, leaned closer and squinted at the map. "There's Charleston, look."

"Need glasses, Nugget?" His face was so close, she could feel his breath on her cheek.

"Nope, I can see fine." She straightened and checked the time. "You've got half an hour, Shutterbug."

"For what?"

She pointed to the blackboard leaning against the backsplash. "You might want to check my message board occasionally. I didn't put it there for my benefit."

Saturday, dance lesson, 4 pm.

"I saw it, but what does it have to do with me?"

Naomi narrowed her eyes and crossed her arms. She didn't say a word but gestured between them with her finger.

"Are you shitting me? You were serious about dance lessons?" he jumped off the barstool and towered over her.

"What made you think I was joking? It's for the good of Stella and David, remember? Madame Estelle is waiting for us, so don't dally!" Naomi blew into her coffee cup before taking a long sip. She looked over the rim at Rev to see one of his temple veins bulging slightly.

"Madame Estelle? Wait...wasn't she your dance teacher as a kid? You always referred to her as an old fossil back then...is she still able to move?"

Naomi tsk-tsked. "Be glad she can't hear you. I think she has a young assistant who's teaching with her. If you prefer, you can practice with him." She put her cup in the middle of his map and tapped her wrist. "Twenty-five minutes, Shutterbug. Time's flyin'."

"I'm not dancing with a man."

"See, then you'll dance with me. I'll go change, then we're heading out." She clapped her hands and ran upstairs, suppressing a giggle when she heard Revan saying something rather unfriendly.

He was still muttering when they left the house. Halfway to the dance studio, Naomi stopped walking and looked over her shoulder. "If anybody saw you, they'd think I'm escorting you to your execution, Revan. Speed it up a little and put a smile on your face. It'll be fun."

"Fun? Is it possible we have different definitions of the word *fun*?"

God, he could be infuriating!

Naomi started walking again until they reached the bright red door to the dance studio. How many years had she and Jo come here for weekly dance lessons? Too many to count, and sometimes she felt the way Revan did now. There were only so many arabesques, pliés, and pirouettes one could do while feigning interest when there were more exciting things waiting outside.

But overall she must not have left too bad an impression, because when she called and told Madame Estelle about a friend who needed a crash course in basic dance steps, her former teacher agreed to meet with them for two, maybe three private classes.

"Naomi, child, it is so lovely to see you," Madame Estelle greeted them. "And you must be the young man in need of help. Welcome, and come in."

Naomi gave Rev a little poke with her elbow and walked into the studio after him. A young, slender man, maybe in his twenties, walked over to them—or rather tiptoed over, she thought—and took her hand. "I'm Alfredo, welcome to Studio Lightfoot." He kissed the knuckles of both her hands, then reached for Revan's.

Revan stepped back and pulled her against him. He looked from Madame Estelle to Alfredo and said, "Thrilled to meet you both. I'm sure you're terribly busy, so let's get started."

He murmured in her ear, "Nugget, you are going to pay for this."

After thirty minutes of practicing the very basic combinations of left-right-left, right-left-right and one-two-three, two-two-three steps individually, Madame Estelle announced, "Oh, Revan, you've been hiding your talent. I don't think this is the first time on the dance floor for you. Are you ready to put it all together?"

"Yes, we are!" Naomi rubbed her hands together and looked at Rev. "But watch where you're putting your hooves, Shutterbug. I got a pedicure yesterday." She held out her sandaled right foot for him to see her nail polish. "Wanna know the name? I'll tell you anyway. 'Hot Affair.'"

Alfredo tapped the outside of Revan's left leg. "You are starting with this leg." Pushing the hand off, Rev said through gritted teeth, "Got it, Alf, got it."

As soon as the first beats of "Thorn in my Side" by the Eurythmics started playing, Naomi put her left hand on his shoulder.

"Whoever picked the song hit it perfectly," he said while glaring down at her.

"No idea what you're talking about." She wiggled her hips. "Let's do it, Shutterbug. Show me what you got."

When he pulled her to him, she almost melted in his arms. Then he put his lips to her ear, "Try keeping up, Nugget."

Revan led her through the cha-cha as if they had danced together countless times before. To be so close to him for the duration of an entire song was more than she was prepared for. And she started to question the wisdom of booking several lessons with Madame Estelle.

"We'll work on the waltz when I see you two again in a few weeks. Don't forget to practice what you learned today. Naomi, child, I saw you mixing up your feet a few times. You have to pay better attention," Madame Estelle said as she waved goodbye.

Once they were on the sidewalk again, Naomi put her fists on her hips and said, "You. Bloody. Dirty. Liar." She stretched to her full height and her nose almost touched his chin. Darn those four inches he had on her. "You said you can't dance."

"I said I *don't* dance. Never said I can't," he grinned. "And if my memory is correct, I also pointed out to you how I've been complimented on my moves."

She stormed off, calling over her shoulder to him, "Let's go. Gram Annie is waiting."

"Tell her I said hi." He began to walk in the opposite direction.

"You're coming with me. She asked to see us after the dance lesson. I guess she's bored and desperate for company, even yours. I promised her we'd swing by before we go out to dinner."

"We're going out to dinner? Since when?" He caught up and fell into step with her.

"Do you have to repeat everything I'm saying? And yes, dinner. You can't take a girl out to dance and not feed her. Dating 101, Shutterbug."

"I didn't take you out to dance, you steamrolled me into it. And we're not dating," Rev said grumpily, but continued to walk with her.

She ignored his tirade. "Yeah, yeah, get it all out now. We don't need your negative energy around Gram Annie." She knew he liked her grandmother and didn't mind spending a little bit of time with her. Gram might be old and gravely ill, but she was still sharp and witty.

Naomi's skin still tingled where his hands had touched her through the soft fabric of her dress. Having been in his arms was totally worth listening to his complaints.

She couldn't wait for their next lesson.

"There you are, my dears," Gram Annie called from the lounge chair in the shaded backyard. Dixon and Scarlett, the family's rambunctious, eighteen-month-old boxer dogs, chased each other around a tree but stopped to greet them as soon as they walked into the yard.

Revan squatted to scratch Dixon behind his ears. "Good sit, Dixon. Good boy. A man needs to show some dignity and restraint," he praised the male dog, who drooled heavily in his eagerness to please and held up a paw for his dog-version of shaking hands. "Wow, you learned a new trick?"

Scarlett followed her brother's lead—and rolled onto her back to expose her belly to Rev. "Look at the little tramp. She knows no boundaries when it comes to getting Rev's hands on her. Well, if I were a few years younger..." Gram Annie announced with a shaky laugh. "What do you think, Naomi?"

Naomi saw Revan grinning. She couldn't believe what her grandmother just implied. To cover her irritation, she coughed and walked toward her apartment. *Former apartment*, she corrected herself. "I think I need something to drink. Gram, do you want anything? Rev, you?"

"Since it's after five, a healthy shot of whiskey would be nice. But put it in a water glass with a lot of ice. Your mom doesn't need to see me having a grand old time with my dear boy here," Gram Annie smirked at Revan.

"I can't let Gram Annie drink by herself. The same for me, please. But a little less ice," he said with a wink in Gram Annie's direction.

"How did the dance lesson with my girl go?" Gram Annie asked as soon as Naomi was out of earshot.

"Great. The Dancing Queen and her young Romeo were quite entertaining."

"I bet you're right. Madame Estelle—bless her heart—used to go by Miss Elly back in the sixties and seventies when my daughters took dance lessons, but maybe when you're an old spinster you have to make yourself more interesting by changing your name," she giggled. "But she could always dance. I saw her perform a few times and have to admit she was good."

"I was told we have at least one more lesson lined up with those comedians. Hopefully Alfredo will keep his hands to himself next time."

"Just send him the right message and hold hands with my granddaughter when you're walking in. Maybe he's bright enough to notice it."

"Well, I tried a similar tactic today."

"Maybe you haven't made it clear enough," Gram replied.

"What are you talking about?" Naomi asked as she joined them, carrying two whiskeys along with a glass of wine for herself. "Wait until you dance with Rev at Stella's wedding, Gram. He's not half as bad as I expected."

"It will be enough for me to watch you dance together. My old bones aren't for dancing anymore. But I want to discuss something with you. Come and sit with me."

She glanced up to the living room windows and took a sip of her whiskey. "Much better than the herbal teas your mother is forcing on me. Lisa means well, but the whiskey won't kill me, since the cancer is already taking care of that. Anyway...I have a favor to ask, my dear."

"Sure, whatever you want, Gram."

"I want to see my brother one more time before I meet my maker," she looked heavenward. "And since you're going to Charleston for the travel industry meeting, I thought you could bring Charlie with you on your way home. He'll be happy to get out of that old farts' home for a bit."

"It's an assisted living facility. Do you think he's well enough to travel?" Naomi asked.

"I haven't heard otherwise. I asked your Aunt Mary to talk to his sons about it. Mary offered to have him stay with her since she finally has a guest room with bathroom on the first floor. And when she makes house calls to her patients, she'll bring him over here to visit me."

"Seems as if you've figured it out. But I'm flying to Charleston. Is he okay with going on an airplane?"

"No. He said years ago that he doesn't trust airport security anymore and those young hotshot pilots even less."

Naomi laughed, "He's watching too much TV."

Gram Annie continued, "Besides, flying would be a hassle with all his medical equipment. You could take one of my cars and drive."

"Gram, honestly, it's easily ten to twelve hours each way without stops. I have tons of things to do here and wasn't planning to take any more time off than I need for the meeting."

"When's your meeting?" Gram looked straight at Naomi without showing any signs of illness or weakness.

"Thursday afternoon and most of Friday."

"Then you leave on Tuesday or Wednesday, stop somewhere nice in between, go to your meeting, then leave on Saturday, take your time again, and be back on Sunday," Gram Annie patted Naomi's leg. "It will do you good to get out."

"I just told you I can't take much time off."

Naomi noticed Revan's wide grin. He seemed to be enjoying the conversation. Now he asked, "Gram Annie, which of your cars are we talking about here? I know you have two sitting under tarps in the garage, and I don't see how Naomi will be able to get Charlie into either one. Not if his walker is going to make the trip with him."

"Good question, my dear boy," Gram Annie pinched her lips together and looked at Naomi. "As much as I love you, but I'm not loaning you the Porsche. Your grandfather was so proud when he bought it, but every time I see you driving your Volkswagen Beetle, I'm scared. I don't see how you can handle the Porsche."

"I told you I don't want to drive to Charleston," Naomi repeated with little hope that it would get through to Gram Annie this time, either.

At the same time Revan coughed and said, "No offense, ma'am, but... Are we talking about the Porsche 356B that only comes out once a year when a collector is knocking on your door? The one I've offered to buy how many times?"

"Don't you '*ma'am*' me, my sweet boy, and I've told you just as many times why I can't sell the car to you. My husband insisted it has to stay in the family. Whenever I took Lisa out in the car, people waved to us. Back in the 1960s, long before car seats," she looked at Naomi, "you should've seen your mother sitting on her knees so she'd be able to peek out. And after Mary was born in 1965, she came with us too, since they were able to squeeze into the back seat together. I just never told their father about our outings."

Gram Annie looked upward again. "Once we had our two girls, my husband insisted I drive something a little more... hmm, what did he call it? Oh yes, *family appropriate*...so he bought the Thunderbird Roadster. You could take that one, Naomi."

"How do you expect her to maneuver that albatross?" Rev asked.

"If I may say something..." Naomi interrupted. She had no desire to drive that old tank, but Gram and Rev were discussing this issue like she was totally incapable. "I see no problem driving it. If I'm only going straight ahead and don't make any turns, it'll be easy. There are plenty of Walmart stores along the way, and they have huge parking lots. Charlie and I can stop there, then shuffle in together to use the restrooms, get a coffee and a donut to go, and be on the road again."

"No!" Revan said. "Are you nuts?"

"No, my dear," Gram Annie said at the same time.

"Well, then we'll have to put Charlie on the train. I'm not sure how much he'll like it, but I can't change it," Naomi got up. "Be right back, speaking of bathrooms... I have to pee."

"Thanks for sharing, Nugget."

While Naomi was gone, Revan and Gram Annie sat in companionable silence. The dogs had finally settled down and rested under a tree—until a chipmunk entered their territory and they jumped up again to chase it.

Suddenly, Revan broke out in a big grin. "I think I have the solution, but Naomi might not like it."

"We don't give her a choice, then. What is your plan, my boy?" Gram's eyes sparkled with mischief.

"About what?" Naomi asked. She carried a glass of water for her grandmother. "Mom caught me and said to tell you you've had enough to drink. What plan were you talking about?"

"We take my new car. The Explorer is big and comfortable enough for Charlie and his walker, and even your suitcases fit easily in the trunk."

"What do you mean, *we*?" *What is he talking about?*

"How quickly you forget, Nugget! I told you I'm leaving on Monday for a job in South Carolina and Georgia. But I can wait until Tuesday and be your chauffeur. I can take care of my business in Charleston while you're at your meeting, and we'll pick up Charlie on Saturday. I'm not on a deadline and can switch a few things around. Besides, I have the whole summer to work on the project and can go back later to visit the other places on my list," he explained. "One of the advantages of freelance work."

Gram Annie smiled and held out both her hands to him. "Oh, you sweet boy, what a wonderful idea."

"Yeah, Shutterbug, *sweet boy*, it's indeed a wonderful idea," Naomi fumed. "Twelve hours in the car with you sounds a-ma-zing."

"Nugget, again you weren't paying attention. We're taking Gram Annie's suggestion to stop halfway for a night.

Maybe in Norfolk or Virginia Beach. I'm sure you can find us a motel."

She knew a road trip with Revan wasn't the smartest idea. But...on the other hand...it meant quality alone time with him...

She wanted to wipe the smirk off his face, but her hands were tied. Especially in front of Gram Annie, whose smile was similar to Revan's. Gram knew Naomi couldn't refuse her wish to see her brother again.

"Why don't we discuss our little adventure over the dinner you insisted I'm treating you to? Where do you want to go?"

"I've made reservations for seven thirty at Clarke's, even though I kind of regret it now," she said with a pout.

His loud laughter was answer enough. "You've made reservations? You must've been mighty sure."

"Shut up," she said through her teeth.

"Where are your manners? This sweet boy just saved us and is going to fulfill one of my last wishes," Gram said and smiled at him again. "Naomi, give me a copy of the reservations and I'll take care of the bills. I'm old-fashioned, so make sure to print out the information, including address, phone numbers, and room descriptions. Make one for the way home, too. Charlie will appreciate it if he doesn't have to sit in a car for too long."

"Nugget, look for something in Richmond on the way back. With Charlie, we'll take the direct way home, even if it means going through DC. But, Gram Annie, I'll pay for my own room."

"I don't think so, sweet boy. You're doing me a huge favor, and this is not up for discussion," Gram patted his cheek.

"Yes, Gram. Thank you, Gram," Naomi kissed her grandmother and beckoned for Rev to follow her. "Bye, Gram."

She didn't want to hear her grandmother calling Revan *sweet boy* even one more time.

But worse, she had a sinking feeling she'd just been played.

CHAPTER 12

Revan—June 2019

On Tuesday morning, as soon as they were out of Philadelphia, Naomi reached behind the driver's seat and pulled a huge, fat binder out of one of the many bags she brought along.

"What have you got there?" Revan asked after a sideways glance.

"My binder with wedding preparations, of course. I hardly see you at home, and since we have at least five hours till Virginia Beach, I thought we could discuss the twofer party."

"The *what* party?"

"I'm sure you've heard about Jack and Jill parties—at least I hope so. In case you haven't, it means that instead of having separate bachelor and bachelorette parties, the happy couple combines them and celebrates together."

"Is there a short version?" Revan kept his eyes on the traffic but was fully aware of Naomi sitting so close. His right elbow and forearm occasionally touched her arm on the console between their seats. Every nerve ending in his body was on edge, and a lengthy explanation about party protocol was something he wasn't even remotely interested in hearing about. Unfortunately, Naomi had other plans.

"But normally Jack and Jill parties are intended to raise money to help pay for the wedding or the honeymoon. Since Stella and David don't need any cash donations toward whatever, theirs is called a co-ed Bachelor and Bachelorette party."

Looking to the right before changing lanes, he saw her lips touch the rim of her thermal mug. She sipped slowly and continued, "I thought we'd call it a 'twofer party.' Doesn't sound as stupid, right? You can use finger signals so you don't have to say it out loud every time." She juggled the mug, then held up two fingers on her left hand and one on her right hand.

"Yeah, much better," Rev said. "And what do you mean by 'every time?' I'm not planning to spend a lot of time on the subject. We'll call an event planner and let them deal with it."

"Huh? Two of our best friends are taking a life-altering step, and you want to hand over all control to a stranger? Oh no, Shutterbug, it's our responsibility to plan every-thing down to the last detail. If you're uncertain about your duties, ask me," she said and flipped through pages in her

94

binder. "And imagine...one day soon they're going to ask us to be the godparents of their first baby! How much fun will the baby shower be to plan?"

He almost drove into the guardrail on the side of the road. "Why would they ask *us*?"

"Is there anybody else?" She leaned forward, pretty much blocking his view, and shook her head. "Think, Revan. Oh, I can see it already."

For the next sixty minutes, he half-listened to Naomi debating the advantages and disadvantages of tea lights versus votive candles, and real candles versus flameless candles. He tried to make appropriate noises every so often to signal he was paying attention. And, more importantly, he nodded his agreement to everything she suggested.

Two hours after leaving his house, he was seriously second-guessing his offer to drive her to Charleston. Seeing the exit to Rehoboth Beach in Delaware, his fingers twitched to flip the turn signal. He glanced at the navigation system...at least three more hours to go.

After pulling over at a rest stop so they could grab a sandwich and use the facilities, he took his time washing his hands. The noise from several electric hand dryers had a soothing effect on him.

Once back on the road, he was grateful when the next hour went by without him having to make any earth-shattering decisions, until Naomi said, "Oh, we haven't talked about what color candles we want," and flipped back to the respective tab in her binder. "White, off-white, ivory, or cream?"

"White, unscented," Rev growled. He thought of the hand dryer and imagined its noise. It was likely to become his Zen place before this trip was over.

"You're a genius. We haven't discussed scented versus unscented. Thank you for bringing it up."

"And we won't. Let's talk about something else, please." He couldn't believe it. They had talked for at least two hours now about fucking candles! No, not *they*—*she* had.

Naomi sighed and reached for another file separator in her binder-from-hell. She pulled out a round plastic object and waved it in front of him.

"Get that out of my face. I'm driving."

Surprisingly, Naomi complied and was quiet for a few minutes. Unused to her silence, he glanced to his right. Her left foot was on the seat while she held the plastic thing over it.

"What are you doing?" he asked, against his better judgment.

"Have you never seen a nail polish color wheel?" she waved it in front of him again.

All he could see were shades of red—a lot of them.

"Look, Shutterbug, it has eighteen artificial nails. And each one is painted a different shade of red. Wanna hear the names?"—*no, I don't!*—"There's Scarlet, Imperial Red, Spanish Red, Carmine, Ruby, Crimson, Rusty Red, Red Cosmos, Cardinal Red, Chili Red, Fire Brick, Redwood, Dark Red, Maroon, Barn Red, and Vermillion." Instead of turning the plastic wheel, she tilted her head while reading the names. She probably turned maps in the direction she was going, too.

"And the last two are called Blood Red and Lust."

Now there was a color name he could've done without...

"If I can't decide which shade I want to get at my next pedi, I play with the little wheel and hold the color samples over my toes." She demonstrated it while she babbled on.

"But there's only red on this one. I've seen you wearing other colors." *Shoot.* Why did he admit to checking out her nail polish?

"Yes, well observed, Sherlock, but for the wedding, I'm wearing red...I think. Maybe I'll change my mind. I haven't bought my dresses yet. And of course I have more of those color wheels at home."

Dresses. Revan heard the plural loud and clear, and prayed to the gods of sanity that his input wasn't needed for those decisions. He glanced at the time. Still another hour to drive.

As soon as they got to the hotel, he would go for a run, then go to the pool, followed by a double whiskey. At some point they'd have to get something to eat. Hopefully their dinner conversation wouldn't revolve around candles or eighteen shades of red.

"Rev, do you mind if I charge my phone?"

"No, go ahead," he pointed to the USB port.

As soon as she hooked up her phone and his car's stereo system connected to it, a painfully familiar song from her play list came on, bringing back memories of their dance lesson and the cha-cha. Memories of her body against his. Of holding her in his arms.

Why again did I offer to drive her?

97

He should have let Naomi drive in her little tin can. Or better, he could have offered to pick up Gram Annie's brother himself on his way back to Philly. But no, he had to go ahead and create this mess. Although Naomi didn't seem to consider it a mess. She seemed totally content to sit in his car, listening to music and looking out the window. At least she was quiet—for now.

When he finally pulled into the wide parking area of the hotel in Virginia Beach, he was at the end of his patience. All he wanted was some time by himself to regroup.

As he pulled the first of their bags out of the trunk, he looked around. Their hotel turned out to be a sprawling Inn & Spa resembling a Colonial mansion. He had to give her credit for picking it. It was a gorgeous building and the setting was beautiful.

After checking in, they went to their rooms. "Oh, nice, our rooms are next to each other," Naomi said while she pulled her suitcase into her room. "We can send each other signals through the wall. One knock for hello, two knocks for good night, three knocks for good morning."

"I'm not sending anything," Rev grumbled. "Do you need help with your luggage? There are still two suitcases in the car."

"No, those are my clothes for Charleston and for the way home. They can stay in the car," she answered. "I'm color-coding my luggage, didn't you notice? The ones with flowers are for the first part of the trip, the ones without for the return trip."

"Don't travel agents usually pack lightly?" Rev asked. "One suitcase, one carry-on?"

"Well, I need several pairs of shoes of course, and nightshirts, and all the other stuff. So what are we doing now? We have a few hours to kill till dinner. Did you see the restaurant downstairs? We can eat there."

"I'm going for a walk, then for a swim," he said, no longer in the mood for a run or finding the gym. As long as there was a glass of whiskey waiting for him at the end of whatever he ended up doing.

"Pool sounds good, I'll meet you there," she said and closed the door in his face.

After changing into running shorts that doubled as swimwear and a T-shirt, he pulled out his camera and searched through the camera bag for his macro lens, then attached a polarizing filter and was set.

As he meandered through low-cut boxwood hedges, he began to relax and admire the well-manicured English garden. In the distance he saw a gazebo being readied for a wedding, with people arranging chairs and flower decorations.

By the time he arrived at the outdoor pool area an hour later, he wondered whether Naomi had saved a lounge for him.

Carrying his camera bag in his hand, he searched for her.

And almost dropped the bag.

Sitting in a lounge chair, she wore a black one-piece bathing suit with a halter top and an oversized black-and-white sun hat. He watched as she produced sunscreen lotion from her enormous beach bag—*who brings a beach bag on a road trip?*—and squeezed a generous amount into her hand, then slid up and down first one leg, then the other, taking extra time to apply lotion between her toes.

At least she's wearing a decent bathing suit.

Revan couldn't stand here any longer, he had to get in the water. He was sweating, and not because of the heat and his walk. His newfound inner calm was a thing of the past.

"There you are, Shutterbug, perfect timing! Would you mind putting sunscreen on my back? I wanna make sure to be equally tanned front and back."

"Then sit in the shade, Nugget."

"It's not the same. And I would still need sunscreen. Pleeaassee, Rev. Look, I saved you a lounge."

"Okay, give me the bottle." He put his camera bag under the lounge next to hers.

"Ready when you are!" Flat on her stomach, head resting on her folded forearms, she wiggled her shoulders and said, "Don't miss a spot."

Revan massaged globs of sunscreen into her shoulders and her back, trying to ignore how the contact with her skin affected him.

Until his fingertips grazed the sides of her full breasts.

He couldn't pull away.

This would be the first and the last time he ever touched her there. And because he knew it, he took his time massaging in the last bit of lotion.

"All done, Nugget," he wiped his hands on a towel, then pulled his shirt over his head and tossed it on his lounge. On the way to the pool, he grabbed a pool noodle.

There was no time to use the outdoor shower first. He needed to float for a long, long time. He didn't dare look over to where Naomi sunbathed, blissfully unaware of the battle raging within him.

CHAPTER 13

NAOMI—JUNE 2019

Face down on her lounge, Naomi closed her eyes and tried to take a few deep breaths, but all she managed were irregular puffs.

Her cousin Jo was into all the mind-body mumbo-jumbo and would tell her to pick an object to focus on. What should she envision?

The only mental picture she got was of Revan's hands sliding over her back and accidentally touching the soft side of her breast. Naomi had wanted to roll over and pull him down to her, to whisper in his ear where else she'd like to feel his hands.

Reaching into her beach bag, she blindly searched for her cell phone. She needed to text Stella. But what was she going to tell her? *Rev just put sunscreen on my back and ran away. Now he's in the pool.*

She tossed the phone back and stifled a frustrated scream. This couldn't go on much longer. At some point she had to talk to Revan about this new weirdness between them. Was it only her, or did he feel it too?

But not today, and not on this trip. They were still stuck spending a few more days in each other's company, and Naomi didn't want it to become even more awkward.

Wait a minute... she didn't have to stay with him. She could rent a car big enough to fit Charlie's equipment and drive him back with her. Then Revan could finish his job in the South as he'd planned.

The last thing she wanted was to be a burden to him. She'd tell him at dinner.

Naomi got up and dropped her sunscreen in her beach bag. Walking along the pool, she called out, "Rev, I'm going to my room to shower. Want to meet for drinks at six thirty?"

Without looking, he flashed a thumbs-up.

Standing under her shower, she switched back and forth between the gentle rain setting to the power massage function until she could feel some of her tension draining away. After toweling off, she applied the complimentary citrus-scented body lotion on her arms and legs, put on a black maxi dress, slid into black flip-flops, and pulled her hair up into a messy bun.

Before meeting Rev for drinks and dinner, she wanted to walk in the garden. What she needed was a plan.

The crushed shells and small stones covering narrow paths through a low-growing labyrinth of hedges made crunching sounds under her feet, and a wedding ceremony was taking place in a gazebo.

Naomi sat on a bench and listened to the voices and soft music drifting over to her. In less than three months, Stella would walk down a similar aisle to marry David, and Naomi wanted to make her best friend's wedding as beautiful and unforgettable as possible. Stella had hired the event manager at the venue Naomi suggested, but as maid of honor, she had some influence over a few details.

She watched the ceremony. Besides the bride and groom, the maid of honor and the best man were standing in the front, as was usual, flanked by the rest of the brides-maids and groomsmen.

One of the groomsmen signaled and winked to someone sitting among the guests. She hoped David's groomsmen had better manners than this guy.

Oh, no! What if Revan brought someone to the wedding?

If he brought a plus-one, she'd have to make sure she wasn't there by herself. Should she call Frank and ask him to accompany her? They had a friendly parting of the ways. No...with her luck, he'd drop out at the last minute or simply not show up. And then she'd really be screwed.

She needed to bring up the issue with Revan directly. And—unlike the other *issue*—this question couldn't wait until later. At least it would make for an interesting dinner conversation.

Actually, let's give this a little twist! An idea began to take shape...

She checked the time on her phone. Just enough time to run back to the room and grab her purse before she met Rev. Naomi felt pleasantly revived—she was on a mission.

Five minutes later, in her room, she debated where she should wait for him. Her eyes fell on the connecting door between their rooms. Without thinking, she pushed down on the door handle.

Oops! Maybe she should have at least knocked before she opened it?

Revan came out of his bathroom, wearing a pair of dark jeans, but no shirt. The jeans were unbuttoned and hung low on his hips, showing the waistband of his gray boxer briefs. He rubbed a towel over his wet hair and looked up.

Their eyes met.

Naomi could only stare, couldn't even manage to apologize for barging in.

"I...I wanted..." she stuttered when Rev tossed his towel on the floor and crossed the room to stand in front of her.

"Do you always show up in men's rooms uninvited, Nugget?"

"I... No..." All she could think of was running her hands over his chest and then letting them trail down.

His eyes bored into hers, the green turning darker. A sign she began to recognize as annoyance and something else she couldn't name.

"I..." she began again.

It was embarrassing, how she just stood here, stuttering and staring. No wonder he didn't think of her as desirable.

She wanted to disappear into her room, lock the door behind her, and forget the past few minutes.

Before she could turn away, he touched her arm and asked in a hoarse voice, "What did you want, Nugget?"

"I...I wanted t-to see...if the...door...is l-locked."

"And aren't you glad to have the answer to the mystery?"

"Did you ask the hotel to unlock it?" her voice got stronger again. "Shutterbug, don't tell me you had dirty plans for tonight!"

He looked at her hard, his expression unreadable. "No, I didn't have anything to do with the door. But if I had plans to visit you in the middle of the night, a locked door wouldn't keep me out."

She giggled, "Ooh, are you channeling your inner Rhett Butler? I'm surprised you know that detail. Did you watch the movie or actually read the book?"

"Unfortunately, I had to suffer through the movie," he muttered.

"Hmm, but tell me, who would I be to you? Scarlett O'Hara or Belle Watling? The one who Rhett wants more than anything, or the one who's his loyal, forever friend?"

Naomi didn't wait for him to answer her hypothetical question but saw him flinch. She pulled her arm out of his hand, "I'm ready for a drink whenever you're dressed, Shutterbug. Meet me in the bar."

Closing the door behind her, she walked through her room. Still rolling up the sleeves of his button-down shirt, Revan came out of his room at the same time she left hers. His door slammed shut, like thunder rolling in.

"All dressed up?" Naomi asked him while they waited for the elevator. "Have plans for later?"

"Yup, I have a date with a glass of whiskey. Can't hurt to look decent."

She waved her hand at his untucked shirt. "You've got a very classy look going. Need help tucking it in?"

"I can manage without your assistance. Thanks for offering to help, though."

"It's what friends do."

As soon as they stepped inside the elevator, Rev said, "Turn around."

"Excuse me?"

"I want to tuck in my shirt but can't do it while you're watching."

"Then why didn't you finish dressing in your room?"

"After your surprise visit, I thought I'd better hurry. Now turn around."

"Nothing I haven't seen before," Naomi said, but complied.

"Not mine. Why are we even having his conversation?"

The elevator bell *dinged*, announcing their arrival on the first floor. "Are you decent, or do you need to hide behind me?" she quipped.

He took her elbow and said, "Let's go."

They settled on two chairs at the bar and ordered their drinks. For a while, Revan stared at one of the wall-mounted TVs while Naomi poured nuts from a complimentary bowl on a napkin and sorted them by size, popping one in her mouth every now and then, washing it down with a sip of wine.

When her glass was almost empty, she said, "Can I ask you something?"

"Sure."

"You're a man, right?" She made a show of picking out a peanut and tossing it into her mouth.

"I hope that's not the question," he raised an eyebrow.

She ignored him.

"I'm in this...situation, and I'm stuck at an impasse."

"Are you in trouble?" Now Revan was on full alert.

"No, not in trouble, but there's something I've been struggling with. For a long time. And I simply don't know what to do about it," she looked at him while she ate half a walnut, "and since we're sitting here, two old friends chatting nicely, I thought I'd ask you—"

"Just say it," he interrupted her.

"Okay, well... I've kinda been in love with a guy for a pretty long time." Naomi drew out the sentence, then popped another peanut.

"Wait, are you asking me for dating advice?" he looked at her closely.

Naomi didn't answer as she went on, "But he doesn't know it, and he doesn't seem to see me."

Peanut...pop.

"Why not? What's wrong with him?" Revan snatched her cocktail napkin and discarded it, including the remaining nuts.

Naomi threw her hands in the air, "See, I've been asking myself the same question. The other question is, should

I do something to make him notice me, or wait until he wakes up from his stupor? Which could be...never."

"Do I know him?"

"You may have seen him once or twice." *As in, every time you look in the mirror.*

"Want me to talk to him?"

"Thanks for the offer, but he wouldn't listen to you. He's very stubborn."

"He sounds like a dumbo."

"I know! But he really isn't. Anyhow, until I decide what to do about him, I thought I'd sign up with Tinder."

Revan slammed his hand on the counter. "Are you out of your mind? What did you just say?"

Naomi shrugged and pushed her hair behind her ears. "Maybe they'll be able to pair me with someone who's looking for something more serious than a little bit of fun in the sack. Don't they match character traits and all that stuff?"

"Nugget, who do you think the guys who rely on a dating service to find a girlfriend are?"

She pursed her lips and pretended to think. "I guess I'll find out."

"You and Frank just broke up. Are you sure you don't need time to get over him?"

Naomi noticed how Revan's forehead veins began to show again.

"I'm over him. I always knew he wouldn't stick around."

"Plus, right now you're busy with the wedding planning stuff. You don't have time to meet other men."

Naomi wanted to laugh but kept her poker face in place.

"It might come as a surprise to you, but I can concentrate on more than one thing at the same time. And imagine that, now I remembered one more thing we need to discuss."

Revan pierced her with a questioning look. "Not sure I wanna hear it. But let me tell you one thing. Forget about Tinder. You might as well delete your account right away."

"Yeah, well, sorry. But, as you told me a few weeks ago, I'm neither your mother nor your wife. And, likewise, you are neither my father, husband, nor brother," she put extra emphasis on the word *brother*, "and therefore I can do whatever I like."

She raised her eyebrows and silently challenged him, *what are you gonna say now?*

CHAPTER 14

─◦◦◦◦◦─

REVAN—JUNE 2019

R evan didn't pay attention to the layout or décor of the restaurant. He blindly followed the hostess to a table near the windows and buried his face in the menu.

When the waitress came to take their orders, Naomi said, "I'll have the burger with sautéed mushrooms and onions and fries. Thank you. Oh, I'd like the burger well done, please."

"The ribeye steak for me, medium, and I'd like a baked potato with it." Revan ordered the first item he saw, then looked at the wine list. "Naomi, how about some wine?"

"Sure. You pick."

"Bring us a bottle of the Australian Shiraz. Thanks." He closed the wine list and menu and gave both to the waitress.

"So, anything else we have to discuss? No, wait, let me guess…it's either the color of the napkins for the party, whether they have to be cloth or paper, which way they are to be folded, or whether we have to prepare small bags with party favors."

"Revan Forrester, what did I do wrong to be forced to work with you on that kind of thing?" she shook her head. "But the damage is done, and those are really good points. Thanks for bringing them to my attention. Especially the party favors."

"How about I let you make those decisions? I'm responsible for getting a playlist together for the music, and you're responsible for the really important things." He leaned back in his chair.

"No, we have to do it together. But you may take care of the music. I'm delegating it to you. Since you insist on it," she smiled. "But here's something I really need to know. Are you bringing someone with you?"

"Like who?" He had no idea where she was going with this. "There'll be plenty of people to talk to."

"Shutterbug…try to follow me. If you are bringing a lady friend, I have to ask someone to accompany me, too. I can't show up all by myself. And if Tinder doesn't produce a decent guy, I might have to ask Frank to be my guest."

"You can't expect him to neglect his new clients. What if one of the athletes needs a shoulder massage and he's not available? I can't imagine," Rev smirked. "Did you have anybody in mind whom you'd like to see by my side?"

"Not really. But Barbie would probably love to come along."

"If I didn't know better, I'd say you're jealous, Nugget. How many times do I have to tell you, I'm working with Barb, nothing else?"

"And how many times do I need to tell you she might have other plans for your *collaboration*?" Naomi made air quotes with her fingers, then put her forearms on the table and leaned over her arms, pushing her breasts up just enough to make him stare at them.

She copied something Barb had indeed done more than once in front of him. Something he never honored with a second look because he didn't think of her in a sexual way. Naomi, on the other hand, was different. Her breasts were perfect, full without being...

He shifted in his chair and said, "Well, back to your question. Right now, I don't plan to bring anyone, if that's what you want to hear."

"It's exactly what I want to hear, so I won't be looking for a plus-one either. I'll keep you company, then."

"I'm sure we can manage somehow, Nugget."

Later in the evening, Revan sat by the window in his room and looked out over the garden, recalling Naomi's comments about Tinder and the mysterious guy she was in love with.

He wanted to know who the man was. Could it be someone who was happily married and therefore not interested in her? But no, she didn't say he was married. She said she'd known him for a long time, but he never noticed her. Maybe he played on the other team? He knew a few women who had secret crushes on gay men. Naomi also hadn't said anything about whether she was still in touch with the man or not.

Who could it be?

She said I've seen him once or twice. But when and where?

Nobody came to mind. He'd ask her again tomorrow for the guy's name. And maybe he would call him secretly and set them up on a blind date. The idea rubbed him the wrong way, but it was at least a little better than Tinder. What had possessed her to sign up with them?

Should he check out her profile? The thought of Naomi on a date with some other guy bothered him.

Revan had no idea what to do about her. He was at a point where thoughts of her consumed every hour of the day, and a good portion of the night, too.

For a while now, he'd been hesitant about even greeting her in their usual way, with a quick peck on the cheek. He felt a powerful urge to pull her into his arms and not let her go. And to kiss her for real. But kissing her was one of the invisible lines between them.

And the first line was as important as the others.

Applying the damn sunscreen lotion this afternoon had set off a major inner battle. With any other woman, it was a mechanical, natural action, but with her, it had turned into not-so innocent foreplay and stimulated far more than just his fingertips.

The air coming in through the open window was mild. Too bad they weren't closer to the beach. If it wasn't almost nine, he'd suggest driving there for a walk. But he knew it was a twenty-minute drive each way.

He could ask her if she wanted to go for a late evening stroll in the garden.

Instead of running away and avoiding her, maybe he should try to find out what would happen if he touched her hand while they walked next to each other. Revan rubbed his neck.

Man, I've got it worse than a kid who's trying to work up the courage to kiss a girl for the first time.

Somewhere not too far away, music played softly. Rev stood up and leaned over the windowsill. "Sweet Dreams" floated out of the open window next to his. Her room!

Listening to a Eurythmics song for the third time in a week, all connected to Naomi, was a little too much of a coincidence.

Taking a few long strides, he reached the door between their rooms and stopped. He wouldn't barge in as she had done earlier.

He grinned at the memory of the moment. The look on her face was priceless when she saw him coming out of the bathroom. She seemed shocked to see him only half-dressed, and he couldn't deny the satisfaction of watching her trying to retreat to her own room in embarrassment.

He knocked once, then opened the door.

"Okay, see you tomorrow evening at eight. I'm sure we'll have a lot to talk about. Bye, Marcus." Naomi tossed her phone on the bed next to where she lay on her stomach.

Revan didn't need to hear one more word. He backed up into his room, grabbed his keycard and iPhone, and pulled his sneakers on. He'd tie them once he was out of here.

"Did you need something, Shutterbug?" Naomi asked from the open door. She was barefoot, with slightly tousled hair, still in the dress she wore for dinner, and the light behind her accentuated her body.

"Yeah, fresh air. You better leave me alone," Revan said through his teeth and left his room. He didn't wait for the elevator, instead taking the stairs and speed-walking out into the evening.

The air was fragrant with the mingled scents of roses and lavender, but he didn't want to be plagued by that kind of fragrant stimulant right now. A pile of cow manure would've been a better match for his mood.

Laughter from the gazebo reached him, and soft classical music came through outdoor speakers lining the stone paths in the garden. The speakers doubled as outdoor lighting and dimly illuminated the hedges and paths.

He couldn't believe it... It was a tie who he was madder at—her for talking to some guy and making plans for the next day, or himself for wanting to join her on her bed and peel that tempting dress off her.

"What do you think you're doing?" Naomi's angry voice came from somewhere behind him. Revan hadn't even heard her footsteps on the stone and gravel path. "You barge into my room, then run out and tell me to get out of your face?"

"Go back, Naomi. I really need to be alone right now." It was impossible for him to talk to her. He shouldn't be surprised that she followed him, though. She'd never been one to avoid a confrontation. But for the first time, he was on the receiving end of her wrath.

"Not until I know what's going on." She reached for his arm and pulled on it.

Seriously???

He whipped around. "What's going on? Come on, you really have to ask?"

"Rev, listen…"

"No, you listen to me! Our plan was to visit your uncle, great-uncle, or whatever Charlie is, after arriving in Charleston tomorrow. To let him know we're there and to talk about Saturday with him. I thought we're doing this together. Instead, you turn around and make dinner plans with some jerk? I don't care whether I'm eating by myself, but I expect to be treated with some respect."

Revan was furious. He stepped closer to Naomi, but then turned his back on her again. If she so much as looked at him with her big eyes, his paper-thin defenses would crumple, and he didn't know what he'd do next.

Through gritted teeth he said, "Go back to your room. We'll meet tomorrow at eight thirty in the lobby. Make sure you've had breakfast by then." He turned and strode away.

"Oh no, no, no, you are not dismissing me this way." Naomi caught up with him and poked his shoulder with a finger. "Look at me when I'm talking to you."

It was more than he could take. He spun around and hissed, "Don't. Touch. Me."

She stood too close to him. As if the force of his barely-contained anger whipped up the air around them and unleashed its fury, Naomi stumbled while trying to back away from him.

His hand shot out. The only way to steady her was to pull her against his chest and wrap both arms around her.

His heart was beating at twice its normal rate, and he could feel hers trying to catch up with his. She was breathing heavily, her breasts swelling against him with every intake of air. He buried his face in her hair and inhaled her heady scent, tightening his hold on her.

He wanted to kiss her so badly it hurt. His body craved hers so powerfully, getting his heart ripped out alive couldn't have been more painful. One kiss—if only he could allow himself one kiss.

Her hand gripped the front of his shirt, making a fist.

They stood motionless under the clear night sky, not hearing the songs of the crickets and frogs, not seeing the moon or stars shining above them.

She pushed away and started to walk to the main house, then stopped. Without looking at him, she said, "By the way, I was on the phone with one of Charlie's sons. Marcus called me to invite us for dinner tomorrow evening to fill us in on his father's medical situation."

CHAPTER 15

NAOMI—JUNE 2019

As soon as Naomi walked through the lobby to get a cup of coffee and check out the choices at the continental breakfast buffet, she spotted Revan sitting at a table reading a newspaper and drinking his coffee. A plate with only crumbs and a banana peel sat to his left.

She put a pastry on a plate and filled a mug with steaming coffee and joined him. "Good morning."

"Nugget, good morning, come and sit down. We don't want you spilling the coffee on your pretty shirt."

Naomi didn't need to ask him how his night was. He looked as tired as she felt.

All night long, she replayed the evening's events in an endless loop. First, she told him her fib about signing up with Tinder. Then he came into her room, only to retreat as if he'd caught her *in flagrante delicto*. Which made her—almost—laugh.

But his reaction in the garden, when he acted like a jackass, was anything but funny. Especially when he pulled her into his arms and she thought he was going to kiss her.

At that point, she had no choice but to break their connection. Who wants to kiss someone when you're spitting mad at them? As much as she longed for him to kiss her, she'd be damned if she'd let him steamroll over her.

She sat down across from him and picked up her pastry. "How long is our drive today?" she asked before taking a bite.

"About seven hours. If we don't take too many breaks, we should arrive around four in the afternoon." He folded the newspaper and set it aside.

"Do you want me to drive for a bit? You did all the driving yesterday."

"No, I don't mind driving, and down here they have express lanes that should allow us to breeze through."

"Okay, let's get back on the road then! I have to get my bags from the room and check out, but it won't take long." She wrapped the rest of her pastry in a napkin.

"Mine are already in the car, so I'll meet you there. And don't forget to refill your coffee. It'll make for one less stop along the way."

Once they were on the road, Naomi noticed Revan didn't put his elbow on the armrest between their seats the way he did yesterday. He was talking as if their argument hadn't happened, but he avoided touching her. It promised to be a long seven hours. She needed to break the ice, to keep him talking, to figure out where they stood.

"You know, Shutterbug, there's not much time, but maybe we can do some sightseeing in Charleston after I get out of my conference on Friday afternoon."

"Yeah, sounds good. I'm sure you'll find something that interests you."

She took out her cell phone and, after a short Google search, said, "How about Magnolia Plantation? It's about thirty minutes outside of Charleston."

"Tell me more about it," Revan said without taking his eyes off the road.

"Their website says it was founded in the 1670s along the Ashley River by the Drayton family, who became immensely rich through the cultivation of rice during the Colonial era. Later, the American Civil War threatened the welfare of the plantation. But it recovered, and in 1870 the family opened their gardens to the public. It's the oldest public garden in America and has lots of magnolia trees, rhododendrons, and azaleas." She put her phone down.

"Doesn't *Gone with the Wind* take place during the Civil War?" Naomi could tell he tried to suppress a smile. "What's so funny?

"You and history, Nugget. A match made in heaven. Yes, it does. And Magnolia Plantation sounds like an interesting place."

123

Naomi rubbed her hands together and said, "I can't wait. Can you bring your camera and take pictures of me in front of the house? I hope it has a wide porch and a staircase, like Tara. I'll wear my black-and-white sun hat."

Revan laughed, "I think I can arrange it."

Then another thought from her restless night came back.

"Oh, forget about it," she put her phone away and looked out the window. "I don't think we can go there together."

"Why not? It sounds like the perfect thing to do."

"Well, I just remembered something. You really don't have to stay in Charleston because of Charlie and me. After last night, I thought you'd like to be able to do your stuff without having to drive us." She couldn't look at him, and instead fiddled with the hem of her shirt.

"Wait a minute..." he started to say, but she interrupted him.

"No, I think it's best if I rent a car and you and I part ways this afternoon. I'll see you back at"—she swallowed—"at home."

"Not happening, Nugget. I offered to drive you, and I will. I'm sorry about the way I went off, and I think we need to talk about a few things, but not while we're on this trip."

Naomi nodded, but then another thought hit her. "Rev, do you want me to move out of your house when we're back in Philly? I don't think this living together is working out so great for us."

When he didn't answer right away, she thought he hadn't heard her. She was surprised when he pulled the car over, flipped on the emergency flashers, and shut off the engine.

He turned in his seat and said, "Don't *ever* ask me about it again. I said you can live there until your apartment is available again, and I hope it's going to be a long time, because I want Gram Annie to live as long as possible."

He rubbed his neck, something he seemed to be doing a lot when he was talking to her.

"I never go back on my promises. After I drop you and Charlie off on Sunday, I'll stay for a day or two and then head back south."

"How long will you be gone?" she asked quietly.

"Maybe eight to ten days." He looked at her with the lopsided smile she loved so much. "I won't forget my presence is required for another dance lesson and there are important decisions to be made, like the color of my tie for the whatever party."

Naomi laughed, "You're right, Shutterbug! Big decisions are waiting to be made. And it's called the twofer party."

Thank goodness they'd somewhat cleared the air and found their way back to slightly more familiar ground.

They checked in at the hotel and, after dropping off the luggage in their rooms, which weren't on the same floor this time, they drove to the assisted living facility.

When she called ahead earlier, she was assured they could simply show up and Charlie would most likely be in his room.

The frail man who shuffled behind a walker wasn't who Naomi had expected, but she hadn't seen Gram Annie's brother for almost ten years. At least he tried to remain mobile and independent, something he had in common with his sister.

"Hello, Uncle Charlie, I'm so glad to see you. Gram says you're excited about this trip," she greeted him and leaned in to kiss his leathery cheek. "Do you remember my friend Revan?"

"Yes, of course I do. We met at Annie's eightieth birthday and discussed his documentary about Vietnam. Glad I didn't have to go there."

The men shook hands.

"So, how are you doing here? This looks nice." She looked around Charlie's small one-bedroom suite, complete with a kitchenette and bathroom and the lovely view of a river and some marshland.

"Yes, it is a nice place. And Helen doesn't have to worry about me being alone when she and Marcus are traveling. I'd like to offer you coffee or tea, but would you mind making it yourself? By the time I get to the kitchen it would be dark and time for other beverages," Charlie chuckled. He went to a recliner and sat down, using both armrests to lower himself slowly.

"I'll have a cup of coffee, thank you. Rev, anything for you? And you, Uncle Charlie?"

"Only water, thanks," Revan answered, and Charlie said he'd like a cup of tea, "with a dash of something else."

"You're just like Gram. I'll see what I can find," Naomi laughed.

"Try the bottom cabinet next to the fridge," Charlie advised her.

Leaving the two men alone, she went to the kitchenette, where she put a pod in the coffee machine and checked the cabinets for mugs and an electric kettle to heat water for the tea. She didn't know if Charlie liked his tea with sugar, milk, or lemon and decided to put everything on a small tray.

After she located his secret stash of whiskey, she poured a small amount in a shot glass, and opened a tin of cookies, which she added to the tray.

As she put the beverages on the coffee table, Charlie looked at Revan and said, "Sir, I have to ask, what are your intentions with Annie?"

"I enjoy her company, and she's a lot of fun to talk to," Revan answered.

Charlie waved his shaky hand, dotted with age spots, at Naomi and said to Rev, "You and my sister seem to know each other well, but I've never heard her mention your name."

Naomi opened her mouth to remind him about meeting Revan a few years ago, but Rev shook his head and motioned surreptitiously for her to sit down next to him.

Charlie went on, "I understand we live in a time where women demand more independence, but in my father's absence, I expect you to be honorable toward my sister."

Then he looked directly at Naomi and said, "I know you're a few years older than I am, Annie, but I'm still your brother, and I'm looking out for you. Always."

Naomi squeezed her lips together. She wanted to laugh out loud. Now she had two "brothers" watching over her.

Marcus and Helen's Greek Revival-era house was located in a desirable neighborhood of Charleston, where many elegant historic homes were within easy walking distance of shops and restaurants. It was narrow but deep, and had only two windows on each floor facing the street, and the typical double piazza on the long side, like so many homes in the South.

Built of solid brick, it was painted in a color neither pink nor orange nor red. Naomi thought in any other city it would've looked ridiculous, but here it fit right in. Inside, original details like heart pine floors and rooms painted in period-color shades such as deep red, blue, and yellow completed the charm.

Helen said to Naomi, "I don't think we've ever met. You and Marcus are first cousins once removed...or something"—she laughed—"but I don't think there were any family events where we were all invited. It's a pleasure to finally meet you, and you as well, Revan." Both Helen and Marcus spoke with a typical Southern drawl. It sounded charming, and Naomi liked it. She noticed it a little bit when Charlie spoke, and even Gram Annie occasionally fell back into it.

For the next two hours they exchanged stories about their work and families. Naomi didn't fully understand what Marcus did for work—it sounded as if he was some big shot consulting engineer at Boeing—and Helen was happy being a homemaker and, until recently, Charlie's caregiver.

Helen said, "We loved having my father-in-law living with us, and he was never a burden, but when he wasn't able to master the stairs anymore and the dementia became more pronounced, we knew it was in his best interest to move him into the new assisted living facility. Hopefully he has many more years to live and will always feel comfortable there. We hear he's quite the ladies' man and prefers to sit with a certain female resident at teatime."

Revan laughed and said, "We already had the pleasure of experiencing his protective side today. He mistook Naomi for his sister and made it clear that he's watching me." He winked at Naomi.

Marcus shook his head, "I'm so sorry. I hope he'll behave when he's traveling with you. He only means well."

Revan waved it off and said, "We're grateful for all the input you can give us. The last thing we want is to upset him unnecessarily."

"He's taking medication for the dementia, and it helps when you play along for a bit. Don't try to correct him. Then let him rest and he comes out of it again. If you have room in the car, we suggest you bring his wheelchair along, even though he likes to walk with the help of his walker or a cane. But the wheelchair makes it easier to get moving, especially if you're pressured for time or the weather is bad," Marcus suggested.

"We'll bring it with us. We have enough room for everything he needs," Revan assured them.

Helen said, "From what I understand, his visit in Philadelphia is open-ended. We'll make sure to have copies of his medical papers included with the medications, in case you have to call one of his doctors. We already added your names to the list of people they can give information to. But hopefully it won't be necessary."

"I'm sure Mom, Gram, and Aunt Mary have everything planned down to the last detail. But we won't hesitate to call you or someone on his medical team if need be," Naomi said. "Aunt Mary will watch over him like an eagle. You know she's a Nurse Practitioner who's doing home care visits, right? I'm sure she's seen it all."

When it was time to leave, Marcus said to Naomi, "Wait a second, please. I want you to take this photo album. Dad might like to have it with him, and maybe your grandmother would like to see it, too." He reached for an old-fashioned photo album on a sideboard and handed it to her.

She flipped through the pages quickly, and her breath hitched. Her own face looked back at her from an old black and white photo. "Wow! This has to be Gram Annie! I knew we have similarities, but this is eerie. Rev, look." She held it out for him, and he leaned closer and lightly placed one hand on her shoulder.

"She's your spitting image, Nugget."

"Well, since I'm her descendent, you should say I am *her* spitting image. But you're right. How old was she in this picture? Oh, it says it was taken in 1963."

"The baby in her arms must be your mom." Marcus said after trying to peek at the back of the photo.

"She was my age when she had Mom," she said. "I can't wait to look through this album when I have more time. Thank you for trusting us with it."

Revan squeezed her shoulder before he pulled his hand away.

"Marcus, Helen, thank you both for a lovely evening. We'll be in touch when we get to Richmond, and of course when we reach Philly, to let you know how Charlie is doing," Revan promised. "And don't hesitate to call or text us anytime."

On their walk back to the hotel, Revan said, "I really enjoyed the evening. Talking to Marcus was fun, and he has his entire family history memorized. Did you know your grandmother is descended from the Aikens, who were a very prominent political family in the nineteenth and early twentieth century in this city? I want to make time to visit the Aiken-Rhett House while we're here."

"Rhett House?"

"Yes, but not *your* Rhett, Nugget, even though your shady hero was supposed to be from Charleston, too," he said and winked at her. "Did you know Margaret Mitchell created his character based on a local Civil War Confederate profiteer and patriot?"

Naomi shook her head and rolled her hand in a keep-talking gesture.

Rev continued, "George Trenholm lost his father young and was forced to quit school and look for employment. He was hired by a local cotton exporting company and worked his way up, until by the time he was in his mid-forties he was the firm's principal owner and senior partner. George was a highly respected entrepreneur, and when the Civil War began, he was possibly the wealthiest man in the South. He owned plantations, hotels, shipping firms, real estate, warehouses, and cotton gins. Then the war and the Union Naval blockade made Trenholm even wealthier."

"And Scarlett?" Naomi asked. "Who was her character based upon?"

"I don't know, but I'm sure you can google it. But isn't it fascinating to find connections between fictional characters and real people after you read a book?"

"Yeah, I guess. You know I don't really read a lot of books."

"But even when you watch a movie, aren't you sometimes curious about a character's background?"

"Only if it doesn't have too much to do with history."

Rev laughed and mimicked Rhett Butler. "Frankly, my dear, then you're in the wrong city. You can't avoid history here."

CHAPTER 16

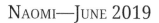

NAOMI—JUNE 2019

Naomi almost bolted out of the conference room where she'd been holed up for the past day and a half, relieved the business meeting was finally over! There was only so long a person could listen to "how agencies can learn from industry experts" and "how to better engage with the customer."

She had thirty minutes until it was time to meet Revan.

Passing the complimentary and always-refilled buffet of fresh fruit and snacks in the atrium, she snatched a chocolate chip cookie and a banana.

In her room, she took a five-minute shower to get rid of the conference room smell, slathered on body lotion and sunscreen, and slipped into a white summer dress. While running a brush through her hair, she stood at the window and looked out at John Wiley Waterfront Park and Charleston Harbor.

Last night, after a never-ending but delicious dinner, her conference group walked back to the hotel through the eight-acre park and stopped at Pineapple Fountain. The meeting organizer talked about how the park was created after Hurricane Hugo's destructive category four landfall on Sullivan's Island in 1989. She explained about pineapples representing hospitality—which wasn't exactly news to Naomi—and added that the city of Charleston allowed weddings to be held there, but limited the attendees to no more than twenty-five, including the bride and groom.

Naomi had glanced around, hoping to see Rev. She wished he'd been with her, wanted to see it with him.

Maybe they could go there tonight.

And do what? There won't be any hand-holding or passionate kisses, missy.

Ugh, it was all so frustrating. But she missed him.

She hadn't seen him since they left Marcus's house on Wednesday evening. He'd been busy yesterday with someone who took him on a day-long tour of Charleston's historic graveyards, cemeteries, and churches. And Naomi didn't know what he had on his agenda today.

But she couldn't wait to see him, to talk to him, and—if she was honest with herself—to touch him. Even if it was only a quick hug to say hello.

Which reminded her to be careful around Charlie. If she'd been aware of his stage of dementia, she probably wouldn't have agreed to bring him to see Gram. Maybe Marcus could have taken him to Philadelphia. But then

Gram's "sweet boy" had to go ahead and throw on his shining armor and declare himself her driver.

She giggled when she imagined him in a black chauffeur's hat.

Naomi plopped her black-and-white sun hat on her head and slipped her feet into sandals, turning in front of the full-length mirror. The dress and sun hat looked fabulous together. Other men, those less ignorant than Revan, would fall to their knees when they saw her like this.

She imagined the scene in a movie...

The idea alone caused a rather unladylike snort, followed by another fit of giggles that made her eyes water. She reached for a tissue when three sharp raps on the door startled her.

Dabbing at her eyes with a tissue, she opened the door to find Rev leaning against the doorjamb with a camera backpack flung over his shoulder.

"Nugget, you never cease to amaze me. Are you crying because you missed me?"

"If you really want to know, Shutterbug, I've been imagining herds of drooling men falling to their knees when they see me like this." She waved her tissue-free hand up and down in front of her.

He pulled her to his side and planted a kiss on top of her sun hat. "This is a pretty wide brim. Not sure any of your suitors would be able to find your face if they wanted to kiss you."

"They could ask me to take it off."

"Which would be very frowned-upon. I doubt ladies removed their hats and bonnets in company," he grinned.

"Let's go. The plantation closes at five thirty, and we want to be able to take our time there, am I right?"

"Absolutely."

The thirty-minute drive took them through a few run-down neighborhoods, then past some amazing Southern mansions. Street signs pointed to places and developments named Magnolia This or Magnolia That. After they missed the entrance to Magnolia Plantation once and had to do a U-turn, they drove along a tree-lined road to the public parking area.

"Can you imagine driving here in an open carriage, with those trees providing shade from the hot sun?" she asked.

"Yes, I can feel the sand between my teeth and the dust irritating my eyes."

After buying their tickets, they followed wide paths through a densely planted park until they arrived at the plantation manor. Several groups of people stood on either the covered porch or the gravel in front of the steps, and more people walked in and out of a gift shop in the basement of the building.

Rev checked a brochure and said, "A guided tour of the house takes thirty minutes, do you want to do it?"

Taking in the number of people already waiting, she shook her head, "No, let's skip it and spend more time in the gardens."

Wherever she looked, she saw huge old Southern magnolia trees with plenty of flowers still on them, enormous Southern live oaks heavy with Spanish moss, azalea bushes in yellow, red, white, and pink, and blooming hibiscus larger than she'd ever imagined. The sheer abundance of fragrant flowering trees and shrubs at the plantation was almost overwhelming.

Like a butterfly, she flitted from plant to plant, smelled the flowers, and didn't notice Revan taking photo after photo of her. After a while they sat down on a bench in the shade. He offered her a bottle of water from his backpack, then opened one for himself.

"We can go down to the banks of the Ashley river, then follow this loop around one of the ponds," Rev showed her on the map they got at the ticket station. "Then go back to the house and take your picture in front of the porch."

"Sounds good. Oh, Rev, this is so beautiful," Naomi said and waved her hand around.

"I agree," he said but looked at her. "Have you tried to imagine how it looked a few hundred years ago, when rice was grown here?"

"To be honest, it surprised me to read about the rice. I thought the South is all about cotton." They started walking toward the river.

"Oh no, they grew much more. But it was mainly cotton, rice, tobacco, and indigo."

"The Spanish moss is another thing I can't get enough of. I've seen it in pictures, but to see the real thing is so much better." She took a few pictures with her phone, then fanned herself with her sun hat. "But I could do without the humidity."

"Imagine your heroine wearing layers of clothes, including a tight corset, in weather like this," he pointed out.

"Oh, how horrible. I wouldn't have worn a corset if I'd lived then," she said and took a few steps off the path to get closer to the edge of a pond. The calm water, surrounded by lots of greenery and flowering plants, looked so peaceful.

"Naomi, no! Step back," Rev said and reached for her elbow.

"Why? Look at the water, there's not a ripple in it." She pointed to the middle of the pond with her other hand.

"Naomi. Now," Rev said through his teeth and pulled her toward him.

"What are you doing, you...you—" she started to say, until she spotted the alligator only eight to ten feet away from her. Its hooded eyes were motionless, but she could see the length of its nose and had no desire to see the rest of the beast.

"Why didn't you warn me?" Naomi squeezed closer to Revan.

"Why didn't you pay attention to the signs? They're posted every few yards," he said and pointed to one. "Or listen when I asked you to step back from the water?"

"I think I've seen enough of this garden—and thank you for saving my life," she let go of his arm. "Oh, look, look at the pretty white bridge." She hurried toward the wooden structure spanning the pond.

Halfway to the bridge, she made a sharp, ninety-degree turn, "And there's a red bridge, over there, look!"

He followed her with a grin. Naomi stopped walking, put her hands on her hips and asked, "What exactly is so funny?"

"You, Nugget. I'm glad we found something that excites you. And in a place steeped in history. Let me take a picture of you on the bridge."

She stepped on the red bridge and held her sun hat in her hand. With her other hand, she shaded her eyes to look across the water.

"Why aren't you wearing your lovely hat?" Rev asked while he snapped photos.

"I'm afraid it'll fall in the water. And we don't want to have to send you in to pull it out."

"I would do a lot of things for you—but I'm afraid jumping into the swampy home of alligators and snakes isn't among them," he chuckled.

"What? Snakes? Where? Let's go to the house." She marched off over the bridge and called over her shoulder, "Aren't you coming?"

"No, because the house is this way," he pointed behind him. "Unless you want to see more wildlife. Have I told you about the fire ants here in the South? Nasty little creatures, I saw plenty of their mounds in the cemeteries yesterday and today."

On their way back to the old plantation home, Naomi said, "I read the plantation is often used for weddings and other events. I'll have to contact the management for details. It would be a good location for the destination wedding packages I'm starting to offer."

Since she and Stella had gone on a promotional tour of romantic places in France last year, she'd been plotting and planning. She wanted to offer something different... And

Charleston, one of America's most romantic cities, simply had to go on Naomi's list. It was so divers.

"Plantation weddings have ended up in the crosshairs lately. There are some very vocal opponents who are saying plantations are reminders of slavery and therefore human rights abuses," Revan said.

"Hmm. I don't want to offend anybody, but it's sad if such picturesque places can't be appreciated for their beauty. And many of the plantations can only be maintained and preserved with the money they make from tourists and weddings. Some charge up to twenty-five thousand dollars per event."

"A few years ago, I worked on a feature about slavery for *National Geographic*. As part of it, I met with a group of doctoral candidates studying plantation tourism and interpretations of slavery. Owning slaves was wrong, the violence and dehumanization unforgivable, and that's indisputable. One of the PhD students said many people get upset when they see former slave quarters in the background of wedding photos.

"Another group member said the deep-rooted beauty of plantations must be placed in context. With a different historical background, everybody would simply admire these plantations for their beauty. But the gardens wouldn't exist without the slaves who started and tended to them. The slaves used their knowledge of plants and made the gardens what they are today. I think their work should be honored, and the wrongs done to them must be recognized, too."

Naomi nodded, but didn't know how to answer, so just looked around the parklike garden. "I'll keep it in mind when I work on my packages."

"Another student in the group had a good point. He said our whole country was more or less built by slaves, and it won't be easy to find a venue which hasn't been touched by slavery," Revan added.

"Even up North?"

"Yes, the original colonies had household slaves, servants, and indentured laborers who helped build their economies."

The issue of slavery dampened her mood, and she looked at him from under her sun hat. "Oh, Rev, I don't know what to say."

"I didn't want to make you sad, Nugget. It's just something you should be aware of."

They walked around another gigantic rhododendron and found themselves in front of an enormous wooden porch that wrapped around all four sides of the manor house.

Naomi walked up the stairs and spun around halfway. She waved her arm in a half-circle—and smacked Revan on his shoulder.

"You're hitting me, after I've saved you from the beasts in the pond? Since when are you so violent?" He raised his eyebrows and smiled his heart-stopping, lopsided smile. And his green eyes sparkled like the dark green magnolia leaves when they caught the sunshine.

Naomi wasn't sure if it was because of the heat and humidity or him reaching for her hand, but the air felt unbearably sticky.

"Where do you want me to take your picture with the house?" he asked and rubbed his thumb over her knuckles.

She sat down and adjusted her dress. "I guess here is fine."

He took at least twenty photos of her, from different angles and playing with different camera settings. When an older couple walked by and offered to take a picture of the two of them, he handed them his iPhone and sat down on next to her. "Okay, last picture. All right, Nugget?"

"Sit a little closer," the man said in accented English. Revan scooted closer to Naomi.

"Put your arm around the beautiful *signorina*. Make it a picture of love." The man smiled and kissed his own wife, "*Ti amo, bella*."

Naomi offered her cheek to Rev and tapped a finger on it. In reply, Revan tapped the brim of her sun hat, "I told you kissing isn't possible when you're wearing this wagon wheel."

She whipped it off and offered her cheek again, but he turned her face toward him. Sweat pooled between her breasts and ran down her spine.

His lips lingered on her cheek for a moment, then he said to the Italian, "Enough love for today, thank you." He stood, took his phone back and checked the time.

"Nugget, unfortunately we don't have time for any other visits in the area. Everything closes soon."

"Where else would you like to go?" She got up too and dusted off her backside. Sitting on steps in a white dress probably hadn't been the wisest decision. Too late now. She slammed her sun hat back on her head.

"There's Drayton Hall, another antebellum plantation from the 1730s. It's preserved 'as is,' meaning they don't plan to renovate it to look as it would've back then. And there's also Magnolia Cemetery."

"I thought you've been poking around graveyards for two days," she tilted her head back so she could see his face.

"I was, and they are quite fascinating. I think you'd enjoy them. Some of those old tombstones are works of art and tell amazing stories." They started walking toward the visitor center and the parking lot.

She glanced back at the mansion once more, "You know what? I'm glad we came, but the plantation is different from what I expected."

Rev laughed, "I know...I noticed the lack of smitten suitors, too. Unless you want to count the sleepy alligator."

"Picture of love," Revan fumed while they settled at a corner table in a cozy restaurant. "Who did that guy think he was?" Charleston had no shortage of places to eat, and Naomi loved the variety of restaurants. This place advertised itself as a French bistro with Southern charm, and she liked it immediately.

It wasn't big, had maybe ten tables indoors, half of which were already occupied when they arrived shortly after 8 pm, and a man in his sixties walked around greeting guests warmly before taking drink orders.

"Why are you getting so worked up over it? It was harmless," she said and reached for her glass of pinot noir.

"How awkward would it have been if we were just coworkers on a business trip together?"

"Duh, then we would've said no when he asked," she sipped her wine and licked her lips in approval.

"He could've kept walking," Rev grumbled.

"Just forget about it. But would you please send me the picture he took?"

Lately Revan's moods had changed quickly, and often she simply ignored them. After he typed something on his phone, hers rang. She silenced it immediately.

"You have the *Indiana Jones* theme song as my ringtone?" Revan asked with a strange look on his face.

"I don't know how it got on my phone. Maybe something got messed up when I downloaded the latest iOS." She hoped she wasn't blushing.

"Yeah, maybe," Rev chuckled.

When the owner of the restaurant approached their table and told them about the daily specials, Naomi could've kissed him. She didn't want to have to explain her choice of ringtones to Revan.

The man looked at Revan, "You were here for lunch yesterday with Ruth. Welcome back."

"Good memory," Rev replied. "And because I like the food and the atmosphere, I thought my friend and I should have dinner here."

"What's your reason for visiting Charleston?" The man leaned casually against the empty table behind him.

"Business, mostly," Revan said.

"If you've had business with Ruth, then you were in the best hands. I've known her for many years." The man laughed and took in their almost empty glasses. "Would you like another glass of wine?"

Naomi said, "Yes, please, this is very good."

"Why don't you bring us the bottle? We might be here awhile," Rev added.

"Stay as long as you want, take your time, there's no rush," the man said. "Have you decided what you'd like for dinner?"

After glancing at the specials menu on the wall, Naomi said, "I'll have the chicken piccata on fettuccine, please."

Revan asked for the same, and before the man left, he said, "If you need anything else, let me know. My name is Rabih."

Only moments later, a woman who'd been running between bar and kitchen brought the bottle of wine and refilled their glasses, a little more brusquely than necessary. Revan opened his mouth as if he wanted to say something, but closed it again and only raised his eyebrows when she stomped off.

Naomi played with the stem of her wine glass and said with some hesitation, "There's something I want to ask you."

"Sure."

"Why are you helping me with this trip? It messed up your whole schedule."

He took a big sip of his wine, "I thought I made it clear that I didn't like the idea of you and Charlie on the road all by yourselves."

Reaching for the dessert spoon, Naomi fiddled with it. "I appreciate it, but..." She took a deep breath. "You know, it was very admirable when you and Luca thought Stella, Jo, and I needed your protection from older boys with questionable intentions when we were teenagers, but that was a long time ago, Rev. Times have changed. We've grown up."

"Nugget..."

"Give me your phone," Naomi held out her hand for it and wiggled her fingers.

"Why?"

"Let me see a photo of Dinah."

"Why?"

"Is *why* the only word in your vocabulary tonight?" she gimme-gestured toward his phone. "Just do it. Show me a photo of your sister."

A few taps later he held up his phone. Naomi snatched it out of his hand and put it next to her face.

"Notice a difference? Sixteen," she pointed to Dinah. "Thirty-one," she pointed to herself. Holding the phone out to him, her finger touched the screen and swiped to the next picture.

She saw herself, smelling a bouquet of roses. "What's my photo doing on your phone?"

"Must have accidentally synced with something," he mumbled, and ran a hand over his hair and down the back of his neck. "Naomi, I have to apologize for the other night. When we were in the garden."

Naomi's stomach did a flip. Right now he looked like a much younger version of himself. Like a little boy caught with his hand in the cookie jar, and totally uncomfortable. *Like a son of his might look...* Naomi's heart and stomach squeezed tight.

"You've already told me you're sorry. But you didn't tell me why you came to my room."

"It was... I don't know what to say. Quite frankly, I'm trying to work through some shit right now—and I don't know what to do." He looked at his hands. "But I know one thing, Nugget. I can't lose your friendship."

What is he trying to say? Why would he think he'd lose her as a friend?

"I don't know what our friendship has to do with what you're trying to work through, but is there anything I can do to help you?"

"No, you can't," he rubbed the back of his neck again and looked around the restaurant.

She couldn't remember ever seeing him so uncomfortable. Leaning back in her chair, she watched people strolling down East Bay Street, and listened to the music in the background. "Listen to Your Heart." *How fitting.*

Almost absentmindedly, she played with the fine gold chain and gold nugget pendant around her neck. Ever since she found the small gold nugget a few years ago and had it made into a pendant, she considered it her good-luck charm and wore it every day. She used to whisper her deepest wishes to it and hoped, because it rested so close to her heart, it had the power to fulfill them.

Naomi reached for Revan's hand and squeezed it. "My friendship isn't going anywhere, Rev. But I'm going to the bathroom now, if you'll excuse me."

Walking away, she wiped a hand over her face.

CHAPTER 17

Revan stared at Naomi's back. Was she crying?

The evening had abruptly taken a strange turn. But why—after the fun they had at the plantation? His heart started beating a little faster at the memory of her running back and forth between the flowers—almost childlike. For a brief moment she was once again the little girl who couldn't sit still, her blonde pigtails flying in the wind.

Everything was fine until she found her own photo on his phone. After she pointed out the difference between herself and his teenage sister. A fact he was fully aware of.

Picking up his phone, he looked at Naomi's picture again. Why didn't he just admit he liked it? Instead, he gave her a half-witted answer.

But then he remembered the ringtone she had assigned to him on her phone. His friends knew what a big *Indiana Jones* fan he was, especially of Harrison Ford, whom he met a few years ago while working on an environmental documentary. But Naomi's explanation about the personalized ringtone was just as lame as his about her photo.

"What are you thinking about? You look lost, for lack of a better word," she interrupted his musings while she sat down again.

"I was thinking about Charlie. It'll be interesting to see how the two days with him in the car will go. I hope we can make it comfortable for him. What are our arrangements at the hotel in Richmond again?" Rev improvised quickly.

"I've booked three rooms at a Suites hotel. Two of them should be connected, and I thought Charlie and I could take those rooms. In case he needs something in the middle of the night."

"Let me take the room next to his," he said and added, "it'd be easier if he needs to be lifted." The reminder of adjacent rooms made him uncomfortable.

"We'll decide when we get there," she reached for her napkin and twisted it. "I'm sorry I questioned you earlier. And thank you for making this possible for Gram."

Revan took the napkin out of her hands, laid it on the table next to her flatware, and said, "You're welcome. I love her like my own grandmother. Do you remember when she insisted we all call her Gram Annie? She said her heart is big enough to love more than her two granddaughters."

"You're right, she always considered you, Luca, and Stella her honorary grandkids. She's a remarkable woman."

Naomi's eyes got misty, but she blinked it away. "Ugh, I hate crying. Tell me something uplifting. How were your graveyard tours?"

"You call that uplifting?" he laughed. "It was actually a great experience. Ruth, the lady who showed me around, is a specialist in the history of churches in Charleston. I think you would've enjoyed listening to her. The way she talks about the details on gravestones and the background information she has about cemeteries was informative, but also entertaining."

"Did you notice how many churches there are in this city?" Naomi asked. "I saw steeples and spires everywhere."

"Nugget, why do you think the city's nickname is Holy City? Today there are over four hundred churches and houses of worship in a variety of denominations. And more than twelve historic churches, some going back to the 1700s."

"Sounds like you've been in paradise, then," Naomi teased.

"It was amazing, yes."

Their dinner was seasoned with small talk, and Naomi said, "Great job finding this restaurant, Shutterbug. I love the atmosphere, and the food is delicious."

A moment later, a grin spread over her face. "I just thought of something. Did you ever look up the meaning of your name?"

"I doubt Shutterbug is in the dictionary."

"I mean your real name. So, did you?"

"No, of course not. But I get the feeling you did. You're about to burst. Please, tell me. What's the meaning of my name?"

"In Hindu, it means star, or—are you ready? Horse rider. Do you like it, *Ranchero*?"

He held up his hand. "Please, Nugget, please continue calling me Shutterbug. And what's the meaning of your name?"

"You won't be surprised, it's totally fitting. My name's origin is Hebrew and means..." she pursed her lips, tucked her hair behind her ears, then put her elbows on the table and steepled her fingers.

"Please, tell me! I can't stand the suspense," he said.

She put her chin on her fingertips and whispered, "... pleasantness."

His roaring laughter made other guests look up.

Rabih waved to them and grinned.

Naomi leaned back in her chair, reached for her glass, and took a slow sip of wine. She shrugged, "What can I say?"

CHAPTER 18

NAOMI—JUNE 2019

When Revan and Naomi arrived at the assisted living facility on Saturday morning, Charlie was already in his wheelchair, ready to go. Naomi picked up his supply of medicine and necessary instructions at the nurse's office while Revan pushed the wheelchair to his car.

"Uncle Charlie, do you prefer to sit in the back where you have more room for your stuff?" Naomi asked after she joined them.

"I don't have *stuff*. And I'm sitting in the front with this young man, where we can do man talk."

Naomi didn't know what kind of *man talk* he had in mind, but sitting in the back gave her a chance to work on a few things—and watch Revan without him noticing.

For the first two hours she pretty much tuned out their conversation about politics and history. But every time her attention wandered to the driver's seat, Revan's eyes met hers in the rearview mirror.

"Shouldn't you focus on the traffic?"

"Nugget, you'd be surprised how good I am at multi-tasking," he smirked.

After a while Revan asked, "Sir, do you mind if I play some music?"

"Of course not, young man."

Revan took a CD from the middle console and pushed it in the stereo system.

"My Pamela and I danced to this song at our wedding." Charlie moved his head to the rhythm and belted out, "Be my, be my ba-a-by."

Naomi reached forward and rubbed his shoulder. "I'm sure you two looked amazing. Revan and I are taking dance lessons." She watched Revan for a reaction, but he stoically kept his eyes on the road.

"Why do you need lessons?" Charlie asked.

"We're both in a wedding soon. And we need to make sure to be in sync...don't you agree, Rev?"

"Mm-hmm...so I've been told," he muttered.

Charlie shook his head, "In my days, dancing came naturally. Take her out a few times and swing her around, no need to pay for expensive lessons. Maybe we'll find a place with live music tonight. I wouldn't mind trying my luck myself, ha-ha," he chuckled.

"We've heard about your lady friend," Naomi said. "Tell us about her."

"Did Helen tattle?" Charlie asked. "Well, Clara is a fine lady. She's much younger than I am, only turned eighty this year. We enjoy teatime together and, ahem...other invigorating exchanges." Charlie winked at Revan, "Some guys in there are too doddy and don't cherish a woman's company. Not me. Life is short."

Revan burst out, "What?"

"Oh, yes sir. Now, if you'll excuse me, I'll snooze for a bit," Charlie said.

Naomi shuddered. "Do you think he was serious?" she asked when loud snoring came from the front passenger seat.

"Nugget, I don't want to think about it," Rev chuckled.

"Well then, let's talk about the twofer party. I've been wondering if we should make it a themed party."

"Come on, really? We're not in kindergarten."

"It has nothing to do with age. Think, Shutterbug! What brought them together?" Naomi challenged him. "What's something important in their relationship?"

"They love each other? Okay, so hang up a few red hearts and balloons."

"Too boring," she waved him off. "Think romance... Where did Stella see David for the first time? What's a place with a special meaning for them?"

"You want to put a park bench in the restaurant? How romantic. Do we all get a turn to sit on it?"

"Okay, I'll tell you. Are you listening?" she leaned forward as far as the seatbelt allowed.

"Your voice is loud and clear."

"A masquerade party," Naomi said with a satisfied expression. "Brilliant idea, isn't it?"

"Absolutely amazing. I can hardly contain myself, and I'll tell you one thing right now. I'm not wearing some dog ears or a bird mask. Forget about it."

"Who would you like to be?"

"Me."

"I guess we could hang a camera around your neck. But listen..."

"Still am..."

"What if we decorate the room in a theme, like the masquerade ball in *The Phantom*."

"Don't you think David is done with it? He's been impersonating the dude for how many years?"

"It made him famous," she countered. "Maybe I'll email his manager. It can't be too difficult to find him online. Aaron might be able to set me up with someone who can help with a few props. I think it would be fantastic."

"If you think it's fantastic, I won't stop you. But I'll be out of town frequently and might not be able to help a lot."

"How long are you gone for?" she asked. "I know you told me, but I can't remember."

"A week, maybe ten days," Rev said. "But I'll be back for our next dance lesson—I wouldn't dare miss it. Then I'll go to New York for a week to see Luca and meet my publisher for the book project Barb and I worked on."

"Ugh, you had to mention her, did you?" Naomi slumped back in her seat.

"What's up with your reaction, Nugget? What did she do to you?"

"Nothing. I just don't like the way she…oh, forget about it. Can we stop for a restroom break and coffee refill?"

"Sure, Charlie probably needs to stretch his legs too."

"Damn right, young man," Charlie said.

"Uncle Charlie, I thought you were sleeping," Naomi said.

"I wanted to, but your gabbing kept me awake. Nice idea about the masquerade ball. I like it. Maybe I'll stay in Philly until the party," he laughed. "Never said no to a party. We should've asked Clara to join us on our little trip."

A few hours later, Revan maneuvered his Explorer down tree-lined Monument Avenue in Richmond. While he and Charlie glanced at the controversial monuments of Southern heroes in passing, Naomi took in the mansions on both sides of the wide street.

"We're almost at the hotel, and it's only 4 pm, so what's the plan for the rest of the day? Would you like to relax in your rooms after we check in, or would you like to stretch your legs a bit?" Rev asked.

"I wouldn't mind taking in the sights," Charlie said.

"Where do you want to go?" Naomi asked.

"Our hotel is not far from the James River. We can't do the Canal Walk with the wheelchair, but there are some historic factory buildings and the American Civil War Museum. We could refresh your knowledge of history, Nugget."

"I'm impressed. Why, you're turning into quite the tour guide," she teased him. "I can't wait to find out what you've planned next."

"Me neither. I've been surprising even myself."

"I'd like to visit the museum," Charlie said. "If you don't mind pushing my wheelchair, Revan."

"Sure thing," Revan said and pulled into the drop-off area in front of their hotel. "And here we are, we've reached our destination for today."

After loading their suitcases, bags, and Charlie's equipment onto a luggage cart, they entered the foyer.

Naomi approached the check-in desk. "Good afternoon, we have reservations for Winters. Three rooms, two of them adjoining."

"Let me have a look," a young man said. "Here it is. I have two rooms under this name. And yes, they are adjoining as requested."

"What do you mean, *two* rooms? I booked three rooms." She opened the confirmation email on her phone. "Here, see? I assigned names for each room with my booking."

"I'm deeply sorry, miss, but the third room was cancelled this morning."

"Excuse me? Who cancelled it, and why didn't I receive a cancellation confirmation?" she glanced at the man's name tag, "Peter."

"I took the phone call myself. The lady who called asked me to send the confirmation to a different email address than the one we have on file," he looked extremely uncomfortable and frequently peeked into the back office.

Naomi felt bad for him, but she had to know what had happened.

"Can you tell me the name of the person who called?" she asked.

"Her name was Naomi Winters," Peter said reluctantly.

"I'm Naomi Winters, and I didn't call. But why don't you just give us the third room back?"

"I'm very sorry, but we're fully booked."

"Are you kidding me?" Naomi fumed. "You had our room reserved until a few hours ago."

"Is there a problem?" Revan joined her.

After she summarized everything, Revan asked Peter, "So what exactly do you have for us?"

"I have two rooms, and they are adjoining as the reservation requested. One has a queen bed and a handicapped-accessible bathroom, the other one has a king bed and pull-out sofa."

"We'll take it. But we'd like a printout of the cancellation confirmation," Revan said.

"Of course, sir. I apologize for the problem. How many key cards do you need?" Peter asked.

"Three," Naomi snarled.

Walking back to Charlie, she said through her teeth, "I can't tell you how mad I am. Now I know why Gram Annie insisted on getting hard copies of the reservations. This has her handwriting all over it. I don't know what she's up to, but I don't like it."

"Relax. We'll give Charlie one room, and I'll sleep on the sofa in your room. We can do this."

"Relax? She's forcing us into an uncomfortable situation. Now the adjoining rooms and unlocked door in Virginia Beach make more sense, too."

"What do you mean?"

"Well, when I checked out on Wednesday morning, I asked them why they don't make sure the doors are locked. They assured me they do but they received a phone call—apparently also from me—to keep them unlocked," Naomi raged. "Wait until we get home tomorrow. I want to see Gram's face when I ask her about those *coincidences*."

Revan let out a loud, deep belly laugh.

"I don't think this is very funny," she said and handed Charlie his key card.

"Everything okay, children?"

"Your sister is in trouble! Big trouble!" Naomi growled.

"Wouldn't be the first time," he said and laughed. "I don't know what she did, but I'm sure she had her reasons."

"Come on, Nugget, let's go to our rooms and get Charlie settled," Revan said. "If you push the wheelchair, I'll take the luggage cart. Didn't you tell me when we left Philly how much fun we'd have?"

Naomi was so mad she couldn't say a word. Under different circumstances, she might have enjoyed the idea of sharing a room with Revan, but how dare Gram Annie force this situation on them? She couldn't wait to confront her grandmother. *Before* Gram even got a chance to say hello to her brother.

Both rooms were spacious, with small kitchenettes and views of a park, and to Naomi the pull-out sofa in the king room looked comfortable enough—especially since she didn't plan to be the one sleeping on it.

"I guess this will do," she said after they helped Charlie with his luggage and left him to unpack a few things. She checked to make sure the door to his room was unlocked—this time on purpose—and busied herself by carrying her cosmetic bag to the bathroom, checking to see if there were complimentary guest soaps and shampoo in the shower, placing her phone charger on the table next to the bed, until she finally walked toward the kitchenette.

Revan interrupted her roaming when he stepped in front of her and put his hands on her shoulders. "Stop buzzing around like a tipsy bee. Pretend we're at home and this is the living room. It's not so different, and it's only for one night."

Naomi wasn't so sure. Mostly because at home their bedrooms were separated by a brick wall. Here she'd only have to lift her head and see Revan sleeping a mere few feet away from her. She wouldn't get any sleep.

Leaning her forehead against his chest, she closed her eyes for a second. "You're right. We're adults and can do this."

"I hope you're not afraid of me. I promise to be on my best behavior," he squeezed her shoulders.

What if I don't want you to be at your best behavior? Or what if I do something I'll regret? Naomi wanted to scream at him.

"Let's get Charlie and go for the walk by the river." Taking a deep breath, she stepped away and knocked on Charlie's door before opening it.

"What were you two doing in there?" he demanded as soon as they entered his room.

"We're here to pick you up for our walk, Uncle Charlie," Naomi said, ignoring his rant.

"Next time the door stays open, Annie. I will not accept any funny business. The same goes for you, young man."

"Understood, sir. There's nothing to worry about, though. We've only talked about our walk and dinner later," Revan told him calmly.

"Next time do it in front of me," Charlie ordered.

Naomi had noticed before how Rev automatically switched between calling her great-uncle "sir" when Charlie was confused, and "Charlie" when he was lucid. She couldn't imagine any of the other men she'd been with being so accepting.

But you're not with him, Voice One said.

Maybe she should try and change it, Voice Two whispered back.

Naomi wanted to tell both voices to shut up.

As they walked toward the James River, Revan said, "Unfortunately, it's too late for the Civil War Museum since everything here closes around five, but the Tredegar Iron Works site is right next to it and they have old machinery on display outside, if you're up to it, Charlie."

"Oh, bummer," she muttered and let Charlie and Revan take their time at the historic landmark. Sitting down on a metal bench, she listened to a waterwheel churning and watched the two men, total strangers to each other, discussing the mechanics of cannons, presses, and turbines of the late nineteenth and early twentieth centuries.

Charlie abandoned his wheelchair and walked around the old objects, carefully reading the descriptions for each machine. Leaning on his cane, he said, "Revan, did you see this? The factory was founded in 1837 and was one of our country's largest industrial sites before the Civil War and the largest in the Confederate States. They supplied about half the artillery used by the Confederate States Army!"

Revan called over to her, "Nugget, did you hear Charlie? So many connections to your favorite movie."

Naomi replied with a thumbs-up signal. She wasn't in the mood to let him tease her.

When Charlie had his fill at the Tredegar site, they wheeled him through a park toward a modern pedestrian and bicycle bridge. Naomi read aloud, "T. Tyler Potterfield Memorial Bridge, built in 2016."

From the bridge they enjoyed a great view of Richmond's skyline while Revan pointed out the remnants of an old, dismantled bridge scattered in the middle of the river. "Those remnants over there belong to the former Ninth Street Bridge. It was built in 1878 to accommodate horse-drawn carriages and was also known as the Singing Bridge. When tires rolled over the metal plates of the bridge, they gave off a humming sound. Unfortunately, the bridge sat very low over the river, and suffered damage through the years, mostly from being submerged during flooding. In the 1970s, it was replaced by a much higher bridge."

They strolled halfway across the pedestrian bridge, stopping at markers with historical tidbits or explanations about sights. Charlie wanted to read them all, but after the fifth or sixth description, he asked Revan to give him short summaries.

Naomi noticed historic quotes embedded in some of the planks on the bridge and took photos of some of the more inspirational ones. The late afternoon sunlight reflected off the water and sparkled like a million little glass shards. Eventually she sat on a bench and waited for Charlie and Rev to catch up before the three of them turned around and strolled past Brown's Island to the Virginia State Capitol.

She was grateful for Rev's willingness to push the wheelchair over the uneven cobblestone streets and sidewalks while they walked uphill toward the massive, bright white building. Once there, she scurried up the wide marble steps and paused between the tall columns to enjoy the panoramic view of the James River and Richmond.

"This building reminds me of an ancient temple," she called to Rev, who had remained with Charlie.

"You're not far off. When Thomas Jefferson designed it in the 1780s with the help of a French architect, they modeled it after an ancient Roman temple at Nîmes in southern France, the Maison Carrée," Rev called back.

"I don't know how you remember these things," she said after joining the men again.

He only shrugged and grinned.

"Let's take a quick look at the Washington Monument since it's on our way, and then we'd better find somewhere we can get something to eat and drink," Rev suggested and pushed Charlie's wheelchair through the park around the State Capitol until they reached the bronze statue of George Washington on horseback, also looking out over the river. At the base of the monument were six statues of Virginians who took part in the American Revolution, Thomas Jefferson among them.

Later, over dinner at a Scottish pub, the men talked about Revan's visits to countries with travel bans, and how journalists coped with the horrors confronting them. A veteran himself, Charlie shared some of his own experiences.

Naomi welcomed the chance to sit back and let her thoughts wander to Revan. Despite the strangeness that had crept between them, she really enjoyed playing tourist with him and Charlie. But she wanted the awkwardness out of the way—and for them to get back to carefree territory.

By the time Charlie was settled for the night, she was also dead on her feet. At home she would've taken a long bath with a glass of wine, then snuggled into her bed and slept for the next nine hours.

But a relaxing bath wouldn't happen. Not with Revan in the same room. The irony of their situation wasn't lost on her. She was about to spend a night with Revan, but the reality of the next eight or nine hours was quite different from her dreams and fantasies.

Hopefully he'd already pulled out the sofa bed, and was tucked in, ideally covered up to his nose, and preferably sound asleep.

But the sofa bed wasn't pulled out, and Revan wasn't asleep. Far from it.

CHAPTER 19

Naomi—June 2019

He sat on the sofa, casually resting one foot on the side of the coffee table, while holding a glass of whiskey in his hand. "How about a nightcap?"

She saw a bottle of wine on the counter of their kitchenette, next to a bottle of whiskey. "Did you get the wine and whiskey at the bar downstairs?"

Revan looked around conspiratorially and fake-whispered, "Don't tell anybody, but I smuggled it in. I bought both in Charleston yesterday. It's the wine Marcus served on Wednesday night. You said you liked it. So, want some?"

She plopped on the sofa. "I'd love some wine, thank you." It shouldn't surprise her how observant, how attentive he was.

In the kitchenette, he took a glass from the cabinet, checked it for cleanliness, and poured a generous amount before bringing it to her.

She turned the glass in her hand.

"I love stemless glasses. And they're everywhere nowadays. Maybe I should buy a few for at home. What do you think?" Naomi wanted to smack herself but only rolled her eyes.

Sitting down next to her, he asked, "What's going on?"

She shrugged, "Forget what I said. I have no business buying glasses for anywhere. It all just seems too much."

"Try and enjoy the moment. You're doing a wonderful job juggling the extra work at the office and Stella's wedding. And now you're stuck here with me, and Charlie in the next room. Don't be so hard on yourself, Nugget."

"Thank you." She sipped her wine. "Oh, did I tell you Stella, Jo, and Sabrina are coming to Philly next week? We're going shopping on Saturday for Stella's dress, but we're also looking for ours. Dinah is sending me lots of ideas for what she wants. I haven't told her we're getting pedis first because I want to surprise her."

Then she held out her feet and wiggled her toes. "I wish I could get a foot massage right now. We walked a lot today."

"Don't look at me. I'm not a licensed foot masseur," he firmly wrapped both hands around his whiskey glass. "Want to watch a movie? It's still early, barely after nine."

"No movie, and frankly I don't want to talk, either. How about just sitting here?"

Rev looked at her questioningly.

"Oops, I guess that came out wrong," she rested her head on the back of the sofa and didn't say anything for a moment. All day, she'd been thinking about what he said at dinner last night. "Working through some shit."

She shook her head, then sat bolt upright. "No, you know what, Rev? I can't keep quiet anymore. Let's talk. We need to address a few of the things you and I have said in the past few days." She looked at him but couldn't read his expression. He ran a hand over his hair and grimaced.

Before she was able to continue, her phone rang. Maybe she could ignore it. Nope...

"Oh-oh... Mom usually doesn't call me at this time."

"Pick it up," he said and set his whiskey glass down.

Naomi nodded. "Hi, Mom, what's up?"

"Honey, I'm sorry to call so late, but Gram was admitted to the hospital and I thought you should know," Lisa said.

"Oh, no! What happened?" She could feel Revan watching her intently.

"She complained about being in a lot of pain when Mary came to see her this afternoon. Adjusting her pain meds didn't help much, so we called the doctor."

"But why? What does she have? Well, besides the cancer."

"She has an obstructed bowel, which apparently isn't uncommon at this stage of her illness and they're doing everything they can to make her feel comfortable."

"How long does she have to stay? Will she be home when we drop Charlie off tomorrow?"

"I don't know. Maybe. It depends on how effective the treatment is. Right now we're hoping she doesn't need surgery. I'll let you know if there's anything new, hopefully positive, but I want you to call or text me as well. If you can't reach me, try Mary. And don't say anything to Charlie yet. How is it going with him?"

"Well, when we saw him on Thursday, he had moments of confusion and thought I was Gram. But today he's been doing well. I think he likes Revan." Naomi saw him patting his own shoulder.

"What can I say, I'm irresistible?" he laughed.

"Oh, is Revan with you?" her mom asked.

"Yes, we're having a drink before calling it a night. There was a mix-up with our rooms. It's a long story, but Gram Annie had something to do with it. Maybe that's why her bowels are twisted."

"Honey, please, don't make jokes about it."

"Sorry. But I'm not happy with her. Anyhow, we're fine. Right, Shutterbug?" she winked at him.

"Hi, Lisa," he called out. "I already promised to behave."

He reached for his glass and took a sip, using the other hand to give one of her toes a quick tug.

"Be careful, honey. I love you," her mom said quietly.

"I love you, too. See you tomorrow. Bye, Mom."

"What's going on with Gram Annie?" Revan asked as soon as she ended the call, his tone laden with concern.

After she told him everything, he said, "I agree. Hopefully she'll be feeling better soon and can celebrate her reunion with Charlie with apple juice or ginger ale."

"I wouldn't be surprised if she tried to stretch the ginger ale with something else," Naomi laughed. "Okay, I think I'm going to bed. It's been a long day, and this phone call was just about all I can take. Our little talk has to wait a few more days, I guess. Do you want to use the bathroom first?" She finished the rest of her wine and carried the glass to the sink.

"Why don't you go in while I get my bed ready?" Rev said. He pushed the table away and pulled out the couch, then went over to the built-in closet for pillows.

After changing into sleep shorts and a tank top in the bathroom, she took in her choice of nightwear. Perfectly fine for a hot summer night alone in her bed, but too skimpy and revealing with Rev in the room. She slipped her arms into the too-thick, too-warm, knee-length terrycloth bathrobe hanging behind the door and knotted it. Peeking again into the mirror, she gave herself an approving nod. Nothing screamed mood-killer more than looking like an overstuffed hot dog. Even if there wasn't a *mood* to begin with.

Pretending it was how she normally dressed for the night, she strolled out of the bathroom and climbed into bed.

"Are you cold, Nugget?" Revan chuckled as he made his way into the bathroom.

"Hm? Maybe." She tried to get comfortable in the stupid robe. Why did she have to wrap it around herself almost twice? Sweat already began to pool between her breasts, but she couldn't help it. Maybe she could take it off after she heard his slow, even breathing.

As soon as the bathroom door opened again, she closed her eyes, squinting just a bit, and watched him cross the room in pajama bottoms and a T-shirt. She groaned—now she wasn't just sweating, she was also frustrated. And it was her own fault. She should've paraded around, showing him what he was missing by ignoring her...

"Good night, Nugget. You can close your eyes now. End of the show," he said and pulled the flimsy flat sheet over his lower body. "And please don't snore too loudly."

"I don't snore," she reached for a pillow and threw it in his general direction. "But here, put this over your ears."

It instantly came flying back, giving her no choice but to jump up and launch the next one. Which he caught in one hand and came to stand behind the sofa bed.

"Do you need to hide behind the couch?" she teased him.

"Nope, I can fight you standing in the middle of the room with my eyes closed. But why don't you come off your perch and fight fair?"

"Are you accusing me of playing unfair? Eat. Your. Words, Shutterbug," she jumped off the bed.

"Ouch, ouch, ouch. Shit, shit, shit." Sitting on the floor, she rubbed her ankle.

Revan was by her side in a flash and pushed her hand away. Holding her foot in one hand, he placed his other hand around her ankle. Carefully, he turned it first clockwise, then counterclockwise before he slowly moved it up and down.

"I don't think it's broken. Let's get you off the floor and then I'll run to the ice machine." He helped her up and put his arm around her terrycloth-padded waist. "Here, why don't you sit on the bed and put some pillows behind your back?" He also placed one under her throbbing ankle.

Then he grabbed the ice bucket and his key card. "Be right back."

He returned within seconds and, using the plastic ice bucket liner, filled it with cold cubes, tied it at the top and covered it with a spare towel. After wrapping it around her ankle, he pulled the bed's flat sheet over her legs.

She would've laughed if she weren't in so much pain. Her ankle was wrapped as tightly as the rest of her body, white terrycloth galore. The only thing missing was a towel around her head and she'd look like a snowman at a spa.

"I'm so sorry, Nugget." He sat down on the mattress and looked at her.

"For what? It's not your fault. I was the one too clumsy to jump off the bed without messing up my ankle."

"Can I get you anything else?"

"How about another glass of wine? I don't think I'll be sleeping anytime soon. I might as well sit here and get tipsy."

"Glass of wine coming up right away, ma'am," he laughed and got up. "Mind if I join you?"

"Doing what?"

"Having a glass of wine."

"If you behave, you can sit next to me." Her whole body was thrumming with all different kinds of energy, almost making her forget the pain in her ankle.

"I already promised to behave like a gentleman. Can I trust you to be a proper lady?" He poured them each a glass of wine, then sat down next to her and shoved a pillow behind his back. Sighing deeply, he said, "Ah, much more comfortable than that worn-out sofa."

He clinked his glass to hers. "Cheers, Nugget. To you and safe landings."

"Don't remind me. But thanks," she sipped her wine, then studied the color and said, "This is really good wine."

"Then I'm glad I bought a whole case. You need something to put in the new glasses you want to buy."

"You really wouldn't mind if I buy them?" She didn't wait for his answer, "Okay, I'll buy the glasses before the girls are coming."

"Of course you should," Revan said, and smiled his irresistible smile.

Naomi wished she had the nerve to rest her head on his shoulder. She wasn't normally shy, but for some reason she wasn't herself around him. Especially lately.

"Why don't you pull up some music on your phone, and we'll dim the light a bit. I have a feeling neither one of us is going to get a lot of sleep, but maybe we can at least doze," he said after they sat for a while in companionable silence.

She picked a playlist without asking Revan if he had a preference—he'd let her know when he reached his limit. But she turned the volume down a notch and put the phone on the bedside table.

Before she got settled, she carefully wrapped herself deeper into the robe and—for good measure—double-knotted it. *Since when are you a Miss Prim?*

Turning her head to the side while listening to ABBA, she slowly relaxed. Stella told her last year how much those songs helped her through emotionally difficult times, and right now Naomi agreed.

Knowing Revan was so close to her—yet out of reach—was painful.

Listening to "When All Is Said and Done," Naomi saw herself standing at the crossroads they sang about.

She was through running.

CHAPTER 20

Naomi—June 2019

The weight of an arm over her waist made her wiggle closer to the firm body behind her. She didn't want to move any more than that, didn't want to open her eyes. Because if she did, the illusion would vanish. Pop like a balloon meeting its inevitable fate in a sharp, fine needle.

She had never woken up in these arms—but had dreamed of them many times. In those dreams, she always slid her hands over his chest, to his face, into his hair, pulling herself closer.

But she didn't open her eyes, didn't want to watch her dream man morph into a large pillow. Making out with a body pillow would be an all-time low when it came to dream sex.

She could feel his breath on her neck.

The arm remained around her when she rolled over. Warm lips touched her forehead. Day-old stubble rubbed deliciously against her skin.

The contact was brief—much too short.

Her hand crept to the back of his head. His lips touched the tip of her nose.

"Good morning, Nugget. Did you sleep well?" Revan asked in a raspy voice.

"Hm?" Her eyes flew open.

Pop.

But no large pillow. The dream was real.

"What are you doing—" she whispered.

"I'm holding you," he whispered back. He pushed a strand of her hair out of her face.

"But—" her voice still barely audible.

"You snuggled up against me after I changed the ice a few hours ago, and I thought you were afraid of falling out of bed."

"I was dreaming," Naomi said quietly. "But we can't do this."

"We didn't do anything."

"Shutterbug, why did you—"

"Do you always ask so many questions first thing in the morning?" he asked, reaching for her face.

A loud crash, instantly followed by Charlie's voice, came from the other side of the door. "A little help over here!"

Revan mumbled, "Thanks, Charlie."

Naomi's head dropped to his chest.

He stroked her hair and said, "Nugget, just one thing. Don't overthink everything."

What was that *supposed to mean?*

"Hello? Anybody there? Help!"

"Charlie, I'll be right there," Revan called back. Getting out of bed, he put his hands on his hips, bent forward, and took a few deep breaths. "I'll go check on him and see what he needs before he wakes the whole hotel. Do you need help getting into the bathroom?"

"I'll manage, thanks," she said and hobbled off, holding on to the backs of chairs along the way.

As soon as she closed the door behind her, she glanced in the mirror. Disheveled hair and flushed cheeks looked back at her. As she did every morning, she automatically reached for her toothbrush.

Eww...

Please...say it isn't so.

They almost kissed, and—she held a hand in front of her mouth and blew air at it. *Okay, it could've been worse.*

Her whole body was vibrating with energy. The memory of Revan's lips on her forehead and tip of her nose was still fresh. Her earlier frustration battled with new anticipation.

Only one thing was certain—she had no clue what to make of the past few minutes.

CHAPTER 21

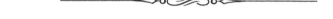

R<small>EVAN</small>—J<small>UNE</small> 2019

They left Richmond around ten in the morning, after a hearty breakfast in a café across the street. Traffic wasn't too bad for a Sunday, and once they were out of the Richmond vicinity, Revan was able to set the cruise control. Hopefully the four-hour drive would go smoothly. Traffic around Washington was always iffy, but there was no way around it.

He was grateful for Charlie's company. Talking to the old man distracted him from thinking about Naomi. Yet his eyes were constantly drawn to his rearview mirror, and he had to force himself to concentrate on the traffic around them instead of looking at the woman who'd managed to sneak behind his defenses. Never mind that he'd opened the gates all by himself, thanks to his impulse to snuggle with her. Why didn't he go to his sofa bed after he iced her ankle for the last time between three and four in the morning?

He couldn't ignore his attraction to her any longer, and had been on the verge of acting on it when Charlie interrupted. It took a herculean effort last night to just look at the beauty next to him...who trusted him to be on his best behavior.

She called to him like a siren out in the vastness of the ocean when a ship of poor lost souls floated by a cursed island. Even bundled up in that ridiculous bathrobe.

After he helped Charlie out of bed—the loud crash being his walker falling out of reach—and made sure he was safely settled in the bathroom, grateful to be told, "the day I can't wipe my own ass will be the day I take my last breath," Revan went back to their room and waited for his turn to take a shower.

He wanted to go to her, to hold her, tell her how amazing she looked in her sundress, but it was safer to keep his distance until he figured out for himself what had happened.

"How's your ankle, Nugget?" he asked when she tried to elevate her leg sideways as far as the seatbelt allowed. "Is the ice still cold?"

"Yes, it is. I think if I take it slow for a few days, it'll be fine. I'll talk to Aunt Mary, too. But she'll only say RICE."

Charlie, whose eyes were glued to the monotonous landscape along the highway, said, "Rice? You're hungry already? We had breakfast not even two hours ago."

"No, Uncle Charlie. It means Rest, Ice, Compression, Elevate. I'm talking about my sprained ankle."

"Well, this traveling makes me hungry, too. I wouldn't mind stopping and refueling," he cackled at his own joke.

"Let's drive for another hour," Revan said. "Then we'll stop and also get new ice for you, Nugget."

"Okay," she buried her nose in her monster wedding planning binder again.

"Any more important decisions to make?"

"No, I'm only going over my notes. Stella and I are meeting with the event planner on Friday evening, and I want to be prepared. Who knows how much I'll be able to get done this week?"

"I'm sure you've got it figured out, Nugget. When am I needed again?"

"Wednesday after next for our dance lesson. I hope my ankle is better by then."

"Okay."

When she turned back to her binder, Revan thought about the next ten days. Today, after dropping off Charlie at Mary's house, he'd drive Naomi home, and then he'd go visit his parents. Tomorrow he'd spend the whole day in his rooms, sorting through photos and getting the pictures for work organized.

And he'd book a flight. He didn't care where he went as long as it was by plane, so he couldn't jump into his car, turn around and drive back as soon as he missed her. Which would pretty much be right after leaving his house.

A truck in front of him changed lanes without signaling, and Revan had to step hard on the brakes. Glass bottles rattled in the trunk. The case of wine he bought in Charleston.

Talk about being hit hard. He couldn't remember ever buying a whole case only because a woman said she liked a certain wine. He didn't do romantic shit like that.

But—Naomi wasn't just any woman.

And buying a few bottles of wine was about as unromantic as buying matching glasses.

She had sounded excited about them. Her instantaneous apology surprised him, though. What was the big deal about buying glasses?

He tried to see everything from her perspective. She didn't even know how long she'd be living with him. She was in limbo.

And the last thing she needed was a new relationship. Not with losers like lover boy, and especially not with him—Mr. No-Commitment.

Wait, who said she was looking for a relationship with him? Just because she didn't slap him after finding herself in his arms didn't mean anything.

But it meant a lot to him. Which scared him.

Yeah, he'd stick to his plan and leave town again, as soon as possible.

An hour before they reached Philadelphia, Naomi received a text message. "Aunt Mary says to bring Charlie directly to her house. We'll discuss everything else there."

"Okay." He knew Lisa had texted her in the morning, saying Gram Annie was staying in the hospital for another night for monitoring, and Mary wanted to give Charlie time to get settled before he saw his sister tomorrow.

Close to midnight, Revan returned home from his parents'. All lights in his house were turned off, except for a nightlight in the kitchen. Good...he'd rather not run into Naomi. He knew running away wasn't the solution, and they needed to talk. They made a few attempts, but never got far. But, frankly, he was sick and tired of the prospect of talking.

He walked through the living room, dimly lit by rays of moonlight shining through the large French doors. A stack of magazines sat on one of the side tables. Naomi was the first one to admit she didn't care to read books, but she devoured magazines. Travel magazines, women's magazines, occasionally gossip magazines, and—to his surprise—magazines featuring his work.

One of her sweaters was tossed carelessly over the back of a chair, and he picked it up and held it to his nose. It still smelled of her citrus-scented lotion, and he wanted to bury his face in it. Instead he folded it and put it back over the chair.

Despite his earlier musings in the car, he couldn't lie to himself anymore. What he told Luca and David at the tavern was the honest truth.

He wanted Naomi like he had never wanted any other woman. The idea of not being around her didn't sit well with him. He wanted to wake up with her every day—like today, but ideally with fewer clothes between them and real, meaningful kisses instead of pecks.

She had felt so good in his arms.

Like she belonged there.

Making his way to his staircase, Revan saw the bowl of gummi bears she always kept filled for him on the kitchen counter, and a wine glass next to the sink.

She left small marks everywhere—visible and invisible ones—probably without even knowing. The house would feel lonely when she moved out. How would he cope with her absence?

And why had he gone to his parents' instead of staying at home with her?

CHAPTER 22

NAOMI—JULY 2019

On Friday afternoon, Naomi spotted the guy who'd been bugging her sitting on a bench in the little park across from the Red Owl. Their eyes met. His stare followed her, making her feel uneasy. Vulnerable.

Today was not the first time she'd seen Ronnie. A day or two before she went to Charleston, she saw him outside the travel agency. She had forced herself to stay calm, tried to tell herself it wasn't him, that he didn't know where she worked, but the icy sensation at the back of her neck told her this was creepy and maybe it was time to involve the police.

It was almost a week since she sprained her ankle, and it was still tender, but she moved as fast as her foot allowed.

Holding her head high, she forced herself to look straight ahead and not show any fear around Ronnie. But deep down she was beginning to worry. Did he stake out her whereabouts? Ignoring her own advice, she glanced in the shop windows to see if he was behind her. So far she couldn't see him.

Under different circumstances she was confident of her ability to outrun him if need be. He didn't look athletic and physically fit. But with her still-recovering ankle, she wasn't so sure. Last year she met a woman who said she always carried pepper spray. Or, if she was flying, a travel-size can of hairspray, which she swore worked almost as well. Maybe Naomi should do the same. It wouldn't hurt to have some kind of protection with her.

Turning onto her street, she checked the surroundings one last time. Nothing. All clear. She breathed out slowly, then shook her arms like a rag doll and told herself to focus on something fun. Like spending the weekend with the girls.

Before she could insert the key, the door swung open and Stella said, "If I didn't still have my key, I'd have been sitting on the front stoop like a child in time-out for the past fifteen minutes."

Naomi hugged her friend. "Yeah, sorry, I had to run by my parents and take the dogs out. And then Gram and Uncle Charlie wanted to chat, and so on."

She couldn't wait to sit down and open a bottle of wine. She had to tell someone about Revan. "I'm so glad you're here, I need to get a few things off my chest."

"Uh-oh. Do we need to cancel our appointment with Sandy?" Stella asked.

"No, let's get the meeting with your wedding planner behind us, then we'll chat," Naomi said. "Let's go."

"Your wedding is ten weeks from tomorrow," Sandy said to Stella an hour later, "and we have you booked for a reception the day before. The suite and all fifteen rooms of our inn are reserved for you and your guests for the nights you requested. Are there any other questions I can answer for you?"

"Everything you presented to us today looks lovely, and I can't think of anything else right now," Stella said. "Naomi, do you have anything we need to address?"

"No, Sandy and I have been in touch, and I'm sure we'll talk more as we get closer to your big day." Naomi gave Stella a huge smile, then hugged her. "Don't worry, we'll make sure you'll have the best day of your life! And tomorrow we'll buy The Dress!"

Stella laughed. "Wait a second! We're looking at dresses, I'm not sure I'll buy one right away."

"You have to, because all the girls will be here." Naomi knew she wasn't playing fair, because Stella would never want to disappoint her bridesmaids, especially Dinah. Then she said to Sandy, "I'll be in touch if anything comes up."

"I hope my friend is not driving you crazy, Sandy," Stella laughed. "Naomi is not known for taking no for an answer if she has her heart set on something."

"Nothing to worry about, Stella. Naomi and I have been seeing eye to eye." Sandy shook their hands. "Have fun dress shopping tomorrow!"

On their way back to the house, Naomi asked, "Want to pick up something at the deli and eat at home?"

"Perfect. I'm sure there's a bottle of wine waiting for us too, right?"

"What do you think?" Naomi laughed.

"I miss our hangouts and this food," Stella said when they sat down in the backyard and spread out their dinners.

"Please don't tell me living with the Troubadour is getting boring already," Naomi said and reached for the bottle of wine to fill their glasses.

"Do you think you could call David something else?" Stella laughed, and added, "But no, of course I don't regret moving in with him. I love him. But I also miss our girl time." She took a sip of her wine. "Mm, this is nice." She read the label. "I don't remember this one."

"Rev bought a case in Charleston because I like it. We had it at my cousin's house."

"And are those glasses new?"

"Rev said I should buy them because I admired them in our hotel in Richmond."

"Anything else Rev said or did or approved?" Stella raised her eyebrows.

"He's using a new shower gel," Naomi laughed. "I think he's been using Old Spice since...forever, so he was due for a new one, in my opinion. I put it in his shower one day and he hasn't commented on it yet."

"You went into his bathroom? Didn't he make you memorize his unwritten rules?" Stella gasped, then mimicked him, "Stay out of my rooms, do your own laundry, and do not touch my camera."

"Well, yeah, he did... But I happened to find a Calvin Klein shower gel, and it smelled so sexy and reminded me of him, so I bought it and put it in there when he wasn't around."

"You could've left it on his stairs."

"I guess so," she shrugged off the comment, "but too late now. And my nose tells me he's using it daily. But he's been away a lot, so I don't see him every day."

"My friend, I wanna be a fly on the wall when he questions you about it. Not much slips by Rev unnoticed."

Naomi scrunched up her face. "M-hm." *Just me.*

Stella reached for a sandwich and took a bite. "I found some good delis not far from where we live. I'll take you there when you come visit."

"You only need to tell me when. I'm sure there are a few weekends between now and the twofer party where I can get away for a night."

"The *what* party? And why aren't you eating?"

"In a minute." Naomi took a sandwich and put it on her own plate. "Rev and I are referring to your combined bachelor/bachelorette party as a twofer party. Well, I do. He isn't too interested in all the details. So, I do my planning, then tell him what we're doing. Like the dance lessons."

Stella almost spit out the food and pressed a napkin to her mouth. "The..."

"Dance lessons, missy." Naomi grinned and pushed her sandwich around.

"Why? You know how to dance! And Rev must know how to sway left and right."

"Turns out he's been holding out on us. I thought it would be fun to sign up for a few lessons, mostly to see his reaction. Which was exactly as I expected. He sputtered and tried to weasel out of it. But he got the last laugh when he proved after thirty minutes of excruciating basic dance step practice that he knows how to do a mean cha-cha."

"Ha, serves you right. And you said lessons, as in plural?"

"Yes, our next one is coming up on Wednesday. The waltz." Naomi rolled her eyes. "He'll probably make me look like the biggest klutz when I step on his toes."

She held up her left foot and said, "At least I have a good excuse. Thank goodness he was with me when I hurt my ankle in my room in Richmond."

"Stop right there and go back to 'in my room.' How exactly did you hurt your ankle?" Stella put her chin on her fingers and smirked.

"We had a pillow fight, and he accused me of not fighting fair, well... I accused him of hiding behind the sofa first, and anyway, I jumped off the bed and twisted my ankle."

"Pillow fight? Bedroom? Why do I have to pull those tidbits out of you?"

"It's a longer story. We had three rooms reserved, but Gram Annie had called and cancelled our third room. So we gave Charlie one room, and Rev offered to sleep on the sofa bed in my room." She bit into her sandwich and washed it down with a healthy sip of wine. "And later, when we were chatting in bed, Rev said I should buy the stemless glasses."

"In bed? I thought he slept on the sofa bed. What else are you not telling me?"

"There's not much more to tell. After I got hurt, he got ice for my ankle, and the whole trip was completely messing me up, and we'd already gotten into a big argument on our way down to Charleston, and I was tired, so we sat on the bed, drank this wine, and listened to ABBA."

"This is getting better and better, even though it's hard to follow you. You're jumping all over the place! Let me summarize. You listened to ABBA, and Rev did too?! On the bed."

"Yup," Naomi glared at Stella.

"Anything else?"

"No...yes... I fell asleep eventually, and when I woke up, an arm was draped over my waist. Then I rolled over and someone kissed my forehead and my nose. And when I opened my eyes, there was Revan."

"Oh, Nam, finally! Aren't you happy?"

"No! Because before he could kiss me for real, Charlie called for help. And then he left on Tuesday for who-knows-where, and I have no idea what to think. I'm getting so many mixed signals."

"Start by taking a breath. At least now you're both aware of your feelings for each other, which is good, right?"

"I don't know. Really, I don't. In Virginia Beach, Rev said he's trying to figure something out. His exact words were, 'I have to work through some shit.' I offered to help him, but he wouldn't tell me what it is. Oh no, Stella, I hope he's not referring to me. What if he's trying to find a nice way to get rid of me?"

Naomi's gut clenched. "This whole week, I haven't had an appetite. I can only think about him. If he was here, I would've cornered him already. Or thrown myself at his feet...I don't know... But I also don't want to cause bad blood between us."

Stella got up and pulled Naomi into a hug. "It will work out. For him to kiss you is huge. Did it feel like a forced kiss?"

"No, and it wasn't a real kiss, anyway," she said and tried to hold back tears. "I want him so much it hurts."

"I know, Nam. Let me know if there's anything I can do to help you."

"Could you ask him how he feels about me?"

"We're not fifteen anymore, so no. But I'll watch him closely and tell you what I see. And I can ask Luca if he knows anything."

"Yes, great idea. Ask David, too. Revan and David must talk sometimes, don't you think?"

"We'll do some brainstorming tomorrow with Jo and Sabrina. But we need to be careful what we say in front of Dinah," Stella returned to her chair and rubbed her hands together. "Let's get this ball rolling. Mission Let's-Get-Revan is now officially in full swing."

"Yes, thank you so much." Naomi smiled and took another large sip of wine, then finished her sandwich in three bites before she reached for the next one. "Mm, these are really so good. I'm so glad I told you everything."

The women were exhausted by the time they left the bridal store late Saturday afternoon.

Sabrina said, "Thank goodness you found The Dress. David will be blown away when he sees you in it."

"Thank you," Stella said. "Dress shopping is absolutely not my favorite thing to do."

"You could've fooled us in there, missy. How many did you try on?" Naomi asked, "Ten? Fifteen?"

"Ten, I think... So, what's next, girls?"

"Let's go home, order pizza, and hang out," Naomi suggested. "Revan's not home till tomorrow, so the house is ours."

A while later, Stella, Jo, and Sabrina lounged comfortably in the backyard and flipped through magazines when Dinah asked, "Naomi, can I stay over tonight too?"

"Fine with me, but where are we going to put you? Stella and Sabrina are camping out in the smaller guest room on air mattresses and Jo is sleeping in my bedroom. Did you bring anything to sleep in or clothes for tomorrow?"

"I thought I could borrow one of your T-shirts. And I could sleep in Revan's room."

"No!" Stella, Jo, and Naomi shouted at the same time.

Sabrina laughed, "You guys, why not?"

"His bedroom is his sanctuary," Stella said, and Naomi nodded.

"Here's an idea. I'll sleep on the sofa in the living room, and Dinah and Jo, you two can have my room," Naomi suggested.

"Okay! Thank you so much. I'll let my mom know later," Dinah gave her a hug. "Can we order pizza now? I'm starving."

Thirty minutes later, Naomi opened the door to accept their pizza.

"Pizza delive...hello, sweets! So, this is where ya live?"

"What are you doing here?" she was barely able to get the words out while a clammy feeling slid like slime over her whole body.

"Gotta make a living, sweets, and one of my jobs is at Pizzeria Palermo. Maybe I'll always get to deliver your order now." He winked at her. "Ask for me. Ronnie, remember?"

"Naomi, do you need help?" Dinah came to her side and held out her arms for the pizza boxes and salad containers.

"Thank you, put them on the counter, please," she said and paid Ronnie before closing the door in his face. "Shit." She rested her forehead against the door and took a deep breath. Now he knew where she lived.

"What happened?" Stella asked from the kitchen, where she took out plates.

In a few sentences, she told them how she met Ronnie. "I've seen him repeatedly over the past few weeks, and yesterday he was watching me from a bench in Signer's Garden."

"It was really weird how he stared at you. And what a creepy grin he has," Dinah said. "I got goose bumps."

"I don't think I'll order pizza again anytime soon."

"Are you going to tell Rev?" Dinah wanted to know.

Naomi shrugged. "No, I'm hoping the guy will leave me alone if I ignore him long enough. I'm usually not spooked this easily."

They sat down at the large kitchen island and helped themselves to pizza when they heard something slam outside the door. Naomi jumped up and pressed her hand to her chest.

The door swung open and Revan strode in. Putting his bags down, he grinned. "Just in time for the party. Hello, lovely ladies."

A chorus of four voices called out, "Hi, Rev."

"Why are you back already? I thought you'd stay until tomorrow," Naomi asked at the same time.

"Change of plans, Nugget. Luckily I could change my ticket for an earlier flight. I can't believe you're having a pizza party without me. Did you order one with pepperoni?"

He walked over and gave Stella, Jo, and Sabrina each a hug and kissed their cheeks before he hugged his sister and kissed the top of her nose. "Hey, Peanut. Let me know when you want to go home later, I'll take you over."

Dinah beamed at him, "No need. I'm sleeping over tonight. Jo and I are sharing Naomi's bedroom."

"And where does Naomi sleep?" he asked and looked at her over Dinah's head and Naomi wasn't sure if she imagined it or not, but for a split second, she thought he winked at her. It must've been a tic.

"On the couch," Dinah babbled on. "Because Stella and Sabrina are in the smaller guest room."

"Why don't you sleep in my second bedroom, Peanut? Let Naomi sleep in her own bed."

Dinah snorted. "No thanks. I want to be with everybody else. This is a girls' weekend."

"Well, sleep wherever you want," he said and tousled Dinah's hair.

Naomi followed the exchange. He had said hello to everybody but her. Instead of standing there, she went to get a plate for him. Passing the pizza boxes, she plucked a ring of pepperoni and lifted her hand to her mouth when he appeared next to her. "Stealing pepperoni again, Nugget? I doubt that's what you ordered." He raised her hand and ate the pepperoni slice from her fingers, then leaned in and kissed her cheek, close to the corner of her mouth. His lips lingered for a split second longer than necessary.

Naomi scowled at him and said, "It wasn't yours either, Shutterbug."

He laughed and said to the other women, "Ladies, please eat before the pizza gets cold. I'll join you after taking my bags upstairs. I can't wait to hear about your pedicures and dress shopping today."

He smirked at her. "See how interested and involved I am, Nugget? Did you bring your little color wheels?"

She reached for her wine glass, "I knew they'd fascinate you."

Stella was watching her, and Sabrina and Jo stared intently into the salad bowl in front of them, trying to hide their grins. Only Dinah seemed unfazed and dug into her pizza.

CHAPTER 23

REVAN—JULY 2019

Revan woke up to voices outside his open bedroom window. A glance at his phone confirmed his suspicion—seven o'clock on a Sunday morning.

He'd put an end to this gab fest right now. The women had stayed up long after midnight, laughing and calling out to each other while he sat brooding in his own rooms. Listening to the dress stories and everything else had been entertaining enough for a while, but then he excused himself under the pretense of catching up on emails. Just so he could stop staring at Naomi.

And now this.

He threw back his sheet, and got up to call down to the chatterboxes to please consider other people's desire to sleep in. In all fairness, they were talking very softly, but he wasn't in the best mood after a restless night. Before he reached the window, he heard his sister's voice. "Naomi, do you like my brother?"

"You know I like him, and we're friends."

Well, this could be interesting. Maybe he'd sit here and listen for a while.

"He's looking at you a lot. Like this..." she must have made a face because Naomi laughed. Dinah continued, "You're looking at him, too. I saw it yesterday when he went to his rooms. I think you should date him."

"Being friends and looking at each other isn't enough reason to be together."

"Well, it looked to me as if he kissed you when he came home," Dinah said. "And why did he eat the pepperoni from your fingers if you're only friends? He isn't doing it with anybody else, not even me. Thank goodness."

Go ahead, Peanut, you're asking excellent questions. Maybe you can help me figure out what I should do.

"You know, Dinah, as much as I'd love to give you a satisfying answer, I can't. Maybe you'll have to ask him."

Please don't, because there's no way in hell I'm telling you a thing, Peanut.

"He won't tell me anything. He'll say 'You're my little sister, Peanut. I never have and I never will discuss my love life with you.'" *Damn right, Peanut. Glad you already know that.*

Dinah went on, "You should hear when Mom nags him about settling down and giving her grandkids. He goes bonkers." *Enough, Peanut, no need to spill all our family dinner conversations.*

"Why are you asking me those questions this morning, Dinah? Any special reason?"

"Can this be our secret? You can't tell anybody."

"Okay, let's hear it." Revan could tell she was hesitant to make promises.

"There's this cool guy. Trevor is the older brother of my friend Tricia. When I'm at her house, he's often there. We talk, and sometimes he touches me a little."

"Umm, how is he touching you?"

Revan almost jumped out of the window to ask his sister a few more questions. Like, "does he have a death wish?"

Dinah said, "He puts his hand on my arm when I'm walking by, or he touches my shoulder. Like Rev does with you sometimes. A few times, he played with my hair or pulled me in for a hug. He asked a few days ago if he could kiss me."

"Do you mind it when he does these things?"

Naomi had ignored Dinah's comment about him touching her, Rev realized.

"No, I really like Trevor and think he's cute, but other girls are saying all he wants is sex. But maybe he would be different with me? If he wants to hold me and kiss me, doesn't it mean more?"

Hold it right there, Peanut! Not happening. Nugget, tell her to forget about it.

"Dinah, look at me," Naomi said. "Yes, usually kissing, holding each other, and cuddling are things you do with someone you have feelings for, and are the first step to more. But for some people it's just a natural thing to do

201

and it doesn't mean anything more than having friendly feelings for the other person."

"You mean like Revan and you?"

"Yeah, I guess," Naomi said. "Dinah, I don't know this boy, and I don't know if what you've heard through the other girls is true or born out of jealousy, but I ask you to be very, very careful."

"But I want him as my boyfriend. And I'm sure he wouldn't hurt me."

"I'm not talking about him hurting you physically, but he might want more from you than you're willing to give. It's normal to think about a boyfriend at your age and how far you would go with him. But asking me for advice tells me you're hesitant about this, too. I have a feeling it would be your first time, am I right?" He didn't know what Dinah's response was since she didn't confirm or deny it. "Please don't rush into something you're not sure about. You're still young, and when you find someone special, you'll be glad you waited and saved that moment for him."

"When you were my age, did you have someone you really wanted to be with? Did you wait for him? What was the longest you waited for a boy?"

And this is the moment when I should log out of this conversation.

When Naomi didn't answer right away, he wondered if she would even reply to his sister's nosy question. Then he heard Naomi say very quietly, "Now I'll tell you a secret. Yes, there's been someone special since I was only a few years older than you are, and I've been waiting for him for more than ten years."

"Ten years is *forever*. You've never had sex with another boy, or man, because of him?" Dinah's voice was a mixture of awe and disbelief.

"Well, this is really getting a little personal, but..." Naomi paused before she continued, "You know I've been in relationships, but they are all short-lived because I compare every man to this one guy. And yes, I've had sex with my boyfriends, but I would've waited for him if he had given me only one sign that he wanted me, too."

"Why did you never tell him about your feelings?" Dinah asked with an audible gasp.

"Because I don't think he ever thought of me in a romantic way. I was afraid he wouldn't return the feelings and I couldn't deal with his rejection."

Man, what does she see in such a loser? Revan thought.

"He sounds like a jerk." Dinah confirmed his thought. "Do you still think about him?"

"Yes, all the time."

"Why don't you go after him? You know, fight for what you want and blah blah blah," Dinah asked.

"My reasons haven't changed," Naomi sighed.

"Then maybe you really should just hook up with Revan," Dinah suggested.

"Now there's an idea," Naomi's laughter sucked the air right out of Revan's lungs. And how dare his sister offer him as a consolation prize? He never had—and never would—play second fiddle.

"Come on, Dinah, let's go inside and wake up the others. We have a few things to do before they all leave this afternoon."

"Can you and I go dress shopping together again another day?" Dinah asked. "Or get a pedi?"

"Absolutely. I still haven't decided on a dress myself," Naomi laughed. "So another pedi and lunch on me are a sure thing."

Revan heard chairs being pushed around and teaspoons dropped into empty mugs.

"Naomi?"

"Yes?"

"Thank you for not telling me to forget about Trevor. Because I can't."

"Oh, sweetie, I know. I know exactly how you're feeling."

Revan had heard enough. Thornton Wilder must have been delusional when he wrote in his play *The Match-maker* that everybody should eavesdrop occasionally to be reminded that the world outside one's head is different from the one inside.

He hadn't gained any new insights. But he was more determined than ever to find out who the jackass was who held Naomi's heart hostage.

Because he wasn't about to pose as a stand-in as his sister had so graciously suggested.

On Wednesday evening Revan arrived at the dance studio shortly before six o'clock. While he waited outside for Naomi, he checked his phone for messages.

He groaned. Not again. Barb asked if he'd swing by later tonight to go over last details regarding the book project. It wasn't the first time she'd asked to see him in the evening using the flimsy excuse of talking about work. Naomi saw it right away, well before he did.

Rev typed back,

Can't, I have plans. I'll call
you in the morning.

"Did you wait long, Shutterbug?" Naomi called from afar. She was wearing ballet flats, a flowing maxi skirt and a simple V-neck T-shirt, with her hair loose the way he liked it best, and he wanted to scoop her up and run home with her. Instead, he smiled broadly when she hurried toward him.

"Just got here. How's your foot? Should we cancel our lesson?"

"My ankle is pretty good, so let's go in." Before he had a chance to reach for the door handle, Naomi opened the door to the studio and went inside without greeting him with the usual peck on his cheek.

"You seem nervous, Nugget. Are you okay?" He wanted to ask more, but Miss Estelle walked toward them.

"Everything's fine." Her voice had that fake happy undertone. If she didn't want to be here, all she had to do was tell him, and they'd be out in a flash.

"Hi, Miss Estelle. How are you?" Naomi asked.

"Very well, thank you. Follow me, please," Miss Estelle said. As if on cue, Alfredo appeared from behind a door and joined them.

The first thirty minutes crept by...sticky molasses ran faster. Revan counted in his head, *One-two-three, One-two-three, Alfy, keep your hands from me*...until Miss Estelle announced, "And now, we put it all together! Revan, Naomi, take your positions, please."

Finally! The moment he'd been waiting for since...well, since their morning snuggle in Richmond.

For the remaining half hour, they went through the routines, and he didn't even notice when one of them made a wrong move. The way Naomi was pressed against him, he was too busy hiding his physical reaction to her.

"Do you like my shampoo?" her voice shook him out of his daydreams. "You've had your nose buried in my hair for the past three songs. I'll give you a bottle if you want."

"You can put it next to my shower gel." He enjoyed the slightly uncomfortable look on her face and grinned. Too bad—no, thank goodness—they weren't alone. She was adorable. "Did you think I wouldn't notice it? But I like it. So, thanks."

"You're not mad because I went in your bathroom?" she flashed him a big grin. They stood in the middle of the dance studio, Revan with his hands in his front pockets, Naomi with her hands on her hips, and waited for the next song.

"No, everyone is allowed one misstep. This was yours, Nugget." His eyes moved to her mouth.

ANNETTE G. ANDERS

"Your last dance today, so make it count, my dears. Naomi, stop talking! You know I take dancing seriously and don't approve of idle chitchat," Miss Estelle called and clapped her hands. "Alfredo, music please."

Revan had started to like the old woman and laughed. He held his arms in position and waited for Naomi to step into them.

But when the music started playing, it was as if someone had punched him in the chest. Who in their right mind picked this song to dance a waltz? He looked for Alfredo, but the man had disappeared.

While Rod Stewart crooned "Have I Told You Lately," Revan imagined Naomi, as she looked up from beneath him, both moving in sync to another rhythm, one as old as mankind. Where no words were needed, where they let their bodies speak.

After stepping out into the warm summer evening, Naomi immediately scanned the street both ways. She almost speed-walked ahead of him, until he caught up with her and said, "Why are you in such a rush? Want to stop for a glass of wine and something to eat?"

"Where do you want to go?" she asked, but didn't slow down.

"The Red Owl is on our way."

"I don't know. We can decide when we see who else is there."

"Are you embarrassed to be seen with me, Nugget?" he chuckled.

"Nah," she said.

A few minutes later, after Naomi checked out the pub from the sidewalk, she said, "Okay, looks good."

They secured a table, and Revan ordered their drinks at the bar. Naomi was glancing around again, and even craned her neck to check out the tables on the second floor.

"Expecting anybody in particular?" he asked when he sat down.

"No, only looking," she said.

He knew she was keeping something from him. Her eyes were glued to the entrance, supporting his suspicion. But since she shrugged it all off, he had no choice but to let it go—for now.

For the next hour, they sat, ate, chatted, and drank, and by the time they left, she seemed more relaxed.

At home, he asked, "Care for another glass of wine?"

"No, not for me, thanks. I wanna take a bath and go to bed early." She flipped through her mail and separated magazines and bills from junk mail.

"What's this?" she held up a medium-sized manila envelope. It had her handwritten first name on the front but no address.

"I don't know. It was mixed in with the mail. Open it and you'll find out."

"Oh God." She dropped the envelope and backed away from it. A wilted rose fell out with a note. *Picked this at the park for ya today. R.*

Revan picked up both. "Who sent this?" He turned the note around, then reached for the envelope.

"I'm not sure," she rubbed her arms and cleared her throat.

"Did you get others?"

Naomi shook her head.

"If you get even one more, I want to know about it." He moved closer to her, but she held up her hand and said, "It's probably a stupid prank. Let's forget it. Now, I need to go have a bath and get some sleep."

"Nugget…"

"I'll see you tomorrow. Good night, Rev."

Whatever was going on rattled her more than she cared to admit. She didn't even use her nickname for him. And he didn't like that at all.

CHAPTER 24

REVAN—JULY 2019

L uca and Revan sat under one of many yellow umbrellas at a restaurant bordering Battery Park and looked out over New York Harbor. Traffic on the Hudson River and New York Bay was almost as busy as the streets of Manhattan, but well-orchestrated by invisible hands.

"What game do you think you're playing?" Luca asked.

"I enjoy watching the yachts and ferries. Especially on an afternoon midweek when everybody else is working their asses off. Chasing the money," Revan said and pointed with his thumb in the general direction of the Financial District. He stretched out his legs and reached for his beer. He'd prefer a glass of whiskey, but two o'clock in the afternoon was a little too early. But if his friend continued his annoying interrogation, which had been going on for a while now, he might change his mind.

"You know what I mean," Luca said. "What's going on between you and Naomi?"

"Nothing. You know where I stand. Nothing has changed." His eyes never left the harbor. Boat traffic was fascinating...

"Several reliable sources have told me something different."

"Come on, give me a break. Stella is still wearing pink glasses, and probably always will, and Jo is repeating what she gets fed from Stella," Revan said. "They're hearing wedding bells ringing wherever they go. Must be the Christmas in July shit."

A cargo ship, lying low in the river, made its way slowly into the Hudson River, blaring its horn in a deep, booming blast. He wondered briefly where it was going. Probably Albany—the Hudson was navigable by ocean-faring vessels all the way to the capital of New York.

Rev kept watching the freighter.

Maybe he should jump aboard. As one of the oldest surviving European settlements from the original thirteen colonies, and the longest continuously chartered city in the United States, Albany had an interesting historical background, and he had liked it when he went there a few years ago while working on a feature about Tech Valley, New York State's competitor to Silicon Valley.

"I heard something about pizza, pepperoni, and a kiss, all within a few minutes last week," Luca prompted, shaking him out of his musings.

"Why can't you just drop it? What do you want me to say?" Revan looked around for a waiter. He was ready for that glass of bourbon now.

"From everything you've told me, and what I've seen myself when you're in the same room with her, you want her. But the next thing I hear, from you and my sources, is you can't leave town fast enough or are in a questionable mood."

"Tell your sources to worry about themselves. For cryin' out loud, what I do is nobody's business," Rev said heatedly.

"Why don't you talk to Naomi instead of running away? What's holding you back?" Luca turned in his chair to look directly at Revan and pointed his index finger at him. "And do not give me the friendship bullshit you brought up last time we talked."

"Why don't we talk about something else? *Your* love life, for example?"

"There's nothing to discuss. Rev, I've never known you to shy away from a challenge."

"Naomi isn't a challenge. She's the biggest conflict I've ever faced," Rev said and glanced at his phone.

"Something else you've never avoided before," his friend reminded him. "By the way, do you realize you're checking your phone every five minutes? Any other lady keeping you on a short leash?"

"Shit, man, you know I don't want any other woman. Naomi is all I'm thinking about."

"Ah, there we go. Was that so hard to admit? To yourself and to me?" Luca grinned.

"You should've become a lawyer instead of a journalist." Revan rubbed the back of his neck. "How come I never realized how annoyingly good you are at nagging people?"

"Have I finally worn you down? Good, then spill it," Luca challenged him.

Should he tell Luca, to get him off his back?

"I almost screwed up in Richmond. We woke up snuggling, and I started kissing her. If we hadn't been interrupted by Charlie, I would've gone for more."

"Wait a second, you've skipped over some details here. How did you end up waking up together?"

"Messed-up room reservations, long story." He couldn't believe the direction this conversation was taking. And he wasn't willing to rehash every minute of the morning in question. Time to change tracks.

"So, you kissed her. Sounds like step one," Luca said. "Did she kiss you back?"

Or maybe we're not changing tracks.

"Let's just say she was half-asleep, so it was probably a reflex when she reached for me. She said she was dreaming."

"And since?"

"Nothing. I haven't spent much time at home since we got back."

"Running away doesn't solve any of your issues. Avoidance and procrastination are not your friends in this case."

Revan didn't say anything for a moment. Maybe it was time to talk about one of the conflicts he struggled with the most. He trusted Luca to listen with an open mind, despite his teasing. And he trusted his judgement and advice one hundred percent.

"You win. But I need more than beer." He signaled the waiter and ordered two glasses of whiskey.

"Here's the problem. I don't think she's available. She told me she's been in love with someone for pretty much her whole life."

"Hmm… Obviously, he's not around. Do you know if it's anyone we know?"

"She wouldn't tell me…only said I might've seen him a few times. But last weekend I overheard her telling Dinah how she compares every guy she's dating with him."

"Really?" Luca said.

"She said the guy never noticed her, and I've been trying to figure out who the loser is. Can you think of anybody who went to school with the girls? I'd like to try to meet him and talk sense into him."

"You'd go and play matchmaker for the woman you want for yourself?"

"Wipe that stupid grin off the face," Revan snarled.

Luca threw his hands in the air. "I don't know what to tell you. I think you should go after her."

"How many times do I have to say it? I can't! And how can I pursue something with her while knowing she's dreaming about some other guy? The other clowns she's dated didn't know about him, but I do."

"Let me ask you a question."

"Another one?"

Luca ignored him. "What would've happened if you *had* slept with her in Richmond?"

"I wouldn't be sitting here with you, answering stupid questions."

The waiter approached their table and served the whiskey. Revan pushed one glass in Luca's direction. "Cheers."

They clinked glasses and took long sips, and he welcomed the burn as the whiskey slid down his throat. An image came up of him eating the pepperoni slice from her fingers. How she accidentally turned her face when he wanted to kiss her cheek, and he almost got her full on her lips. Under the watchful eye of four overly nosy women.

"So, what would've happened if..." Luca asked again.

Revan sighed. "It's Thursday, so it's her afternoon off, and she'll be walking the dogs, then spending time with Gram Annie and Charlie. She'd normally be home by six, and we'd go to the deli for a bite to eat or I'd call in something."

"Man, I have no more questions. You know her daily schedule down to the hour, and you wonder what's wrong with you?" Luca shook his head. "I take it back. I do have one more question."

"Couldn't prevent you from asking the other twenty..." Revan grumbled.

"What is *really* holding you back from taking this to the next level with her?"

"Weren't you listening? Don't you remember our conversation at the Red Owl a few weeks ago? Three things—the mystery guy, losing her as a friend, and threatening the harmony within our group."

"This is getting old. Come up with something less lame." Luca put his elbows on the table.

Here it comes.

"Let me spell it out for you. The five of us," Luca ticked off the names on his fingers, "Stella, Naomi, Jo, you, and me, have gone through a lot together. You and I have known them since before they started wearing training bras."

Revan didn't want to think about training bras—or any other bras. It wasn't a visual he needed. "Can you get to the point?"

"We've been best friends for most of our lives. But we don't live together like the *Friends'* gang. We all have our individual lives. And I think it's pretty obvious what's going on."

Rev harrumphed.

"You want her. Find out what her feelings are. If you are attracted to each other, fine. And if it doesn't turn into happily-ever-after, then you remain civil, say goodbye, and go your separate ways and—as old friends—see each other twice a year at a party."

Revan rubbed the back of his neck again. "What are you saying?"

"Do you need me to write it out for you? I'm not saying you should go all caveman on her..."

"A little dramatic, don't you think?"

"...and rip off her clothes the moment you see her. Take her out on dates, be a little more romantic. Get a feeling for what she likes as a woman. Woo her...and stop running away from your own feelings and stupid fears."

"I told her she could buy wine glasses for the house."

Luca snorted. "Really, Rev? And was she happy to be allowed to buy six or eight glasses for thirty bucks?"

"She was actually pretty excited. But it was also after Lisa called about Gram Annie being in the hospital. It was all too much, I think. I told you she's vulnerable right now."

"Flowers, Forrester! Start with flowers. When you've mastered step one, maybe watch a movie together!"

"Good idea, maybe a movie night at home. She seems to like movie nights." Revan grinned at his friend. Then he sobered up quickly.

"What now? What's wrong with flowers or a movie?"

"Last week, after our dance lesson," he saw Luca's smirk and said, "not a word, buddy. Anyhow, after we came home from a drink—see, I took her out afterward..."

"Let me guess, you stopped at the Red Owl."

"Of course, she likes to go there."

He received an eye-roll. "Man, try someplace new."

"Hmm, she liked Clarke's when she forced me to take her there a few weeks ago." Rev scratched his chin.

"She *forced* you to go to Clarke's?! Rev, buddy, sorry to tell you, but she's light-years ahead of you," Luca hollered. "Forced you... You seem to have a lot of catching up to do. I used to think you're a smart man, but it looks as if you're pretty dense."

"Happy to entertain you... Anyhow, after we got home, there was an envelope in the mail. It had her name on it, but no address or return address, and when she opened it, a flower fell out with a note. She blanched when she saw it, but then shrugged it off as a prank."

Luca sat up straight. "When was that exactly?"

"Last week on Wednesday. Why?"

"Jo mentioned something about Naomi acting weird when they ordered pizza on Saturday and said the delivery guy was someone who had harassed her at the pub a while ago. Jo also said Dinah saw the guy."

Revan couldn't believe what Luca had just insinuated. "You think the asshole is stalking Nugget? I happened to walk by when he followed her out of the pub and sent him packing. He wasn't happy."

"Do you know of any other incidents?" Luca asked.

"She kept looking over her shoulder when we met on Wednesday, and when I invited her to go for a drink, she wouldn't agree until she could see who was in there. I asked her if she was nervous, but she told me she was just looking around."

Then he remembered something else, "I also saw him when you, David, and I went to the bar the day she moved in. He kept staring at me." He slammed a hand on the table. "Why didn't she tell me? And worse...why didn't I connect the dots earlier?"

"You know her, she doesn't scare easily and is probably trying to deal with it herself. But now you're aware of it and can keep an eye out. Don't hesitate to get police involved, especially because he knows where she lives."

"Thanks, buddy. For everything, really! I'll drive home first thing tomorrow morning." Revan pulled out his wallet and put money on the table.

"As much as I enjoy your visit, I agree. I think you should be in Philly, Rev. Maybe for more than one reason," Luca agreed, checking his phone when he stood and smiled.

"Anybody we know?" Revan asked with a big grin. *Two can play this game.*

"Maybe. Maybe not," Luca pushed his hair out of his face.

"I think we've grown up, man." Revan started whistling "Wind of Change."

"You're the brother I never had, and we'll get through this together," Luca said and slapped Rev's shoulder. "Because I feel a change in the air, too."

CHAPTER 25

≺∘◯∽◯∘≻

Naomi—July 2019

"What do you want from me? Leave me alone!" Naomi snapped irritably. She closed the door with a bang and leaned against the inside of it. This wasn't the first time this week the creep had been waiting near the house when she got home. She saw him hanging out around the corner or sitting on the front steps of a neighbor's house.

He was everywhere.

She really should call the cops, but what could they do? It wasn't against the law to stand on a street corner. But she couldn't go on like this much longer. Maybe she should go online and read about stalkers and how to get rid of them.

She closed her eyes, willing her heart to slow down. Her hands shook.

"Nugget, what's going on?"

Her eyes flew open at the sound of Revan's voice and she pushed harder against the door.

"Oh, geez, Rev! What are you doing here?" she asked and wiped her hands on the sides of her capris.

"I was done early with everything in the city." He stopped a few feet away from her. "Did I scare you? I didn't mean to." He tried to make eye contact.

"No, you didn't. Maybe a little bit. I didn't expect you until tomorrow or Sunday."

She could feel her heart rate finally slowing down and pushed herself away from the door.

"What was going on when you came in? Who were you talking to?"

"Nothing. Forget about it." She dropped her purse on a table and slid out of her sandals. Something dark red on the kitchen counter caught her eye.

"Those roses are nice. Like the ones at Stella's engagement party." She went over and put her nose to them. "And they smell so good. Where do they come from?"

"The little flower shop on Chestnut Street."

"Did you buy them?"

"Yeah."

"Hmm. I know it's not your mom's birthday... Who is the lucky duck?" *Do I really want to know?*

"You," he folded his arms and watched her.

Naomi's head whipped around. He had bought flowers for *her*?

Putting a hand on his folded arms, she leaned in and kissed his cheek. "Thank you. I haven't gotten flowers in... forever."

"You're welcome. Umm...listen...do you want to go out and grab dinner?"

"I'm sorry, but I was looking forward to a quiet Friday evening at home." *What is he up to?*

"Shall I order pizza? With extra pepperoni for the pepperoni thief in this house, maybe?"

"No!" she called, her heart racing again. Then said in a calmer voice, "Mom gave me meat loaf last night to take home. I planned to heat up leftovers and have a salad with it. There's plenty."

"Sounds good. How about a glass of wine?"

"Yes, please. But let me go upstairs and change quickly." Halfway up her stairs she stopped and said, "You know, Shutterbug. I could get used to being treated so nicely when you come home after a few days away. Flowers—"

She heard him chuckle when she continued to her room.

After washing her face and changing into a dress, she sat down on her bed, needing a moment to compose herself and slow her heart rate.

Thank goodness Rev was back! Ronnie was starting to make her nervous.

Should she tell Rev about him? The perfect moment would've been a few minutes ago when she came home. Why did she try to deal with it herself? Naomi snorted.

Because she hoped Ronnie would eventually get the message if she continued to tell him to leave her alone.

The clattering of plates interrupted her thoughts, and tantalizing aromas of warmed-up food teased her nose. By the time she joined Revan, he had taken out plates and filled their glasses. She quickly tossed the salad, and when they sat down at the counter, asked about his days in New York.

Distraction 101 at its finest.

"Work went well, the new book is at the publishing house, and Luca and I had a good time catching up. Yesterday afternoon we sat in Battery Park and looked out at the Statue of Liberty and watched the harbor traffic. It was beautiful, with all the yachts and boats, and made me think how much fun it would be to go back another weekend. What do you think?"

"What does it have to do with me?"

"You could come along, and we can hang out with Jo and Luca. I was reminded this week how much I miss talking to him. Life's keeping us so busy, but we shouldn't neglect our friends. Maybe you and Jo can do some plotting and planning for the party. I'm sure she'd like to be involved, too."

"Good idea, Shutterbug. I'm not saying no to a weekend in New York—or to Jo helping me. There's so much more to organize. Can you believe it's only six weeks away?"

As soon as they finished eating, Naomi asked, "Want to go sit outside for a little bit? I'll clean up the kitchen quickly."

She walked around the island to load the dishwasher.

"Do you realize, Nugget, that you actually put a meal on the table today? I never thought you had it in you," he teased while he scraped the leftovers into the disposal before handing the plates to Naomi.

"I'm sure there's a lot more you don't know about me. But keep watching, I might surprise you again." Naomi raised her eyebrows and reached around Revan for the salad bowl.

He took the bowl from her and set it back on the counter. Then placed his hands on the countertop on both sides of Naomi, framing her in. "I'm looking forward to it, Nugget."

His face was so close, she could see little lines around his eyes and a few golden specks in the irises. She could almost feel his breath on her face, and only a few inches separated them. It was getting uncomfortably hot in the house.

She licked her lips and saw his eyes follow every swipe of her tongue. She wanted to kiss him so badly.

"Let's go sit outside before the bugs get too pesky and start eating me alive, Shutterbu...," she stopped mid-word and grinned, "never mind, they're already here."

Then she ducked under his arm, rushed to the other side of the counter and giggled. "Wasn't that a good one?"

"Hilarious, Nugget," he said drily.

She grabbed their glasses and called over her shoulder, "I'll be waiting outside, and don't forget the wine."

"How about bug repellant?"

Nearing her parents' house after work on Saturday afternoon, Naomi followed the sound of laughter and found Revan chasing the dogs around the lawn. Her grandmother and Charlie were sitting and watching from under a large umbrella.

"Naomi, why didn't you call me about Revan stopping by?" Gram Annie called and pointed to a vase with roses. "And look, he brought flowers. Isn't he such a sweet boy?"

It was indeed sweet of him. "What a nice surprise, Gram."

"Hello, Nugget," he said close to her ear. His voice, combined with the puff of breath touching her neck, sent shivers down her spine. Would there ever be a day when she wasn't so affected by him?

She turned around and patted his cheek, "Such a sweet boy."

When Gram Annie announced her need for a nap twenty minutes later, Naomi and Revan said they'd take the dogs for a walk and invited Charlie to join them. The two boxers ran in different directions and wanted to chase squirrels and birds, twisting Naomi's arms more than once when they changed direction too fast.

"Why don't you give me their leads and you push the wheelchair," Revan offered. He ordered the dogs to sit, reached for the leashes, then said to them, "Now walk."

"Look at them," she complained. "All you do is snap your fingers and they behave."

"What can I say—" he winked at her.

"Revan, Naomi, I want to thank you both for giving Annie and me the chance to spend this time together. Next time we see each other it'll likely be in the afterlife. Or wherever we're going," Charlie said a few minutes later.

Naomi looked at Revan, also grateful for his generosity with his time and devotion to her grandmother and great-uncle. He was a good guy. Always had been.

Charlie's voice interrupted her thoughts. "I want to treat you two kids to a nice dinner, on me, as a thank-you. Annie said you like Clarke's, and I called and made a reservation for you for tonight at eight. If it doesn't work for you, you can reschedule. They have my credit card number, and all expenses are covered. Go and have some fun." He looked at Revan and said in a conspiratorial voice, "I hear there's dancing on Saturday nights. Take her for a spin."

He snickered and had to cough. "Lungs are not what they used to be, and neither are my legs, or I'd take our Annie out myself."

Naomi smiled at him, patted his hand, and said, "Thanks, Uncle Charlie." She didn't correct his lapse. They had become more frequent and lasted longer, but she didn't want to upset him and so played along.

Hours later, after dinner was finished and they both had declined dessert, Revan ordered a whiskey and Naomi another glass of wine to round off their meal. In the background, the band began playing "Fly Me to the Moon."

"Want to dance?"

"Sure! After all, Miss Estelle ordered us to practice."

When he stood and held out his hand, she accepted it, and together they walked to the small dance floor, where he put his arms around her waist and pulled her close. "Let's just listen to the music, Nugget. Stop thinking."

With her arms around his neck, they began to move slowly. His face was buried in her hair again, and she wished this moment would last forever. But after three songs, he said quietly, "Are you ready to go home, Nugget?"

She could only nod.

Revan didn't let go of her hand until they reached their table, where he lifted it to his mouth and kissed her knuckles.

"What a wonderful surprise from Charlie. We have to tell him tomorrow," he said.

Again, she could only nod, and swallowed hard.

At home, Naomi shook off her shoes and said, "I don't want the evening to end yet. I think I'll have one more glass of wine. Would you like to join me?"

"Of course. Sounds like a perfect ending for a date night."

"Date night?" Naomi cocked her head. "It was Charlie's thank-you dinner for us."

"Nice restaurant, delicious dinner, beautiful lady at my table, and don't forget the dancing...what else would you expect from a first date?" He poured the wine.

"Well, in the movies, the boy usually tries to kiss the girl somewhat awkwardly when he drops her off at home," she quipped without thinking, accepted her glass and took a sip.

"Be glad I'm not a boy."

He took her glass, put it on the counter, took hold of her freed hand and walked to the front door.

Naomi laughed, "Where are we going? I'm not wearing my shoes."

"You don't need them." He opened the door and pulled her outside. Stepping down one step, Rev took her face in his hands and asked very quietly, "May I kiss you?"

He lowered his mouth until their lips almost touched. He was so close, what was he waiting for?

One second, two seconds...

It was now or never!

Naomi closed the distance. His lips were soft, the kiss was gentle, until Revan pressed one hand to her lower back and pulled her closer. And deepened his kiss.

Slowly, he walked them back into the house, shut the door with his foot and didn't break their kiss until the kitchen island stopped their aimless wandering. His hand slid over her waist, over her hip, to her butt, and she could feel how powerfully their kiss affected him.

She was burning up from inside. Unlike in Richmond, she was fully awake and knew this wasn't a dream. She needed more, needed to feel his skin under her lips. She fumbled with the front of his shirt.

One button—undone.

Next button—undone.

He started to nibble on her earlobe, then breathed kisses down the side of her neck until he reached her collarbone.

"Nugget, you have no idea," his voice was raspy, "how long I've wanted to do this."

The cell phone vibrated on the counter behind her before her mother's ring tone played.

They broke apart and Revan pressed her forehead to his chest, his arms still around her. Naomi grabbed the phone blindly and answered the incoming call, trying to sound calm, not out of breath and fired up.

"Mom, what's up? Everything okay?" She reluctantly pushed away from Revan and turned her back to him, staring into the dark backyard. She didn't want to be on the phone, she wanted to be back in his arms and getting rid of his damn shirt.

"Honey, I have bad news. Charlie suffered a heart attack at Mary's house this evening. He was pronounced dead when the ambulance arrived."

"Oh, no!" Naomi started shaking and tried to hold herself together with one arm around her waist. Revan's arms came around her and held her tight. He put his chin on the top of her head and waited. "But...he seemed okay this afternoon. He was in a good mood. Why so suddenly?"

"We don't know anything yet, honey. He sat down in a recliner after dinner and closed his eyes."

"Do you want me to come over? How is Gram Annie taking it?"

"She's upset, but is taking it well overall," Lisa said. "We'll talk tomorrow, honey. I wanted to let you know before Gram calls you or in case you hear it from Jo. Why don't you come over for breakfast, around ten, maybe? Bring Revan, too, if he has time."

Revan nodded into her hair.

"Okay, Mom. Good night."

She put the phone back on the counter. "Did you hear everything?"

"I did, and I'm so, so sorry." He turned her around in his arms and held her.

It was all she wanted right now. And it was more intimate than sex would have been. She needed his strength. And tomorrow, she'd rely on his strength for Gram Annie.

A giggle-sob combination escaped her mouth.

Charlie had successfully interrupted them for the second time. Was he trying to tell them something?

CHAPTER 26

———————⊶o〰o⊷———————

NAOMI—JULY 2019

Two weeks later Naomi was looking forward to a quiet evening without any plans or urgent business to take care of.

Glancing over her shoulder as she speed-walked through the familiar streets on her way home had become second nature, and in the past few days she'd spotted Ronnie twice. Both times he watched her from a distance and waved. As if they were old buddies. She tried to take different routes to and from work, but unless she wanted to take huge detours, there were only a limited number of streets to choose from.

Turning the street corner, she froze. There he was again, coming toward her on a bike. Stepping behind a parked van, she mentally scrambled through her options.

A constant uneasiness had crept into her bones and was now joined by anger. Enough was enough! It was past time to do something.

She pulled out her cell phone and peeked around the truck to take a picture of him. Maybe it would help the cops, especially since she also had his first name and knew where he worked.

Where was he? She knew he hadn't passed her hiding spot yet, so she peeked again. There—he'd stopped a few doors down.

Naomi didn't notice that she was sweating until a few drops slid down the side of her face. She was thirsty and hungry. The last thing she felt like doing was crouching behind a van at the end of the day. She peeked once more. Ronnie was talking to the woman who moved in recently, and Naomi was able to get a photo of him.

While she bided her time, she wondered if Revan was home. *I should text him. If he comes out and distracts Ronnie, I can sneak into the house. But what am I gonna say? Stupid me. I should've told him about the creep.*

Naomi licked her lips. The blazing hot kiss at the end of their so-called date night was so promising, as if he'd finally emerged from his hibernation. But there hadn't been any repeats. Of course she'd been spending a lot of time at her parents' house since Charlie's death, and only went home to sleep and change clothes.

Home. One was her parents' house; one was Revan's house. And in both places she was nothing but a tenant.

The past weeks—*months*—had been an up-and-down of mixed signals. Naomi was utterly lost about what she was supposed to think. One day Rev kissed her as if he wanted her. Then he returned to be the jovial and loyal friend he'd always been. He still left town, too, but never for longer than two days in a row.

Something between them *had* shifted, and there was a new underlying tension. She didn't understand which direction things were going. They kept circling each other without making progress in any direction.

Naomi heard whistling and saw Ronnie finally pedal off, back the way he had come. Sprinting to her own front door, she opened it, darted in, slammed it shut—and exhaled with a loud swoosh.

"What's up, Nugget? Did you run?" Rev asked from the kitchen where he opened a bottle of wine. She wanted to go over and feel his arms around her. She wanted to feel safe.

"Oh, hi. Only from the other side of the street."

"And I thought you were eager to see me," he said and gave her his best lopsided smile.

"What are you doing?" *And stop giving me that sexy smile of yours.*

He kept grinning and pointed to the table outside. "I've got dinner for us ready. Pizza and..."

"You had pizza delivered from Pizzeria Palermo?" Naomi interrupted, the shock giving her chills.

"Nope, I went there and picked it up. You never said you don't like their pizza anymore, only that you don't want it delivered."

She hadn't told him why she avoided any food deliveries lately. Maybe it was time to come clean. About food—and a few other items on her plate.

Naomi swallowed hard before she said, "Well, you asked me a while ago why not, and it's because of this guy. Remember the creep from the tavern?"

Revan nodded, giving her a penetrating look. *Why doesn't he seem surprised?*

She cleared her throat, "He's been following me, and since he delivered the pizza when the girls were here, he knows where I live. I don't want to give him a reason to come to the house, so I avoid deliveries."

"And you never thought I should know about it?" The strange undertone in his voice matched the thunderous look on his face.

Naomi held up her hand, went over to the kitchen and pulled the still-warm pizza out of the oven.

"Half pepperoni, half veggie. Yum... Why don't we eat while I tell you everything?"

"About time," he muttered.

After cutting the pizza into smaller sections they could eat with their fingers, Rev reached for the bottle of wine he'd already opened.

"Okay, Nugget, start talking, and I want to know everything." He poured them each a glass.

"You actually know most of it. Tavern, pizza delivery, weird note in mailbox—" she said.

"Shit, Nugget, we should've contacted the cops right then. I can't believe this has been going on so long without you saying anything." He looked furious.

"I thought I could deal with it alone," she said, "but then he started to pop up in the strangest places. I've changed my route to work and home time and again, but he still finds me. And it's starting to make me nervous, Rev. A few minutes ago, I hid behind a truck because I saw him coming down our street. But he stopped a few doors down, where the new couple moved in."

"What were you thinking, Nugget?"

She shrugged. There wasn't much she could say that made sense.

"We're going to the police tomorrow morning."

"I took a picture of him from behind the truck, so maybe that'll help the cops. Do you think he's a stalker?"

"I'd say he fits the description," Rev said in a low voice.

"The police must have a database for stalkers, right?"

"They do. If he's been reported before, he should be in there."

Relief flooded her. She told Rev, and he wasn't mad.

"But enough of that. I'm hungry, and it's so sweet of you to have dinner ready. Thank you," she leaned across the table and gave him a quick kiss on his cheek.

Revan bit into his pizza, then paused as if he was counting to ten. "Remember how we talked about maybe going to New York for a weekend? I'd like to go tomorrow. We can leave right after we're done with the cops."

"Out of the blue? Why?" It sounded fantastic to get away for a day. But she didn't understand why it had to be this weekend and on such short notice.

"Between Charlie's death, Marcus and Helen coming to have him cremated and take his ashes home, constantly running around between the agency and your parents' house, I think you need a break."

"It sounds very tempting. And I don't have to work tomorrow morning, either. It really helps that we hired a new part-time employee. How long do you want to stay?"

"Maybe until Monday morning? I know you don't go into work until noon, and we can be home by then. It would be nice not having to rush home on Sunday evening."

"Hmm... I like your idea. But we'll keep it casual, okay? We won't go anywhere fancy, where we're required to dress up."

"Nope, we'll slum it, Nugget," Rev grinned.

"We don't even need a hotel. You can stay with Luca, and I can stay with Jo. The four of us can hang out during the day and dinner. I wouldn't mind some time alone with Jo to go looking for bridesmaid dresses. Maybe we'll find something different in New York."

"You still haven't found your dress? It sounds to me as if you girls are constantly dress shopping, but sure, if it's what you want. We'll text them later. Now finish up, I have dessert waiting."

"Wow, pizza *and* dessert? What's the occasion, Shutterbug?"

"Do I need a reason? Maybe I simply wanted to do something nice for you," he rubbed the back of his neck. Naomi didn't believe him for one minute, but she let it slide. She was sick of constantly second-guessing his every move. *Just enjoy the moment.*

"Have you ever heard of an incompetent stalker—who comes up with such a term?" Naomi asked Rev while they were driving away from the police department. "And if Ronnie is considered incompetent, I really don't want to see how a competent stalker behaves."

"Let's hope it doesn't get to that point," Rev said as he maneuvered his SUV onto the freeway.

"It is probably good to be out of town for a few days now the cops are going to the pizza place and keeping an eye on our neighborhood. I don't want to be underfoot."

"Good thinking yesterday, by the way! Between the picture and his first name, which the jerk gave you himself, it didn't take the detective long to find him in the database."

"I can't believe he stalked and harassed women in three other cities so far. Annapolis, DC, Baltimore—and now Philly. And he always disappeared before they could take him in," she rubbed her arms, then touched Rev's forearm and squeezed it lightly. "Thank you for helping me."

Then she laughed. "I seem to be thanking you a lot lately, Shutterbug. Don't get used to it."

Rev gave her a sideway look and hummed, "That's What Friends Are For."

A few hours later, Naomi, Jo, Revan, and Luca strolled through City Hall Park, pausing while Naomi dipped her hands in the cool water of the fountain at the south end of the park. The imposing Manhattan Municipal Building dwarfed everything around it and stretched up over the crowns of tall trees and into the dark blue sky. Naomi looked up at *Civic Fame*, the gilded copper statue atop the cupola, carrying a mural-style crown representing New York City's five boroughs.

"Luca, why don't we take Jo and Nugget to the place we went last time for a late lunch? My treat," Revan suggested. He sat on the wide stone rim of the fountain, running his hand through one of the four jets at the centerpiece of the fountain.

"Sure, why not? Maybe we'll have more enlightening conversations about the perils of personal attachments. The ladies can share their thoughts," Luca said with a barely-contained smirk.

"Or maybe not..." Rev mumbled. A strange look passed between the men, and Naomi was dying to know what it was about.

"Which perils?" she asked as they continued their walk. "And since when are you using those pompous words when you talk to each other?" She paused before she repeated, "'Enlightening conversations about the perils of personal attachments'—I hope it's not your nighttime reading assignment."

"I was more thinking about enjoying the views of the harbor," Rev replied, not answering her question. "And why don't we go to Ellis Island and Lady Liberty afterward?"

"Sure. We can include a stop in Jersey State Park. The view of Manhattan from there is phenomenal. Have you heard of the Empty Sky Memorial?" Luca asked.

"No, this is the first time I've heard the name, which surprises me. What is it?" Rev asked.

"A memorial to the New Jersey victims of the 9/11 attacks," Luca said. "I don't get why it's not better known."

Naomi said, "I've never heard of it either. And the last time I went to the Statue of Liberty was on a field trip in high school."

"I remember you were in a shitty mood because Chuck Carter didn't pay enough attention to you and used the excuse of the boat rocking to get a better feel of Ally Shuster's sizable front load," Jo laughed.

"Well, he did behave like a little schmuck," Naomi rolled her eyes and said, "Especially since he'd kissed me a few days before. And then he went and squeezed Ally's boobs when he thought nobody was watching. I mean, come on, Jo, he was supposed to be my boyfriend. We'd already kissed twice!"

"You didn't think of him as your boyfriend until after Ally got his attention. And one or two kisses doesn't automatically mean you're in a relationship with someone," Jo said.

"He wasn't even a good kisser," Naomi grimaced. "He slobbered." Naomi looked at Jo out of the corner of her eye. She was walking so close to Luca, it was amazing that their hands didn't catch fire. She'd have to watch them, since apparently nobody else had noticed what she did.

"Chuckie obviously made bad decisions since he didn't grab his chance with you," Rev said and put his arm around Naomi's shoulder. "Even if it's been...what? Fifteen years since he failed to realize what a treasure he had in his hands..."

"Sixteen years, but who's counting? I hadn't thought about Chuck in ages—until someone," she shot a pointed look at Jo, "had to drag out old stories. Chuck was a nobody."

Rev laughed and pulled her close. "What a relief. We wouldn't want you crying over an undeserving—what did you call him?—slobbering schmuck."

"Why don't you tell us about the first girl you kissed?" Naomi wanted to smack herself for asking, but it was too late to take it back.

He dropped his arm and put his hands in his front pockets. "Nope, nothing to tell," he added a little speed to his step and said, "Oh, good, we made it. Food and a beer comin' up."

Luca laughed, "Touchy subject, Rev?"

"Drop it." He approached the hostess at the restaurant and asked for a table for four.

After being seated, Jo looked at Luca and Rev and said, "What about the most *memorable* kiss?" Jo asked, surprising Naomi. Her cousin usually wasn't so pushy.

"Why don't you tell us yours, Jo? I think you're making those two uncomfortable," Naomi said, even though she was dying to hear Revan's answer.

"I can't think of one. Maybe it's yet to happen," Jo confessed. "Luca?"

"I'm starting to agree with Rev. Let's drop it," he said and scooted around on his chair.

Rev gave Naomi a strange look. She would have loved nothing better than to slide closer to him. Instead, she changed tracks and told Luca and Jo about their meeting with the police, ending with, "And I hope I'll never see the guy again."

"Why didn't you tell Revan earlier—like right after the pizza delivery, for example?" Jo asked.

"Not you, too," Naomi exhaled loudly. "I know, I know, I should've said something."

Rev put his hand on hers. "We'll be extra careful in the next few weeks. If you want, I'll go with you when you're walking around town."

"Thanks, but I don't think it's practical," she replied, "I'm taking up too much of your time already. When you let me move in, neither of us knew this was going to happen. It doesn't feel right to stick you with guard duty for who knows how long."

"We'll see, Nugget," he mumbled and let go of her hand.

Luca asked, "Rev, remember the break-ins in our neighborhood a few years ago, right before I moved to New York? We discussed installing a security system, but never got around to putting one in. There are some great ones out there these days. One tiny camera and you get the live feeds and alerts delivered to your cell phone. Since I still own half the house, I'll pay for half of it."

"Not a bad idea, man. It can't hurt to keep an eye on the house while I'm away. I have to fly to Savannah on Tuesday morning to finish my job there, but I'll get to it as soon as I'm back."

"You didn't tell me you're leaving town again," Naomi said, then bit her lip. She sounded needy and clingy—two traits she abhorred.

"I'll be back either Friday evening or Saturday morning. I have to finish taking pictures for the graveyard feature I'm working on, and then I can do the rest from home." He winked at her and said, "I'll be back before you have time to miss me."

"Well, Shutterbug, so much for escorting me... But it's okay, I told you I don't need a babysitter."

"I'd like to see myself more as a tough bodyguard or guardian..." he corrected her with a grin.

"I don't need a guardian either, thank you very much. Let's eat, or we'll never make it to Lady Liberty."

As they boarded the sightseeing boat, Jo announced that she preferred to sit on the lower level, and Luca stayed with her.

"I'm going to the upper level to channel my inner *Titanic* moment," Naomi said. "Are you coming, Rev?"

Climbing up the steep metal stairs, she looked back to Jo and Luca. Their shoulders touched, and whatever Jo said made Luca smile. To Naomi, they seemed extremely comfortable around each other. She snapped a photo with her phone to send to Stella later to find out what she thought.

On the top level of the boat, Naomi leaned against the railing, and ignored the hordes of people around her. For a moment, she just...let go.

She didn't notice when the boat left the dock, and embraced the summer wind with open arms, letting it play with her hair. She loved the feeling of hair flying freely— one reason why she bought the VW Beetle convertible, not a hard-top. Driving in the summer with the top down and

Bruce Springsteen singing to her was one of her favorite pastimes.

"I hope you're not thinking about that untalented kisser, Nugget. You seem far away," Rev said close to her ear. He caught a handful of her hair and twisted it around his fingers.

"Oh, I was thinking about driving around in the summer with the top down, my hair blowing in the wind, like now. I didn't have much time for it this year," she turned around to look at him. "Maybe in the fall."

She didn't pay attention to the spectacular views of Manhattan, Jersey City, and the Upper Bay. All she saw was the wind tousling Revan's thick, ash-blond hair, and though he probably thought it was getting long enough to need a haircut, she loved this slightly rugged look on him. Her fingers itched to push a strand off his forehead.

"Or maybe we can take the Harley out one day. It'd be fun."

This was the first time he ever invited her for a ride on his precious motorcycle…

"It would, but I meant what I said earlier. I'm taking up too much of your time already. You must have better things to do than hang out with me."

His hand was still in her hair and his forearm rested lightly on her shoulder.

"Maybe…maybe not." His voice was getting huskier. "And do you want to know something else?"

"What?" The butterflies in her stomach fluttered madly, as if they had caught the invigorating scent of a new flower.

More and more often, her usual friendly banter with Rev turned into flirting. She enjoyed it, but at the same time couldn't help analyzing it.

"About memorable kisses," he leaned closer. "There were one or two lately. But I'd be damned if I would tell those two knuckleheads about them." With his free hand he pulled her to him. He slid his thumb over her lower lip and said, "I think it's time to erase the memory of Chuck Carter's slobbery kisses."

His lips barely touched hers before the boat bumped against the dock at the little island around the Statue of Liberty. The voice blaring through the speakers informed passengers of departure times for the next boats to Ellis Island, Jersey State Park, and Battery Park.

Naomi didn't care one bit about boat schedules. She wanted to stay right where she was.

But Rev took her hand and together they made their way to the stairs. "Let me walk down in front so I can catch you in case you stumble, Nugget."

She considered faking a fall. But with her luck, she'd end up on her ass and be bruised for the next few weeks. Nope, safer to hold on to the yucky handrail.

Couldn't the boat ride have taken a little longer? Would she ever get another searing kiss from Revan? Maybe it was time for her to initiate the next one. She never used to hesitate to go after what she wanted. Why was she suddenly so wimpy?

She didn't notice she'd reached the bottom of the stairs until her knees gave way. Clinging to the sticky handrail with one hand, she flung out her other arm, trying to catch her balance. Her flailing hand hit a man who pushed past her, his whole family trailing him in their hurry to get off the boat first, together with at least a hundred other overeager tourists.

"Hey, what's the rush? Lady Liberty isn't going anywhere." Naomi called after him. A crude hand gesture was the only reply she got.

"Asshole," she sputtered and bumped into the person in front of her.

"Can't I let you out of my sight for even a second, Nugget? Crashing into people and cussing at them?" Revan took her hand and said, "Walk with me, and don't let go of my hand."

Does he have to treat me like a misbehaving child? She pulled her hand free. "I think I'm good, thanks."

And immediately could have kicked herself while wondering again why she'd become so reluctant.

CHAPTER 27

Revan—July 2019

Forty-five minutes later, Naomi and Jo declared that they'd taken enough selfies with Lady Liberty, and they rode the ferry to Liberty State Park in Jersey City, where they were greeted by a large red brick building—the Central Railroad of New Jersey's waterfront passenger terminal, built in 1889.

They entered the partially-open railhead concourse between the massive building and remnants of the train tracks. Green iron gates prohibited access to the former platforms, now overgrown with weeds, while departure times to different locations were listed on reproduction designators. The only things missing were the huge engines huffing and puffing, and conductors yelling out to board the trains.

When they walked out of the other side of the building, all four stopped in their tracks.

A hundred feet away, two stainless-steel walls lay on their long sides, pointing toward Manhattan.

Slowly making their way toward them, Revan stopped at a marker and read that the length of each wall equaled the length of one side of the World Trade Center Towers, two hundred ten feet. From where he stood, his attention was drawn to the bluestone-paved path between the parallel walls, which aimed directly across the gently lapping water of the Hudson River to where the iconic twin towers used to stand.

Aptly named, the Empty Sky Memorial pointed to an empty space.

He continued to read. The names of all seven hundred forty-nine New Jersey victims of the 9/11 attacks were engraved on both sides of the thirty-foot tall walls.

These people had said goodbye to their partners and families on that Tuesday morning like every other day, not knowing they'd never get a chance to see them and to hold them again. No more kissing their children good night, no chance to apologize for words spoken thoughtlessly, leaving behind nothing but emptiness.

Revan swallowed hard and shook himself out of the reverie. Naomi was halfway down the bluestone path, wiping away tears while she traced some of the names with a finger. People she never met, but whose deaths she mourned, nevertheless.

She was one of the most empathic human beings he knew. A spitfire one moment, sentimental the next. Caring and nurturing, fun and sometimes exhausting, honest and firm in her beliefs. And, judging by the few kisses they shared, passionate and stimulating like no other woman he'd ever known.

If the victims memorialized in front of him were able to tell him one thing, what would it be?

He looked at Naomi...

They started Sunday with a Circle Line boat tour around Manhattan, followed by a walk on the High Line before Naomi and Jo decided to go shopping and Revan and Luca went to an electronics store to check out security cameras. They met at a steakhouse for dinner, and hours later, after Naomi and Jo left, the men ended the evening at Luca's apartment.

Just as he was about to call it a night, Luca said, "Rev, there's something I need to get off my chest."

"Okay, let's hear it."

"I've never known you to be a coward, but what do you think you're doing with Naomi? You're watching her, you're holding her hand when you think nobody's looking, and I don't think the flushed look on her face yesterday on the ferry was from the wind. Have you talked to her about your feelings?"

Not at all what Rev had expected to hear. "Are you serious? You're quizzing me about Nugget again? Nothing has changed since your last interrogation. Yeah, she's been kissing me back, but she's kissed plenty of other men in the past. And none of them were her mystery guy."

"What's your obsession with him? He's clearly not coming forward or doing anything to encourage her. But she's right in front of you! You just said she's kissing you back. Maybe it's time you stopped looking through your camera and use the eyes in your head."

"What's wrong with my camera? It's my work, my passion." He couldn't believe how invested Luca was in this topic.

"Nothing's wrong with it, as long you take off the cap in front of the lens, buddy."

This camera-talk didn't make any sense to Rev.

"Why are you so adamant about me pursuing her? You and I have always stayed out of each other's relationships. I have to figure this out myself. Maybe I shouldn't have told you about my dilemma."

The whole conversation was starting to annoy him. But because his own reluctance to pursue things with Naomi was starting to annoy him even more, it was easier to get mad at Luca than himself.

"But you did, more than once now. Which gives me the right to comment on it." Luca stretched out his legs and crossed them at the ankles.

Revan downed half of the whiskey in his glass. He watched his friend, sitting there totally relaxed, while a storm of epic portions was brewing inside him.

Then a mental flash went off, opening Revan's eyes wide instead of blinding him.

All day yesterday and today, Naomi's attention had been on Luca!

On *Luca*, who hadn't paid any more attention to her than any other time. He was as attentive to her as to any other close friend. Just as Revan was with Jo.

And all of a sudden, the pieces fell into place. How could he have been so blatantly stupid? Naomi had given him hints when she said, "You may have seen him once or twice," and, "He doesn't seem to see me."

The key to Naomi's happiness was right here, in this room, sitting directly in front of him.

"It's *you*," Revan ground out the words.

"I'm what?" Luca raked his fingers through his hair.

"*You* are Naomi's mystery man! I've seen her watching you, following you around. *You* are the man she's wanted her whole life." Saying it out loud hurt like hell.

Luca slapped his hands on his thighs, grabbed a newspaper off the coffee table, folded it in thirds and smacked Revan over the head with it. Then he said, between bouts of laughter, "Buddy, get your head out of your ass. And maybe stop drinking."

"What the fuck, man? You're telling *me* to stop playing games? Can't you see how gorgeous and special Nugget is? She's perfection."

"Rev, I don't think you've actually listened to a thing I've said," Luca replied and crossed his legs again. "But I'm telling you once and for all, I'm not interested in a relationship with Naomi."

Revan couldn't decide whether it was good news or not. It was only a matter of time for Naomi to accept Luca's lack of romantic feelings for her, and she'd be devastated. Revan vowed to be there for her, to catch her when she fell, and to help her recover.

What would it take to convince her that *he* was the right man?

On Monday morning, cruising along I-95, past the supersized warehouses of New Jersey, Revan glanced over to Naomi. Her right elbow was propped up on the door, and she watched, expressionless, while they passed one industrial park after the next.

Normally, he wouldn't mind the lack of conversation. But he had too much on his mind and needed a distraction. Images of Naomi tormented him most of the night. And his exchange with Luca had left a bitter taste in his mouth.

"Nugget, what's up? I don't think I've ever known you to be so quiet."

"Just stuff going through my mind. This weekend was great, but it also made me think about my life, my future." She shifted in the passenger seat and looked at him. "When we walked through the Central Railroad Terminal on Saturday, I tried to imagine the immigrants who came here. We always hear how those people arrived by boat and went through the agonizing immigration process on Ellis Island, but not much is ever said about where they went from there."

She paused, sniffled, and wiped her cheeks, blinking hard. He watched her out of the corner of his eye but kept most of his attention on the highway.

"They followed their dreams. Most sacrificed so much, when they didn't even know if they'd be allowed to enter the country, or if they would be denied and sent back. They arrived here desperate, but also full of hope that they'd have a better life if they worked hard enough for it."

She paused again, swallowing a couple of times before she continued, "And then there's us, living pretty comfortably. We take so much for granted and easily forget about the important things in life—and yet we still complain."

She took out a tissue from her purse and blew her nose. "Sometimes I wonder if I need a new start. Jo went to New York years ago, and now Stella's left, too. What's stopping me from moving? With my degree in business administration, I can work in any office. Bloomberg's a huge company, maybe Luca can help me get a job there."

Revan almost slammed on the brakes. Couldn't this blasted woman bring up heavy topics at home, not when they were speeding toward Philadelphia at seventy-five miles an hour? Her talk about moving away had to be nipped in the bud.

And to work in the same company as Luca—over his dead body.

It was time to put his cards on the table.

CHAPTER 28

NAOMI—JULY 2019

A silent house awaited Naomi after work on Monday evening. Due to construction traffic delays outside of Philly, they didn't have time to go home before she had to be at work, and Revan dropped her off at the travel agency.

Making her way to the kitchen, she saw her weekend bag sitting at the foot of the stairs. Naomi opened the refrigerator. She wasn't hungry, and some cheese and fruit would tide her over until Rev got home and they could have dinner together. When she saw the selection of cold cuts and an antipasti platter, she smiled. He went to the deli! After fixing herself a small plate, she sat at the counter and flipped through a magazine, then tossed it aside.

It had been interesting this weekend to watch Jo and Luca tiptoeing around each other. Those two seemed to have no idea about the sparks flying between them. But even when she tried to pry something out of her cousin as soon as they were alone, Jo was tight-lipped. "We're friends and hang out sometimes," was all she would say.

Naomi was a little disappointed Revan wasn't home. But maybe it was for the better. His cat-and-mouse-game was tiresome. She thought of herself as many things, but mousy wasn't among them.

One thing she was dead serious about was leaving Philadelphia—at least considering the possibility. What was left here for her? Gram was dying; she was already so much weaker, even if she stoically tried to hide it. Stella was in her happy place with David, and Jo said her future was in the City.

Which left Revan, who traveled half of the year, and who gave her zero encouragement to plan her future around him. They were friends and temporary roommates.

A roommate who really knew how to kiss...

Which led to another frustration. The few times they had some physical contact, he turned into a grouch and avoided her like the plague.

By eight thirty, she decided not to wait for him any longer and heated up a microwavable entrée. Another hour and a large glass of wine later, and still no sign of her *roommate*, Naomi double-checked all doors and windows on the first floor, then went upstairs to her rooms.

Maybe she was getting paranoid, but the new security camera wasn't installed yet, and even though she hadn't seen Ronnie today, she felt as if she was being watched, followed, on someone's radar.

This afternoon she called the police officer who was assigned to her complaint and was told, "He's not working at the pizzeria anymore and he's also not living at the address he gave them. The person who answered the door said she didn't know anybody with the name Ronnie."

"So what's happening now?" Naomi had asked.

"We've increased our presence in your area. Your job is to be cautious and let us know if you see him again. And, most important, don't do anything to encourage him, and don't engage in a conversation with him, which he would interpret to mean you're interested in him."

It wasn't what she wanted to hear, but there wasn't a thing she could do about it. At least she always carried that small can of hairspray now. If he came anywhere near her, he'd get a faceful of L'Oréal Satin Extra Strong Hold.

On her way home on Friday afternoon, Naomi picked up a variety of sandwiches and salads. Revan texted the day before to let her know he'd be back on Friday before dinner but didn't give her an exact time. Exiting the deli, she juggled her purse, the plastic bag with their takeout and an iced tea while holding the door for an elderly couple.

"Hi, sweets, haven't seen ya in a while." Ronnie was leaning against a streetlight and grinning at her.

Remembering what the officer told her, she continued walking without giving Ronnie a reply. Since he already knew where she lived, there was no sense in trying to shake him off. But sweat was beginning to run down her spine.

"Why don't ya say hi to me? That's not nice."

Ignore him...ignore him...do not engage in any kind of conversation!

Naomi reached inside her purse to pull out her cell phone. There was no time to pull up the direct number of the officer, but she could dial 9-1-1.

Why did she go by the deli? Couldn't she have just gone home without the detour? Didn't matter—it was too late now.

Someone zoomed past her on a moped, much too close for her liking. She didn't look up, only tried to focus on getting away from the creep. One more corner, and then only a few more yards.

"Sweets, how 'bout I walk ya home?"

"No!" She was regretting the word before she closed her mouth. She wasn't supposed to talk to him.

"I know it ain't far. It's no problem for me. I'd like to see ya."

Naomi walked faster while glancing around for help. Usually there were customers going in and out of the small shops at this time of the day. But now? Nobody!

Should she scream for help like a lunatic? She had her can of hairspray, but it was buried somewhere deep in her purse, with no way to get it out. Between the iced tea and her cell phone, her hands were full. The takeout dangled at her elbow. She slid her phone back in her purse and reached for her house keys. Maybe she could unlock the door quickly and slip inside. *Then* she'd call the cops, while he was still in the vicinity.

Head down, Naomi speed-walked, making sure she didn't stumble over one of the raised cobblestones, while trying to avoid running into the trees planted every few feet or bumping into bikes leaning against houses. Sweat soaked the waistband of her capris and in between her breasts.

A few more feet, and she'd reach her street corner. But Ronnie was right behind her. She could feel him, hear him, smell him. She could—sense him.

She turned the corner. Three more doors, and she'd be home. Suddenly, a hand firmly gripped her elbow, forcing her to turn sideways.

"Don't touch me! Leave me alone!" Naomi yelled and pulled her arm out of his grip. Something scratched her skin, leaving a burning sensation behind.

Her heart was beating double-time, she didn't know where to look first, where to go, and she only wanted to be in the safety of her home. Tears pooled in her eyes, and she blinked them away.

Spinning around, she set off and ran. Didn't see the ladder in front of her neighbor's house—and slammed right into it. She tried to hold onto it, to stabilize it, to free herself, but to no avail. Together, she and the ladder tumbled onto the sidewalk, where she hit her head on the uneven stones.

"Miss, are you okay?" A man in a painter's uniform, white but splattered with a rainbow of colors, ran toward her. "Are you hurt?"

"I think I'm okay." She touched the back of her head. Nothing sticky or gooey, so she didn't think she was bleeding. "Where did the ladder come from?"

"Didn't you see the sign at the corner?" he asked and offered a hand to help her up.

"No, I was distracted. This guy was following me, and he grabbed me, and I tried to get away as fast as I could."

"Which guy? Where is he?" The painter looked around.

Naomi looked everywhere, but Ronnie was gone.

"I don't know. I'm sorry about the ladder, I hope it's not broken. At least you weren't on it when I bulldozed into it. I live in three hundred seventeen, please let me know if I owe you anything."

The man picked up his ladder and said, "No damage, so you don't owe me a thing."

"Thank you, and sorry again." Naomi grabbed her purse and the bag with the now-scrambled food. Her empty iced tea container was rolling in the street, and her elbow hurt where Ronnie had grabbed it. She needed to get into the safety of her house and check out her arm. Calling the cops had to wait.

Once inside, she flung the deli bag down before she slid to the floor.

And cried.

Her shoulders heaved and her breathing hitched, and she hugged herself to calm down, when two arms reached for her and pulled her up. They closed around her like a vise.

"NO! Leave me alone. Don't touch me!" she screamed, shaking her head, kicking, and pushing against the restricting arms to free herself.

"Shhh... What happened, Nugget?" Revan's voice had an edge she'd never heard before.

Revan! Thank goodness!

"Ronnie...he touched me...he was waiting for me... outside the deli," she sobbed. Relief swept over her with cascades of goose bumps because she was now in Revan's arms. Safe!

"I need to call the cops. They have no idea where Ronnie is, and the officer told me to call when he makes contact again."

"We'll call them in a moment, although I doubt he's still around. Tell me what happened," he said and ran a hand over her hair, down her arm, then repeated it with his other hand. When he touched her elbow, she winced.

"He grabbed me real hard, and he scratched my skin." Naomi started crying again.

"Let's have a look and get some antibiotic cream on it." He led her to the kitchen and pulled out a barstool. Silently, he washed her elbow with a clean kitchen towel and put some cream on the scratch. But his face looked like thunder. If Naomi didn't know him so well and trust him blindly, she'd have been scared and tempted to run for cover. She wouldn't want to be on the receiving end of his anger.

"Rev, s-say something," she hiccupped.

"What do you want me to say? I feel horrible because this happened to you when I wasn't out there to stop the son of a bitch," he said through his teeth. His eyes were pitch black with barely contained fury. "Here's my suggestion. I'll pour you a glass of water, or wine, or whiskey, and you call the officer. Then we'll have dinner…"

Fresh tears rolled down her face, "I went to the deli because I have nothing at home, but it's ruined now because I ran into the ladder in front of the new neighbor's house and fell. I don't want to go anywhere tonight." She whispered, "I'm afraid to leave the house, Rev."

"Nugget, slow down." He put a Band-Aid on the scratch, then cupped her face with his hands. "Does anything else hurt?"

"No, I hit my head when I fell, but it's not bad. The poor painter, I gave him the shock of his life, I think. At least he wasn't on the ladder when I plowed into it."

Revan stroked her cheek with the backs of his fingers and said softly, "So, why don't you make the phone call and let me worry about dinner. I picked up steaks earlier, planning to grill them outside. I wanted to surprise you. And tomorrow I'll install the camera system."

"Okay. Thank you." She slid off the chair. "I'll go upstairs, make the call, and change. And then," she looked over her shoulder as she walked away, "could I have a glass of wine, please?"

Revan was already reaching for the bottle. "It's waiting for you right here, Nugget."

CHAPTER 29

NAOMI—JULY 2019

"I can't eat any more. This was perfect. Steaks, garlic and herb potatoes, and a salad," Naomi wiped her mouth with the napkin and pushed her plate away. "Why have you hidden your high-level domestic talents from me? I had no idea you know how to cook."

"I never had to. Stella always left something in the fridge for me. And when Luca and I lived together, we didn't go hungry, either. But I admit, back then it was mostly thanks to our mothers, who provided us with plenty of leftovers."

He grinned, and Naomi's heart skipped a beat or two. Did he have to be so devilishly handsome and charming?

"You'd be surprised what else I can do. But I can't let it all out at once," he said.

"Do you also have dessert, by any chance?"

"Didn't you just say you can't eat any more?"

"Well, there's always room for dessert. Especially ice cream. So, is there any?"

"Maybe...but let me take in the dishes first," he got up and collected their plates. "It's such a nice evening and not too humid. Want to sit out here till the mosquitos get unbearable?"

"Wait a second. You cooked, so I clean up. It's only fair," Naomi said and reached for the plates in his hands.

As she walked into the house, she asked, "How did it go in Savannah?"

"I got everything done. Working on the photos and putting it together will keep me busy for the next few weeks, but at least I can do it from home."

"Can I see the photos?"

"Sure, but not until I'm done."

Naomi rinsed the plates and leaned over to put them in the dishwasher. A dull pain in her hip reminded her of her tumble, and she rubbed a hand over it. Maybe she'd take a nice, relaxing bath later.

Reaching for the stainless-steel flatware, she was giving them a quick rinse when Revan set the salad bowl next to the sink. "Do you want dessert now, or wait?"

"What is it?" Naomi looked over her shoulder and reached for the wooden salad servers to wash them by hand.

"I bought tiramisu, and we can have coffee with it—unless the machine is broken." His grin went from one ear to the other and he raised an eyebrow with an unspoken question.

Naomi waved a hand and sent soap suds flying, "Oh, no, that only happened when Blondie was in the house." She put the salad bowl in the dishwasher and started the cleaning cycle. "Weird, huh?"

"You have blonde hair." Standing close behind her, he reached for her hair, which was hanging loosely over her shoulders. He gathered it into a ponytail and kissed the side of her neck.

"What are you doing?"

"Something I've wanted to do since last weekend. But I have a confession to make along with it." He hesitated, then kissed the other side of her neck.

"A confession?" She lost her ability to think and simply enjoyed his caresses.

"I don't know if it's a smart thing for me to kiss you like this," he said against her skin.

What the… Naomi had no idea what he was trying to tell her. "Then why are you doing it?" She turned around to look at him. Who followed a kiss with such a statement?

She wrapped her arms around his neck and pulled herself closer to him. His face was inches away from hers, with an unreadable expression. In his eyes, she saw her own reflection.

Putting her mouth to his ear, she said, "Stop thinking."

He had exactly three seconds or she'd kiss him, then pack her bags and be out of here. There was only so much rejection she could take.

One, twenty-one…

Two, twenty-one…

Three…

His lips found hers.

It wasn't a gentle kiss. They were hungry and starving for each other, and their tongues battled and danced around, exploring every inch of their mouths.

Revan angled Naomi's head and deepened their kiss. He pressed her hip against the counter. Naomi could feel his erection, and if his hand should happen to venture between her legs, he'd know she was ready, too.

Needing to breathe, she broke the kiss and snuggled her face against the side of his neck. Rosemary, citrus, and something woodsy. Outdoor essences bottled up in a shower gel. Revan in a bottle.

She closed her eyes and slid one hand under his polo shirt, roaming over his back inch by inch.

He dropped feathery kisses on her hair while he gently massaged the back of her head. She winced.

"Did I hurt you? Let me have a look." He lifted her hair and turned her head to have a better view. "You've got a little bump there. Does it hurt when I'm not touching it?"

"Not really, it's just tender. I'm not worried about it." She reached for his face with both hands.

"Can you explain to me what's going on here, Nugget?" he whispered, his forehead touching hers.

"It's called kissing," she grinned at him. "If you need more practice, I'd be happy to help."

Revan put his arms around her waist. "I think I like kissing you." One of his hands lightly squeezed her hip, and she winced again.

"Did that hurt you, too?"

"A little. I guess I also bruised my hip. It'll go away." She snuggled against his chest and didn't want to talk about her bruises.

"Shutterbug, weren't we going to have dessert?"

"Do you want coffee with it?"

"No, thank you. I think I'll have another glass of wine, though." Naomi tightened her hold on Revan and pressed her full length against him.

"You've got it. Go sit outside, Nugget, and I'll bring everything. But first..." he leaned in and kissed her again. Naomi slid her hand under his shirt.

"I thought you wanted dessert," he said, his lips hovering over hers.

"I changed my mind. Forget the tiramisu," she pushed up his polo shirt. "Maybe later."

Breathing heavily, he stilled her hand and said, "Naomi, as much as I want you, I think maybe we should take it slow."

"Why?"

Three short raps came from the front door.

Naomi began to shake immediately and whispered, "Revan!"

He touched a finger to her lips and said, "You stay right here, I'll check it out." With a few long strides he reached the door and threw it open.

"We're so sorry to disturb you," a woman said. "I'm Carrie Newman, and this is my husband, Marc. Our painter told me about your wife"—Naomi heard the hesitation in the woman's voice—"or girlfriend walking into his ladder today. We want to make sure she's okay."

269

Naomi joined Revan at the door and said, "Hi, I'm Naomi. Thanks so much for checking on me, and I'm fine. A little bruised, but it's my fault. I didn't pay attention to where I was going." She shook hands with Carrie and Marc, and accepted a small basket filled with handmade soaps and little sachets with bath salts.

Revan held out his hand and said, "I'm Revan. Nice to meet you, and welcome to our street. Would you like to come in?"

"We don't want to interrupt your evening," Marc said.

"No, please come in," Naomi said. "We were going to sit outside and have a glass of wine. Why don't you join us?" She looked at Rev, who nodded and rested his hand on Naomi's lower back.

After the wine was poured, Carrie said to Naomi, "My painter also said someone assaulted you?"

"Yes, there's this guy who's been stalking me for a while, and today he was waiting in front of the deli. The police told me to avoid contact with him, but when he grabbed my arm, I tried to free myself and didn't see your painter's warning sign on the sidewalk."

Naomi pointed to Rev. "We're going to install a security camera, but I guess unless someone is with me when Ronnie makes contact again, I don't see how we can catch him." She picked up her glass and said, "But enough about him. Thank you for checking on me, and for the soaps. They smell lovely, and I'll use my first one later, when I have a hot, soaking bath."

Marc and Carrie stayed for an hour, and after they left, Naomi was unsure how to act around Revan. If their neighbors hadn't interrupted, how far would they have gone tonight? Then she remembered he wanted to take things slow. So there was her answer. It wouldn't have gone past kissing.

Was she okay with it? She wasn't sure, but she could hardly force herself on him—mostly because she had no clue where they stood.

After they carried the empty wine glasses to the kitchen sink, Naomi said, "I think I'll go take a bath. Thank you for dinner and a nice evening. You surprised me again."

She leaned in to kiss his cheek, but he put a finger on her lips, then draped his arm around her shoulders and said, "Enjoy your bath and try to relax. Are you working tomorrow?"

"Yes, until one."

"If you want, I'll meet you afterward and we can take the dogs down to the river. I don't think you should be out there by yourself right now."

Relief washed over her. She hadn't thought about taking the dogs out alone.

"Sounds great. They also behave better when you're walking them." She tried for the second time to kiss his cheek, but he stopped her again by running his finger over her lips.

"Must be my magic touch," he wiggled his eyebrows and grinned. "Text me half an hour before you go over to your parents' and I'll meet you there." He took her chin in his hand and tilted her head. "Good night, Nugget."

He closed the distance and kissed her, slow and sensual, making love to her mouth and making her insides go gooey.

CHAPTER 30

REVAN—JULY 2019

Revan adjusted the umbrella to make sure Gram Annie was sitting in the shade and then ensured she had a light blanket within reach. It was another hot afternoon, but she complained about chills. While it pained him to see her physical strength declining, he was also happy to notice that it didn't prevent her from interrogating him.

"Have you finally hooked up with my granddaughter?" She pierced him with her blue eyes, the same shade as Naomi's, and sparkling with the same mischievous glimmer.

"Which one?" Two could play the game.

"Sweet boy, you know I'm talking about Naomi, not Josephine," she giggled and shook a finger in front of his face.

"What if I don't want to hook up with her?"

"Stop playing dumb. I see more than you think. I want her to be happy," she sighed, looked heavenward, and rolled her eyes.

"Don't you think you should let her decide her future by herself? What makes you think she wants me?"

"Some people don't see what's right in front of them and need a little push. I don't think you'd understand what I'm talking about, though," she raised her eyebrows and pinched her lips together.

"So, your little push was messing up our hotel reservations?" He looked directly at her. "Don't you think it was a little too obvious?"

"What? I have no idea what you're talking about. I forget so many things."

"Gram Annie, nothing's wrong with your brain, and we both know it," he chuckled.

She beckoned him a little closer and lowered her voice, "Would you mind bringing me something to drink?"

"Sure, what do you want?" He knew exactly what she wanted, and he also knew Lisa was monitoring her mother's alcohol consumption.

"Surprise me, sweet boy, but make sure it has some taste to it," she wiggled her eyebrows at him. "Bring one for yourself, too. It can't hurt."

Revan laughed and gave Gram Annie a hug. "How can I say no to you, Gram Annie? I'll be right back."

Just as he returned with two tumblers in his hands, Naomi walked into the backyard. He would have liked to pull her into his arms, but he wouldn't give Gram Annie the satisfaction after her little speech a few minutes ago.

"Nugget, do you want something to drink before we take the beasts out?" he called across the yard. He hadn't seen her this morning because he went for a long run as soon as he woke up. By the time he got home, she'd already left for work. Now he couldn't take his eyes off her.

"I'll go in to say hi to Mom and Dad and grab a bottle of water," she pecked his cheek in passing and went to hug her grandmother. "Hi, Gram."

"Pretend I'm not here and kiss my sweet boy," said Gram Annie.

"Gram Annie, I believe we've covered this already," Revan said.

"Maybe you did, but I wasn't finished." The old woman cackled, then reached for a glass.

"Oh no, that's not yours. Nice try, though. But Lisa is watching us, and I don't want to get in trouble with her."

"You should be afraid of getting in trouble with me, not my daughter." Gram Annie waved toward the house.

"Here, this is for you," Revan handed her the other glass. "Take it or leave it."

"I used to like you," she pouted, but still with a touch of humor in her voice.

Revan bent down to kiss her leathery cheek, "You still do, Gram Annie. How can you not?"

"Hmpf…"

Naomi came back with a bottle of water and the two dogs at her heels. She sat down next to Revan, and for a while they chit-chatted with Gram Annie. When the dogs began running in circles, the old woman said, "Take those two out of here. They're making me dizzy"— she gave Rev a long look—"since it sure isn't because of this corn juice."

Two hours later, after dropping off the dogs, Naomi and Revan walked home. "I finished installing the security cameras, so all we need to do is activate the app. I didn't have enough time to do it before I left to meet you. I'll show you everything later and we'll install the app on your phone, too. We can see what's happening in the open spaces of the first floor and in front of the house. The footage can be saved as a video, or a still picture, and we can even communicate with whoever is outside."

"Oh, so when you're not home, you can check on me and watch me clean the house, you mean?" she laughed. "Then you need to show me first how to turn it off. But hopefully we won't need the camera for long."

"I think it's not a bad idea to have a permanent security system, but we can turn off the inside camera and only watch the front of the house if it makes you feel better," he agreed.

"We'll decide after you show me how it works." Naomi stopped walking and looked around. "Funny, when I'm walking with you, I don't feel as if I'm being followed, but even this morning I was constantly checking behind me."

"I should've walked with you, but my run took longer than I planned. Sorry, Nugget."

"Stop apologizing. You can't be around me 24/7, it's just not possible. Or normal. But... Do we still have the tiramisu at home? I would love a cup of coffee and dessert before I do my laundry."

"I didn't eat it, so it should be in the fridge."

They turned onto their street and came to an abrupt halt. Three patrol cars and one ambulance, all with lights on, were gathered in front of their house, and they could see uniforms going in and out.

"What the hell is going on here?" Revan stormed toward his house. "Stay back, Nugget."

"I'm not staying back. I'm going with you." She was pale and started to shake, and Revan stopped walking to pull her to his side.

"Officer, this is my house. What happened?" He approached the first man in a Philadelphia PD uniform. "Do you need to see my ID? Here, let me pull it out," he reached for his wallet in the back pocket of his jeans and took out his drivers' license.

"Thank you, Mr. Forrester," the cop said after glancing at the card. "One of your neighbors called it in. They saw someone who wasn't you or Miss Winters messing with the lock on your front door."

"Where is the person? Who was it?" Rev reached for Naomi's hand and let his thumb run over the back of it.

"If you wait a minute, someone will fill you in," the officer said.

"Thirty seconds would be better, or I'll go in by myself," Revan fumed. Before he could check the time on his watch, a policewoman and an EMT came out of the house, guiding a handcuffed man.

"What's Ronnie doing here?" Naomi whispered. She stepped closer to Revan and clung to his hand.

"I don't know, but I suspect we're about to find out." He started to walk over to the trio, but was stopped by another police officer. "Sir, please step back."

"I wanna know right now what this man did in my house."

"We'll give you the details in a moment. I understand you're upset, but please be patient for only a little longer."

Ronnie spotted them and called, "Ey, sweets, glad ya're here. Tell 'em this is a mistake. And what are ya doin' there with him?"

Revan didn't condone violence, but right now he wanted to beat that creep to pulp. Who did he think he was? Talking to Naomi the way he just did—and way, *way* worse, making her life miserable for the past weeks? He took one step toward Ronnie, but Naomi snuggled closer to him and said, "Don't, Rev. Let the cops take him away."

Rev wrapped his arm around her while they watched the cops guide Ronnie into the cruiser. Before the car door closed with a thudding sound, he called, "See ya, sweets."

Revan grumbled, "Yeah, in court, buddy."

An hour later, after the police left and they were finally alone, he poured them both two generous fingers of whiskey and sat down next to her on the sofa.

"Drink this, Nugget, it'll help."

"How can booze help with this? Revan, the guy broke into our house. I mean, *your* house, and..."

"It's our house, Nugget. You live here too," he said and tucked her hair behind her ear, then left his arm on the back of the sofa while he drew circles on her shoulder with his fingers.

"Okay... So, let's recap what the cops told us," she took a sip of the whiskey. "They think he waited until you left, broke in, and then went into my bedroom and wrecked it." Her voice wobbled. "Rev, he even went through my underwear."

He had a hard time containing his anger. The police took a few of her shirts and dresses, so they must have found samples they connected to him. Did he jerk off on her underwear? God, getting those pictures out of his mind would take a while, and he couldn't imagine how Naomi must feel. "Why don't you throw everything out and buy new stuff?"

"I'm not going to throw it out. I'll wash it, more than once, and eventually wear it again. And until then, I'll resort to the good old Fruit of the Loom cotton bikini panties, which can be bleached in the washing machine."

The image of Naomi in any kind of underwear was too much, no matter how inappropriate the timing was. But he still managed to say, around the lump in his throat, "That's the spirit, Nugget."

He turned his focus to the next matter needing to be addressed. Earlier this week, he called Luca to apologize and make sure they were good. Luca assured him they were, but then immediately reminded him to man up and tell Naomi about his feelings. He had said, "Man, I've never seen you jealous, and I love seeing you squirm the way you have recently." Revan didn't think he was squirming but decided not to argue with his friend.

So, for today he planned to take Naomi out for a romantic dinner. He had never officially courted a woman, but it felt the right thing to do with her. And he'd been serious when he insisted they take things slowly.

He crossed the first of the invisible lines when he kissed her. Not in Richmond, but after their dinner date, when he led her outside and kissed her.

He crossed the second invisible line when they made out in the kitchen yesterday.

And that's why he needed to buy time. To figure things out before there was no turning back.

The time had come to have the dreaded *talk*.

And now, thanks to the unexpected Ronnie stunt, his plans for tonight were in jeopardy, and Naomi's emotional state and well-being were his top priority. What if she'd been home when he broke in?

As if she had read his mind, she said, "I'm so glad neither one of us was here. Imagine what could've happened."

He knew exactly what would've happened if he'd been able to get his hands on that asshole.

"Let's not think about it. I'm glad you're safe." He kissed the top of her head and she leaned against him. "I'm going to get the locks changed as soon as possible."

"I'm so sorry about this. And it's my fault. If I didn't live here, this wouldn't have happened," she said and shook her head. "Everything's such a mess."

For a moment, Revan thought he had misheard her. "Erase those thoughts right now, Nugget. You have nothing to be sorry for. Absolutely nothing."

"Thank you," Naomi smiled at him. "Okay, I better run to the deli. There isn't much to eat in the fridge."

He laughed and said, "If you're thinking about food, you're feeling better. But I planned to surprise you with dinner at La Scala and already made reservations. That way we also don't have to worry about cleaning up afterward."

"La Scala, wow. Hmm, I'd really like to go there and see if it's as good as everybody's saying," she rolled her lips in and out, driving him crazy. "But just so you know, I enjoyed cleaning up the kitchen yesterday."

"Then we'll order the dessert to go and you can clean up the plates." He looked at her mouth and imagined a smudge of chocolate on the corner of it. Ran his tongue over his own lips, then touched a finger to her mouth and said, "I see a chocolate-covered strawberry or two in my future."

"What time is our reservation?"

"At eight, so we have plenty of time."

"Well, then I'll better go check on the upstairs, whether I want to or not. I have to find something nice to wear," she said, then stood and pointed to the coffee cups and glasses, "Leave those for later, too."

"There's a dishwasher in the kitchen, or did you forget?" he grinned.

"I know, but a quick rinse won't hurt them."

Revan laughed and shook his head. How could anyone not love Naomi?!

Wait... *He* loved Naomi!

If only he could kick her mystery man off his pedestal and make sure she never gave the loser a second thought.

CHAPTER 31

❧

NAOMI—JULY 2019

By early afternoon the following day, Naomi was in her bedroom folding her freshly-laundered T-shirts and—*white cotton, urgh*—panties.

She looked longingly at the laundry basket in the corner, where all her finer lingerie waited to be handwashed. For a brief moment she was tempted to throw everything out, but it would be expensive, if not impossible, to replace most of it. Especially the sexy stuff she bought in Paris last year. Hence, hand-scrubbing it would be...

Revan had proven to be a rock, which didn't surprise her. He'd been extremely angry about Ronnie going through her clothes, but never said a word about the fact that Ronnie first broke into his house.

Last night, after dinner at the fancy Italian restaurant, they had coffee and dessert at home. Sadly, the cleanup ended without another steamy kissing session because Revan had to take a work-related phone call, and when it took much longer than anticipated, she decided to end the day with another relaxing bath to soak her still-sore hip.

She spent the previous night in her second, smaller bedroom on an air mattress after stripping the bed. Whatever Ronnie might have touched went in the washing machine at the highest possible temperature. Now her bed was freshly made and she was finishing her laundry.

Naomi couldn't help wondering about Revan and their strange relationship. He sought her out frequently and touched her hand, head, or shoulder in passing. And then there were the kisses…

She grimaced. She sounded exactly like Revan's sister. And actually Naomi's situation wasn't very different from Dinah's.

While she restored her dry clothes to their respective drawers, she noticed two T-shirts that escaped Ronnie's ransacking. When she snitched them last year—thanks to Rev's habit of leaving clothes all over the house—she pretended to be in his arms when she wore them at night. But now she'd experienced the real thing, even if only briefly, and it was time to get rid of them. They had served their purpose, and she didn't need the reminder of what might never be.

How could she return them? She couldn't very well hand them to Revan and say, "Oh, look what I found." Sneaking into his room and tossing them in his laundry basket? She didn't think he'd keep track of which T-shirt was in the laundry and which wasn't.

Naomi took both T-shirts and buried her face in them. They didn't smell like him anymore—one more reason to give 'em back.

She had fully intended to follow his rule to stay out of his private rooms—except for going into his bathroom that one time. But today it seemed to be the only way, so before she changed her mind, she ran down her stairs, through the living room, and up his stairs.

The door to his bedroom stood ajar.

She peeked into the room. Where was his laundry basket? Not behind the door, not in the corner near the window.

Going to the built-in closet, she opened the folding door. No hamper, no basket, nothing! She didn't see a pile of clothes lying around, either. Where did the man keep this laundry?

Oh, well, she'd just put them in any of the drawers. Let him wonder how they got there. Naomi reached for the pull of the top drawer and tugged on it. The drawer stuck, so she tugged a little harder until it opened.

"What are you doing in here, Nugget?" Revan was leaning against the doorjamb, both arms folded over his chest.

"I..." she swallowed hard. "I found two of your T-shirts mixed in with my laundry and wanted to return them." She showed them to him and tried to smile convincingly.

"You could've left them on the kitchen counter."

285

She smacked her forehead. "Oops, didn't think of it." Naomi couldn't tell whether he was angry or not. He only watched her.

"Care to explain to me how they ended up in your laundry?" he asked in a low voice. "I've been missing them for over a year."

"No idea." She shrugged one shoulder.

"Didn't we agree to stay out of each other's bedrooms?"

"Yes, but..." *How can I get out of this?* She wasn't afraid, but his bedroom wasn't the best place to have a conversation. Or, more likely, get into an argument, going by the look on his face.

"We're going in circles here, Nugget." He left the doorway and came into the room, toward her, effectively blocking her path to the door. She moved backwards, until her leg touched the wooden frame of his bed. He moved closer, and she could see his dilated pupils—totally focused on her.

"Give 'em to me," he held out his hand.

She leaned sideways to put the T-shirts on his chest of drawers. Then she ducked and squeezed past him. His arm came down at the speed of light and stopped her midway. He pulled her to him, then tipped her chin up with one finger.

"What's up with the T-shirts?"

Naomi put her hands on his chest and pushed away from him, then walked over to the window and looked out over the backyard. Her bedroom also faced the backyard, and their views were almost identical, so there wasn't anything new to see from here, but she needed a moment to decide how much to tell him.

She said quietly, "I borrowed them last year. Happy?"

"Why did you *borrow* them?" He stood behind her now, his hands on the windowsill, arms bracketing her in. She could smell his familiar aftershave.

"Hmm?" She turned and looked at him. This was stupid, and she could have avoided it by dumping the darn T-shirts somewhere in the house.

"The T-shirts. Why?" His eyes bored into hers.

Naomi wanted to yell, "Because I couldn't have you," but she only whispered, "Please Rev, let it go. You wouldn't understand." Tears threatened to spill, and she swiped them away. She'd be damned if she'd have a meltdown in front of him. And she wasn't going to tell him her deepest secret.

His hands were still on both sides of her, and she lifted one and ducked under it, letting it drop. Without looking back, she hurried away—out of the room and down the stairs.

Pulling out a handful of tissues from the nearest box, she scanned the kitchen and living room. Stay here, or go to her own rooms?

Stupid tears. She turned toward the powder room to hide for a moment, but before she could reach it, she heard, "Nugget?"

Standing in the middle of the living room, Revan held out a hand. She hesitated, then put her hand in his. He pulled her into his arms and kissed her softly. With one hand, he held her as close as he could. His other hand was in her hair and guided her head to a position where he could deepen the kiss.

"All I've been able to think about is kissing you," he said hoarsely.

"You're thinking too much, Shutterbug." Naomi could feel every hard inch of him. "And you're talking too much." She pulled his face to hers and kissed him again.

A low rumble interrupted the kiss.

"What exactly is so funny?" she narrowed her eyes and looked at him.

"*You* are telling *me* I'm talking too much? Nugget, you're a real gem. Come here, give me another kiss."

"No! Who do you think you are? Kissing and then making fun of me? I don't think so," she dropped her arms and pushed against his chest. Nothing, not an inch. She was still firmly encircled by his arms. *Blasted man!*

Naomi looked at his mouth and saw both corners pulled up into a huge smile. Well, maybe one more kiss...

She leaned closer and held up her face. Then she closed her eyes and waited.

Nothing.

She tipped her head back a little more—and waited.

Still nothing.

She peeked just a bit—and both eyes went wide. He was inches away, watching her, and grinning. Unbelievable!

"Didn't you want a kiss?" she snarled.

"Yes, but I like to watch you squirm while waiting for it. You don't always get everything you want," he said and lifted her chin.

"Oh, believe me, Shutterbug, you're not telling me anything new," she answered. "But I'm not good at waiting."

"Really? Could've fooled me."

"Last chance, Shutterbug. Kiss me again or let me go. I have more important things to do."

Naomi snuggled closer to him and let one hand slide up and down his back. She could feel his muscles flexing under the polo shirt, and his breath hitched when her hand slid under the shirt. He finally lowered his mouth to hers and kissed her gently.

"Do you think we could move to a more comfortable place?" he asked after he broke their kiss, his mouth still dangerously close to hers.

"You mean your place or my place?"

"How about the sofa?" He took her hand and led her to it. "Do you want something to drink?"

"Is it too early for a glass of prosecco?"

"Of course not." Revan went to the kitchen and took a bottle out of the built-in wine refrigerator. He opened it, poured two glasses, and brought them over to the sofa, where Naomi sat with her feet on the ottoman.

He handed her a glass, then tipped his glass to hers, "Cheers, Nugget."

"Are you afraid I'll bite?" she patted the place next to her.

"No, but I don't know what I'll do if I sit next to you." He sat down, put his glass on the table and reached for one of her feet. First, he slowly massaged the bottom of her foot, then her toes. "I've wanted to do this for quite a while."

"Hm, interesting, I remember you telling me you're not a licensed foot masseur. But look," she wiggled her second foot in front of him. "Lucky you, there's two of them."

He stared at her feet as if they held the secret answers to all his questions, then said without stopping the massage, "I need to talk to you about something. And I think it's best to just say it without tiptoeing around." He gave one of her toes a little pinch, then set her foot down.

While running a hand through his hair, he took a deep breath. "Over the course of the past year—since Paris, to be honest—you've begun to creep into my head, and I started to see you in a different light. Not as the girl I knew, but as a gorgeous and mesmerizing woman. You have no idea how hard it was to stay away from you when we were on our trip to Charleston."

"Shutterbug..."

Rev shook his head. "Let me say this, please. I've been fighting my feelings. I've always avoided commitment, refused to get involved in romantic relationships. You made me see things differently, and I want you in my life as more than my friend, but I don't know if I can take this step. I'm afraid to lose you if this thing between us doesn't work out. We don't even know what *this* is."

He reached for his glass and drank most of it. "We can't deny our mutual attraction, but where does that leave us?" He moved closer, took her face in his hands, and caressed her cheeks with the pads of his thumbs. Then he leaned in and kissed her. He started at her bottom lip, then let his mouth travel from one corner of her mouth to the other.

Naomi snuggled closer. His arm circled around her waist and he wove his fingers in her hair while they clung to each other.

She should be happy—no, jubilant!—but something still felt off. Time to speak up.

"To be honest," she said, "I'm confused because you're sending me mixed messages. Like now. One day you're kissing me, and the next day you can't get out of town fast enough. Then you come back early, only to retreat again. The weekend when the girls were here is a good example. I don't know what to make of it, Revan."

She peeled herself out of his embrace, got up and walked to the French doors, watching the water cascading down the little backyard fountain. "Would things be easier to figure out if we didn't see each other every day? If I go to live with Aunt Mary so you don't have to leave town to avoid me?"

Revan followed her and leaned his shoulder against the door frame. "You've brought up leaving a few times now. What do *you* want?"

She shook her head slowly. "I want to be here. But I also can't go on being friends who occasionally lock lips. What does that make us? Friends with pick-and-choose benefits?"

He turned her toward him. "Nugget, there's nothing wrong with kissing and holding each other. You know I want to do more, you can feel it when you're in my arms. But I will not rush into anything. Not with you."

He pulled her closer and—oh, yes—she could feel how much he wanted her. "Let's continue to spend time together the way we already do, go on dates, and see where it takes us. Let us both be honest with ourselves and with each other. If we realize in a few weeks that we had a good time, but it doesn't turn into more, then we haven't ruined our friendship by jumping in the sack right away. Or if we choose to take the next step, we'll know we're not just scratching an itch."

Naomi knew exactly what she wanted and nearly told him how long she'd been waiting, but sensing what a huge step this was for Revan to admit to his feelings, she nodded.

And she was convinced something else was still bothering him. She'd eventually get it out of him, and until then she'd do her best to enjoy whatever he was willing to give her.

She snuggled closer and circled her arms around his waist. His erection pulsed against her belly and she didn't think it was easy for him to be sensible. It for sure wasn't easy for her. Sex was an important part of a relationship for her. But she grudgingly agreed it was best to let things develop slowly before crossing the bridge from friendship to something more.

She wanted to ask, "But can we still kiss?"

"I hope we will, Nugget," he said close to her ear. "Very often."

"Oops, I didn't realize I said it out loud," she giggled.

"You must've, unless we're both thinking the same thing," he said and kissed her again. "Do you want to go for a walk? Unless you don't have time...you said you have better things to do."

He kissed her eyelids, the tip of her nose, then hovered over her mouth.

"Yes, let's go get some ice cream. And I said I have more important things to do, not better, Shutterbug." She kissed him back. Then whispered in his ear, "I have to handwash my nice undies, in case I need them in the not-so-distant-future."

His laughter erupted deep in his belly and he pinched her butt. "Okay, thanks to your comment I'll need a few minutes until I'm decent enough to leave the house. I have a feeling it's going to be hard to stick to my own suggestion to take it slow."

She winked at him and said, "Hard is good, Shutterbug. And slow is, too…at least sometimes."

He gently smacked her butt and raked his other hand through his hair, "One more thing, Nugget, and I mean it. Stay out of my bedroom. Because next time you're in there, I plan to keep you there for quite a while."

"Okay, I'll think of nothing else."

He walked away. "Let me get my wallet. I need to treat my girlfriend to something refreshing to keep her cool."

CHAPTER 32

REVAN—AUGUST 2019

R evan held his phone in a death grip. For the past hour, he'd been sitting in his backyard, alternating between reading Luca's email all over again and gazing at the sky. A few puffy white clouds floated across the blue summer sky, but he didn't see them.

He didn't hear the cars and buses honking on the streets of his neighborhood, either. The heady scent of the rose bush next to the small outdoor patio might as well fade off into thin air. And the extra-spicy mustard on his turkey sandwich was nothing but a glob of plaster. His coffee sat untouched in front of him, having turned cold long ago, and not even his newly developed radar regarding Naomi alerted Revan to her arrival.

"Shutterbug, I'm ho-o-me. Where are you?" She came outside and crossed the short distance toward him.

He jumped up and pulled her in a bear-hug. "Nugget, I didn't hear you come in." Then he kissed her, hard and demanding. No gentle foreplay of nipping her lips, no sensual probing to beg her mouth to open for his tongue. He needed to taste her more than ever and to assure himself she was safe in his arms.

"Ooh...what a nice hello kiss," she looked up at him and ran her thumb over his lower lip. "If I get this every time I come home from work, I'll even go in on Sundays."

He crushed her to his chest and burrowed his face under her hair to kiss, starting at her earlobe, down to the hollow spot above her collarbone, then let his lips and tongue trail upward to her earlobe again. His breathing was ragged and when he started to nibble on her skin, she took his face in her hands and said, "Rev?"

"I need to hold you. I need to know you're here," he touched his forehead to hers and closed his eyes.

"What happened?"

"Oh G-god—" he stammered and lowered his mouth to hers again.

But she put her finger between their lips and whispered, "You're scaring me, Revan. What's going on?"

He walked into the living room without letting go of her hand. Sat down on the sofa and pulled her next to him, their thighs touching. He put both his elbows on his knees and folded his hands. Without looking at her, he asked, "Do you remember Scott Butler?"

"Yeah, of course. He went to high school with you and Luca. The three of you got into trouble more than once." She started to rub his back. "I didn't know you were still in touch."

"Luca's been keeping up with him over the years...more than I did, at least."

"Did something happen to Scotty?"

"His girlfriend was killed in an accident a few days ago."

She gasped. "How terrible for him. I... I don't know what to say."

"Scotty told Luca that he had planned to propose to Marnie after dinner. But she never made it there. Got hit by a drunk driver at the intersection across from the restaurant. She saw Scott and waved to him right before a driver ran a red light and took her out."

"Oh no, he witnessed it? Poor Scotty." She reached for Revan's hands and started to massage his palms. "I vaguely remember Marnie. She was a grade or two ahead of us. Jo knew her a little better because they were both cheerleaders. I didn't know she and Scotty had been dating, though."

"They didn't date until she graduated from college and got a job in Washington. Scotty went to DC for college and has stayed." Revan tried to keep his emotions under control and noticed the tears puddling in Naomi's eyes.

"When's her funeral or service?" Naomi asked.

"They're planning a celebration of life here in Philly because her parents are still here." Revan ran his fingers through his thick hair, then blew out a long breath. "It's next Saturday, in the afternoon. Luca thinks he and I should go. At least show up briefly." He saw when understanding dawned.

"What time is it exactly?" she asked hesitantly.

"At four."

"And Stella and David's twofer party begins at six." She pulled her legs up and hugged her knees. "I agree with Luca. You should go. Scotty needs to know he has your support. Stella's party is all organized, and even if Jo is going with you and Luca because of her connection to Marnie, I have Dinah and David's sister to help me with the decorations. Everybody will understand if you and Luca aren't there at six o'clock sharp. Besides, people will be coming and going throughout the evening."

Naomi got up and walked around the sofa to stand behind him. She gently tilted his head until it rested on the back of the couch and stroked the hair off his forehead. He closed his eyes for a moment, then opened them again and looked directly at her. "If it had been you, Nugget...I can't bear to even think about it."

"Don't think, Rev," she leaned down to kiss him upside down, but he pulled her over the back of the sofa, wrapped his arm around her, and rolled them to their sides, facing each other.

"Let me refresh your memory of how much you mean to me," he said in a low voice and kissed her. Long and gentle, pouring his unspoken feelings into it.

After a long time of kissing, caressing, and just holding each other, Naomi looked at Revan and said, "What do you wanna do this afternoon?"

Make love to you like today's our last day. Because there's no guarantee there'll be a tomorrow.

"Nugget, it wouldn't be Saturday without taking you to Napoli's. In fact, they're probably waiting for you already, ice cream scooper in hand."

CHAPTER 33

—◇◦c∽⌒∽◦◦◇—

NAOMI—AUGUST 2019

The next day, Naomi sat in the backyard, enjoying the gorgeous summer afternoon. She had her gigantic party planning binder on the table in front of her but didn't look at it. Everything was all set for next Saturday.

Absentmindedly, she ran the fingers of one hand over the lavender plant in a small pot on the table next to her, then lifted them to her nose and inhaled the strong fragrance of the blossoms. *Or are they called leaves?* She looked at the dark purple flowers. It would have been a great color for her party dress.

But because she chose the Phantom theme for decorations, she asked guests to wear black, white, or red.

Thinking about the party made her think about Scott's girlfriend and the tragic accident. She had never seen

Revan as shaken as he was yesterday. The way he greeted her when she came home shocked her, and he'd been quiet for the rest of the day. After their trip to the ice cream shop, they drove to one of the larger supermarkets to stock up on household staples. Even when he was pushing the shopping cart piled high with paper goods, laundry detergent, bread, coffee, and other pantry items, he hardly let go of her hand.

To distract themselves, they went to the deli for dinner and to a movie afterward, but she had no idea how much of the movie he remembered. They cuddled and stole a few kisses in between scenes, and to other people they probably looked like any other couple.

To think of them as a couple sent pleasant shivers through her. Imagining Revan's naked body hovering over hers made her intimate body parts tingle in anticipation. Should she sneak into his room again and wait for him there, perhaps move things along a little bit faster?

No… After years of pining for Rev, she could wait a little bit longer. She was determined to let him initiate the next step. Or at least let him think he did.

A magazine on the table caught her eye…specifically, the headline "*The Thirteen Types of Kisses.*" She bought it because of the headline and had every intention of making Rev practice each one of them with her. If kissing and hugging were the only things they shared right now, why not make a game out of it? Just as she opened the magazine to find out more, she heard him walk into the house.

"Shutterbug, I'm outside. Get yourself a drink and join me, because I've got to show you something," she called out while beginning to read the article. When she heard footsteps coming closer, she said, "Wanna learn about thirteen different kinds of kisses? We can skip the hand kiss, air kiss, cheek kiss, forehead kiss, and single-lip kiss, and move on to the bite kiss. Come over here," she puckered her lips and looked up—to see Revan leaning against the door frame with his sister standing next to him. His grin was as wide as her eyes went, and she felt her cheeks burning. *Oops...*

"Hi, Naomi, I brought the two final choices for my party dress and hope you can help me pick one. Do you have time?" Dinah asked. She held up two shopping bags and looked from Naomi to Revan.

"Sure, umm, hi, Dinah, I'd love to help you. Let's go to my room." Naomi got up and gave Dinah a hug. Before she could sneak by Revan, he said, "Don't I get a hug?"

Naomi tilted her head toward Dinah and slightly lifted her shoulder, but he solved the problem by pulling her close and kissing her on her mouth. "I think we're busted... Let me read the article you were so eager to share while you and Dinah look at her dresses. I wasn't allowed to see them, so I trust you to make sure she's decently covered."

"Stop it, you moron," Dinah said. "I wanna look sexy like all the other girls."

"I'm not a moron, I'm your brother, and the other *girls*, as you call them, are women in their thirties, not sixteen. Better not forget that, Peanut," he glared at her.

"Dinah is one of us," Naomi said and patted his cheek. "So chill. We'll be back in a bit."

"There will be dozens of David's theater friends, and I don't want them drooling on my baby sister," he said, and Naomi thought she detected a serious undertone.

He looked at Dinah, "If there's only the slightest trouble, you'll go home."

"Who do you think you are? You can't send me anywhere. And I'll have Trevor with me, so I won't even care about any of the other men."

"Trevor who?" Revan folded his arms.

"My boyfriend," Dinah told him and copied his stance, both shopping bags dangling close to her sides.

"Since when? Wait a minute, are you talking about the fellow who can't keep his hands to himself?"

Dinah whipped around and glared at Naomi, "Why did you tell him? It was a secret."

"She didn't. You two were right under my bedroom window when you gabbed about him. So, are we talking about the same kid?" Rev asked.

"Why do you care? Worry about yourself," Dinah looked again from Revan to Naomi, then marched toward the stairs to Naomi's bedroom. "I can do what I want."

Naomi snort-laughed and wanted to follow her when Revan grabbed her hand and pulled her to him. After he kissed her gently, he said quietly, "Find out more about her so-called boyfriend."

"He's not so-called! I love him. We're dating," Dinah yelled from the stairs.

"I trust you, Nugget," he whispered.

In Naomi's bedroom, Dinah pulled the dresses out of their bags and arranged them on the bed. Then she looked at Naomi and said, "Revan is such a pooper. I hope he doesn't spoil it for me when Trevor's there."

"Give him time to get used to the idea of you having a boyfriend. You know he's very protective of you."

"Still... Maybe you can tell him to butt out. And I saw how he kissed you today. I'll grill him. See what he says then," Dinah fumed.

Naomi laughed and put both hands on Dinah's shoulders. "Let him be. He loves you, and he always will. And yes, we kissed, but let's keep it between ourselves, okay?"

"Are you dating him now?"

"It's complicated. But really, don't make a big thing out of it at the party. The weekend is about Stella and David. What happens at the party, stays at the party," Naomi said and winked at Dinah. "Now, let's look at your dresses. Hm, I like both, which doesn't help you much, right? You can go into my bathroom and model them for me one by one."

After Dinah left without saying goodbye to Revan, Naomi joined him on the patio. "She's upset about your big-brother-is-watching routine. And she questioned me about us kissing."

"I don't have to explain to her why I'm kissing you," he said and pulled her down to sit in his lap.

"No, you don't, but I asked her to keep it between us for the time being."

"I doubt it's going to remain a secret much longer, because I don't think I can avoid kissing you at some point on Saturday evening," he drew her face closer. "And I really like some of the suggestions for the different kisses in the magazine."

"Oh, yeah, which ones?" Naomi asked.

"I don't know about the lizard kiss, but we can try it at least once. We've mastered the neck kiss and a few others. Wait, let me practice them to make sure," he started to kiss her forehead, eyes, nose, and both corners of her mouth. "But I'm very much looking forward to," he lowered his voice to a whisper, "the two kisses in more secret spots."

"All in due time, Shutterbug," Naomi said and slid her arms around his neck. And tried to ignore her own fantasies about more intimate places for kisses.

"Remind me again of the timeline for the party weekend," Revan said after a while. By then Naomi was sitting in a chair across from him, a glass of prosecco in her hand, with her feet in his lap while he massaged her toes. She closed her eyes and sighed, "I could really get used to this."

Without opening her eyes, she continued, "Stella, David, and his parents come on Friday afternoon. His sister arrives Friday evening, but late. Apparently, she's coming alone because the boyfriend isn't in the picture anymore—which can change at any time, according to Stella. Luca and Jo are also arriving on Friday, probably midday."

"It'll be fun to have everybody together," Revan said while he squeezed each toe.

Naomi giggled, "Ooh, did you notice something? The list didn't mention toe kisses."

"Which is absolutely unacceptable and totally unfor-givable! You should toss out the offending magazine." He raised one of her feet and breathed little kisses on each toe, then repeated it with the other foot.

"Don't... I've been walking around barefoot all day," she tried to pull her feet out of his grasp.

"Nugget, what kind of boyfriend would I be if I worried about such minor inconveniences?" He gave her a lopsided smile.

"Do you know how sweet it is when you call me your girlfriend, or say you're my boyfriend?"

"Sweet isn't exactly the attribute a man is going for. Try beastly, or heroic, or..."

"Okay, I get it, Shutterbug. Before we inflate your ego any further, let's get back to next weekend. Why are you asking?"

"I told you, to refresh my memory. What time do you need to be at City Tavern for finishing touches? I'm sure you'll find a balloon or two to move to another place or need to change place cards."

"There's no assigned seating. I'm only reserving a table for the happy couple, and for everyone else it's mingle time. Dinah, Sabrina, and I will meet there at four thirty, Stella and David with their parents will arrive by five thirty, and the guests start arriving at six."

"Where's everybody staying? Should we offer someone our guest room?"

"Jo's staying with Aunt Mary, Luca with his parents, Stella and David reserved a room in a hotel, and so did David's parents and sister."

"Okay. Luca, Jo, and I will be there as soon as we can after Marnie's service. I was planning to wear black jeans with a charcoal blazer to the service, so I'll just bring a different tie for the party. Can you take my camera bag with you to the Tavern?"

"You're trusting me with your camera bag? You never let anybody near your equipment." She was genuinely surprised.

"Whoa, what a loaded comment, Nugget. But yes, I trust you blindly with *all* my equipment," he winked at her, and Naomi could feel her cheeks burning for the second time this afternoon. She drained her glass of prosecco in one big gulp.

Their innuendos were getting less and less veiled. And while she tried to look at them as verbal foreplay, she was more looking forward to the real deal.

CHAPTER 34

NAOMI—AUGUST 2019

S hortly after 5 pm on Saturday, Naomi joined Dinah and Sabrina at one of the many round tables in the event room at the historical City Tavern. Because they expected over one hundred fifty guests coming and going, the restaurant had reserved the whole second floor for them. Off-white walls and green windowsills, dark green, velvety curtains, and high ceilings, combined with the chandeliers and wall sconces, created a cozy atmosphere.

Every table was covered in a floor-length white damask tablecloth with two three-inch wide black satin table runners making a large X. In the middle stood a tall, clear cylindrical glass vase filled halfway with black glass stones, holding three red roses of different heights. White votive candles in glass holders were waiting to be lit, and rose petals lay scattered across the tablecloths.

Naomi chugged a glass of infused water and enjoyed the mild flavor of cucumber and mint before she said, "I think tonight will be great. Just look around." She gestured to encompass the entire room. "This restaurant played such an important role in Stella and David's relationship; I knew it was the logical place to have their twofer party."

"What happened here?" Dinah asked.

Just recalling the evening made Naomi want to take out her cell phone and check Adrienne's whereabouts. To make sure she wouldn't be able to barge in like a human wrecking ball and ruin David and Stella's celebration.

"Last November, after David came back to the States, we met here for dinner. Suddenly his ex-girlfriend showed up and made a huge scene in front of the whole restaurant. Stella had just started to trust him again and was confused when Adrienne talked about performing with him again and hinted at picking up their old romance as well."

Naomi didn't mention Stella leaving the restaurant, or that she followed her best friend outside, where she told Stella to march her butt back inside and fight for David. Which Stella did—and the rest was history.

"Adrienne was coocoo," Sabrina muttered, then said, "The Phantom-themed decorations look amazing with the eighteenth-century ambiance of the building, Naomi. I'm sure my brother will love it."

With the help of David's manager, Aaron, Naomi was able to borrow six mannequins and costumes from the Philadelphia Academy of Music's large arsenal of props and decorations. The mannequins were dressed in long, dark capes, and wore either half-face masks or plumed hats on their faceless heads. Naomi had set them up in safe spots where they could be seen without being in the way.

In the middle of Stella and David's table she placed a six-inch water globe with *Phantom* and *Christine* figurines in it. The characters were looking at each other through a two-sided mirror. David and Stella would understand the meaning behind it.

For his proposal last March, David had been allowed to recreate the perfect setting by taking Stella to the underground lake of the Paris Opera House, where the fictional phantom kept the fictional Christine in his lair. The water globe played the song "Music of the Night," which was one of Stella's favorites.

Instead of red roses, their flower arrangement consisted of yellow, salmon-colored, and white roses. Stella had told her how David had tried to convey his feelings and later his apologies through the language of flowers. Yellow for friendship, salmon for desire, white for purity and new beginnings. As a final touch, Naomi put a dark red rose at Stella's place.

Close to the large windows on the opposite side of the room, the band members were busy setting up their instruments and sound-testing their equipment. They had agreed to play music from the 1970s to 1990s, mostly based on Revan's suggestions, but were also willing to fulfill song requests. Naomi had heard the band a few times and knew them to be amazing musicians.

Waiters and waitresses were busy readying the buffets on two sides of the room, where they would keep an eye on the food and refill the appetizers, salads, and platters of sandwiches throughout the evening. A bar was stocked with a selection of alcoholic and nonalcoholic beverages, and guests would also be able to order cocktails from the downstairs restaurant.

Shortly before 5:30 pm, Stella and David strolled into the room holding hands. Pausing in the wide double doors between the two rooms, David put his arm around Stella's shoulders and pulled her close.

Stella hid her face in her hands and shook her head. "David, did you know about this? I thought this was just going to be a get-together, like our engagement party."

"No, love, I didn't. But even if I did, I wouldn't have told you," he kissed her.

Naomi hugged her best friend. "I'm so happy you're here. I've missed you!" Then she hugged David and said, "And you as well, Troub."

He laughed when he heard her old nickname for him. "Some things never change, huh? Thank you for organizing this. It looks amazing."

Dinah and Sabrina joined them, and Sabrina said, "And you don't even have to sing tonight, big brother!"

"What if I want to?"

"Well, in that case, we won't stop you," Sabrina said.

The parents arrived within a few minutes of each other, and Naomi excused herself to change into her party dress. She didn't want to wear it while they were still setting up the room, but now it was party time. Revan texted her to let her know they were on their way, but traffic was terrible, and they wouldn't make it for 6 pm.

She wrote back,

Don't worry. Stella and David and their families are just starting to arrive.

After running a brush through her hair, she pulled it in a low ponytail and touched up her minimal makeup. Only blue eyeliner, a hint of pink lipstick, and a dab of perfume behind her ears. Done!

It was the middle of August, she was tanned from spending lots of time outside with the dogs and walking to and from work every day, and when she looked into the mirror, she was happy with the woman looking back at her. Not only was she happy with the way she looked, but Naomi could also see she radiated happiness.

Could it be because, on this special day marking the beginning of Stella and David's wedding celebrations, she was also allowing herself to dream of a happy ending for herself and Revan?

She slipped into her two-inch strap sandals, put her cosmetic bag and the sundress into her oversized purse, and left the bathroom. The musicians had already agreed that she could stash Revan's camera bag where the band set up and put her purse with it.

By six thirty the room was filling up with people, and she craned her neck to see if Luca, Jo, and Revan had arrived. Since both men were over six feet tall, they should be easy to spot. She was busy looking for them and jumped when someone called her name.

"Naomi, hi!" She spotted friends standing at a table and went over to them. She and Stella met the couple in France last year and had stayed in touch. Stella even more, since she moved to Baltimore, where Sarah and Andrew lived.

"Hey, you two. I'm so glad you were able to come. How are you doing? What's new?"

"We're good." Sarah said and beamed at her husband. Naomi knew they had only been married a little over a year themselves. They shared last year that they'd been in love when they were young, but Sarah married someone else and, after she got divorced, reconnected with Andrew, who had never married.

Andrew looked at his wife and put his hand over her barely rounded stomach, then said, "I'd say we're better than good. This beautiful lady here is going to have our baby in five months."

"WHAT?" Naomi almost screamed. "Does Stella know? How come I don't?"

Sarah laughed, "Yes, she does, since I can't exactly hide it anymore. And I don't want to. Becoming pregnant at forty-two feels like a miracle."

"Congratulations! I'm sooo happy for you. Well, let's get you a virgin drink, and Andrew and I can toast with champagne," Naomi beckoned a waitress over. "Can we please get two glasses of champagne and a...what do you want, Sarah?"

"I'll have a ginger ale, thanks."

When the drinks arrived, they toasted and continued their conversation, which automatically revolved around babies and nurseries and how Sarah's older children, who were twenty-one and twenty-two, felt about the new addition. "They were fantastic when we told them," Sarah said. "I'm hoping Stella joins the mom-club soon. Imagine how much fun we'd have."

Naomi said, "I think that's her plan."

Would she ever be part of the club as well? Were children in her future? She'd never given it much thought. But as Jo reminded them all last Christmas, their biological clocks were ticking.

She excused herself and walked around the room again, greeting newcomers and chatting with others. At the buffet, she filled a plate with cheese, olives, grapes, and small triangles of still-warm herb focaccia. There was more tempting-looking food, some of it much fancier than what she put on her plate, but she needed something familiar right now. She added a few mini peppers filled with hummus, then started to make her way to Stella and David's table.

"Is this for your starving boyfriend, Nugget?" A hand settled on her hip.

Hearing his low, sexy voice, and feeling his warm hand on her body, sent shivers down her spine. She looked at him and swallowed. *He is one handsome man.*

It wasn't really a new discovery for her. Her fingers itched to rake through his hair, and even though she knew he had shaved earlier, new stubble showed on his face again.

Revan reached for her plate and placed a peck on her lips. "Get another plate of food for yourself and meet me at the table."

"My, my, since when are you so bossy?" she asked him but smiled and went back to the buffet. *I do love that man!*

"Nugget, umm...where is our table?" he called back to her. Naomi laughed and pointed to it.

She filled another plate with slightly different food—shrimp, bacon-wrapped sea scallops, marinated mushrooms, and crackers topped with a cheesy dip which was probably loaded with calories but smelled delicious. Two glasses of champagne waited at their table. Revan leaned closer to her and said quietly, "I missed you."

More shivers ran through her. Was there anything he could say or do that wouldn't trigger a physical reaction?

"How did the memorial service go?"

"Somber and heartbreaking. It was brutal to see Scotty so broken, and I know it'll take a long time for him to get over the loss of Marnie."

She could see how much the tragedy rattled him. "We don't have to talk about it now. Sorry I asked," she reached for his hand and gave it a brief squeeze.

"Don't be, Nugget. And it helped me to know you'd be here waiting for me," he squeezed her hand back, then said, "Now I'll eat a bite, and then I've got to do my duty and start taking photos." He helped himself to food from his plate, then from hers, then his own again, and washed it all down with champagne.

All under the watchful and smiling eyes of Stella from across the table. Naomi gave her a quick wink and smirked, which prompted Stella to bump David's elbow. Stella would demand details before the weekend was over.

Revan wiped his mouth with a napkin and said, "Okay, that'll do it for now. I'm sure there's more later. Where did you put my camera?"

"Where the band is. I decided it's the safest place."

"Good thinking, Nugget. See you later," he kissed her cheek.

After watching him until he was swallowed by the crowd, she finished the food on her plate, then got up to enjoy the party and occasionally check to make sure everything was running smoothly.

When she spotted Dinah, she had to hide a grin. Like her, Dinah had changed into a party dress shortly before the guests arrived. The sixteen-year-old looked stunning in her burgundy-red mini dress with a lightly flared skirt that blended with the reddish streak she'd added to her naturally ash-blonde hair. She was a beautiful young lady, and the way Trevor hovered over her and kept his hand on her waist, he seemed to be thinking along the same lines.

I hope Revan leaves them alone and doesn't play the big brother card too much. Especially since their parents were here, too, and Naomi had no doubt that Robert was eyeing his daughter's boyfriend as closely as Revan did.

Next, she saw Jo and Luca on the dance floor. Luca's arms were around Jo's waist, Jo's around his neck, and they talked quietly and shared a laugh while moving to the music.

She looked around for Stella, to point them out to her, but her friend was deep in conversation with someone she didn't know.

Naomi's eyes drifted to her Aunt Mary, who sat with Aaron. Naomi hadn't seen her aunt looking so happy in a long time. After Uncle Phil was killed on the job in a car chase a few years earlier, Aunt Mary kept busy with her work and didn't do much socializing. But here she was, patting Aaron's arm, coyly playing with her necklace, flirting with the man from New York. *Go, girl*, Naomi thought. *Have fun!*

When she looked up, she saw Revan standing on a chair, with his camera pointed at her. Naomi reached for her ponytail and winked at him. Then she tilted her head sideways to tell him to look at Aunt Mary. Rev nodded and focused his camera on Mary and Aaron.

Before he disappeared in the crowd again, he blew her a kiss.

CHAPTER 35

REVAN—AUGUST 2019

He had plenty of material to work with, both for the official photos as well as the ones he planned to use in the personal album he would make for his friends as a surprise.

Throughout the evening he'd watched Naomi being all over the place. When people started dancing, and he saw her going from one man's arms to the next, he couldn't get rid of the cramping in his chest. He should be the only one allowed to have his hands on her hips.

And that dress… He did a double take when he first saw her in front of the buffet. Seen from behind, it was a hip-hugging black maxi dress. The asymmetrical hem of the wrap-style dress ended on her right side in a thigh-high front slit and showed off her gorgeous, mile-long legs, making it a mini dress in the front.

Revan ripped off his tie, shoved it in his camera bag and undid the top buttons of his dress shirt. Time for her to open her arms to a new dance partner—him!

Exchanging a few quick words with one of the band members, he turned around—and stopped dead in his tracks.

The octopus his sister called her boyfriend had his tentacles attached to her hips, and his mouth glued to hers. He was going to put an end to this schmooze-fest right now. But halfway there he saw his mother holding his father's arm with both hands and giving him one of her don't-mess-with-me looks.

Good, if his father was keeping his eye on Dinah, he could focus on Naomi.

Where was she? He looked around and finally spotted her leaning against the wooden doorframe, looking out into the dark night. What—or whom—was she thinking about?

The identity of her mystery man still made Revan wonder if he did the right thing by getting involved with her. The underlying uncertainty that she could end it with him was causing him a lot of anguish, but he still didn't have the guts to bring it up directly—yet.

Enough is enough, his inner voice told him. *Stop your stupid second-guessing and help her forget him—once and for all. What are you waiting for, Forrester?*

"Nugget, do you happen to have an opening on your overflowing dance card?" He put one arm around her waist.

Kissed the side of her neck, then slowly turned her around to look at him.

"I thought you'd never ask, Shutterbug. Hiding behind your camera all night. Tut-tut-tut... Should I be jealous of the Nikon?" her hands slid up and around his neck.

"It's a Canon, Nugget. Huge difference. And you're right, I've neglected you way too long tonight. It's high time to give you my undivided attention," he traced her lips with his thumb. "I want to kiss you so badly...you have no idea."

"I think I do," she licked her lips, then pulled her lower lip into her mouth.

The band finished a song and the singer announced, "Our next song is by special request."

"Come with me, Nugget," he took her hand. They crossed the room to the dance floor, joining a few other couples waiting for the music to continue.

"Did *you* ask for a song? Which one did you pick?" she asked and settled in his arms as the first notes played. "Oh, no, Chris de Burgh? Really?"

Revan put his mouth close to her ear and said, "I want you to listen very closely to the words, sweetheart. No talking until the song is finished, okay? And by the way, you're wearing the wrong color."

Naomi snuggled closer to Revan and whispered back, "I don't know what's wrong with black, but you can't see everything I'm wearing."

There it was again, the crampy feeling in his chest, but this time caused by something else. He put his finger on her lips, then started to move them slowly across the dance-floor, basic foxtrot steps, just enough to be in motion, only half-listening to "Lady in Red."

Throughout the song, he imagined having her to himself, without an audience, alone at home. He grew iron-hard just thinking about her naked, in his bed, responding to his fingers, his tongue, and his boy. He pulled her closer to let her feel how much he desired her, and when he whispered the last three words of the song, Naomi's eyes shone with tears.

"I'll never forget tonight, Nugget." He lowered his mouth to hers and kept swaying to the next song—even though he had no idea what the band was playing.

It was past midnight by the time they got home. Naomi dropped her purse, kicked off her shoes, and said, "Six hours in those sandals was more than enough."

She carried the vase to the sink and filled it with enough water to cover the glass pebbles. "I hope the roses last awhile. They haven't even fully opened yet. It would've been a shame to throw 'em out."

"You did a fantastic job tonight," Revan hung up his blazer and rolled the shirt sleeves up to his elbows.

"Rev, do you think I could have a glass of red wine? I drank seltzer all night except for two glasses of champagne early in the evening, and it's coming out of my ears," she sat down on the sofa and massaged her feet.

"Coming right up!"

After pouring two glasses of wine, he sat next to Naomi and pulled her feet in his lap, studying her dark red nail polish. "What's the name of this beautiful shade, Nugget?"

"Do you really want to talk about nail polish right now?"

"No, but I hope to earn bonus points if I offer you a foot massage. So, what's the name?"

"Midnight Passion," she reached for her glass and took a sip.

"Are you making up those names, Nugget?" With his thumbs, he massaged the bottom of her feet while he tried not to stare at her stretched-out legs. Her dress barely covered her thighs. Suddenly, the air in his living room was getting too thick.

"Can I ask you something?" Naomi asked quietly. Her head rested sideways on the back of the sofa, with her eyes closed.

"Sure," his voice was husky and his throat was dry.

"Did you call me sweetheart when we danced?"

"Did you mind?" His voice was getting hoarser, and he reached for his wine glass and sipped.

"No."

"Did you listen to every word in the song?" His eyes didn't leave her face and he saw the little uptick of her lips.

"I did," she nodded but didn't open her eyes.

"Good, because I couldn't have put my feelings into words any better than shmaltzy Chris."

"Shutterbug," Naomi whispered, "can you stop babbling and come a little closer?"

Letting go of her feet, he took her glass and set it on the table. Then he gently pushed her down on the sofa cushions and leaned over her, kissing her softly and playing with her lips until she opened her mouth and invited him in.

He poured all his raging emotions into this kiss—the fear of losing her, the jealousy he experienced when he saw other men dancing with her, the desire she stirred in him when he saw her in her sexy party dress, and the passion he had so far refused to give in to.

What was he waiting for? Life could get turned upside down in a heartbeat, and he didn't want to waste another day. Whispering that he loved her wasn't enough, he needed to show her how deep his feelings went.

Letting one hand slide down to her hip, he pushed the soft fabric of her dress out of the way and skimmed his fingertips along the top of her silk panties. It wasn't enough. He needed to see her, to undress her, to make her his.

"Nugget...upstairs..." he said into her mouth. They were both breathing hard, their chests touching with every inhale.

She tugged on his shirt. Revan put his hand over hers and said, "Have patience, sweetheart, we have all night. And I intend to make every second count."

"Have I ever mentioned that I'm not good at waiting?" The look she gave him made him laugh.

"Oh, those are fightin' words, Nugget." Getting up, he reached for both wine glasses. "I'm bringing these in case we need sustenance."

"Let me run to my bathroom quickly. I'll be back in a sec." Barefoot, she sprinted up her stairs two at a time.

When they danced to "Lady in Red," he told her he'd never forget tonight. And it was the truth.

Tonight they'd cross the third and last invisible line. And he was determined to make it the most memorable one.

CHAPTER 36

Naomi—August 2019

Naomi paused before entering Revan's room and watched him standing in front of the window, looking out across the dark backyard. A reading lamp in the corner was turned on to a low setting and bathed the room in soft yellow light. The two wine glasses, refilled, stood on a bedside table.

She wanted to freeze time, to memorize this moment, how he looked wearing his shirt unbuttoned and pulled out of his jeans.

"Can I come in?" Instead of answering, Revan crossed the room in a few strides. His lips found hers, his teeth nipped on her upper lip, and his tongue teased its way into her mouth, and started to play with hers.

She reveled in the pleasure of touching his skin, letting her hands slide up and down his chest and abdomen. *Dreams do come true!* She wrapped one arm around his neck to pull herself closer to him. She had longed for this in what seemed like forever!

Revan broke their kiss, his eyes dark, and he whispered, "I really want to go slow, sweetheart, but I don't know if I can if you keep torturing me like this."

"You mean when I do this?" She repeated the soft brush of her fingertips over his chest hair and then slid one hand up and pushed his shirt off his shoulder, following the path of her hand with her lips. First on one side, then on the other, letting the shirt float to the floor. Her hand glided over his arms, which were sprinkled with the same soft brown hair covering his chest and abs. She could feel his muscles rippling and tensing under the skin.

When she reached for his belt buckle, he stopped her hand and said, "Oh, no, Nugget, your turn next," and slid a finger under the one-inch-wide shoulder strap of her dress. He tried to pull it over her shoulder. It didn't budge. His hand went to the back of her dress. "Where's the damn zipper?"

Naomi shrugged. "Hmm…"

His hand continued patting her down, turning her every direction. "Where is it?" It was more a growl than a word. W'r'zit?

She snickered. "There isn't one. You should've seen me wiggle my way into it." She demonstrated a little wiggle with her shoulders and hips.

"I'd rather see you wiggle out of it, and fast." He reached for the skirt of the dress and fisted his hands around the soft fabric. Before he pushed it over her hips, he stopped and lifted her up, only to set her down on his bed. His mouth found hers as he gently pressed her back, putting one knee between her legs. He loomed over her body with his, leaving only an inch or two of space between them. Holding himself up on one forearm, he slid the fingers of his free hand into her hair, then down her arm, along the side of her body, and changed directions at her waist and went up to her hair again, while his kisses turned hot, demanding, and raw.

Naomi matched his fervor with her own. "Rev, take off my dress. Please," she tried to lift her hips to shed the dress, but he stopped her. "I like how you say please. Raise your arms, Nugget."

This time, he didn't stop her when she raised her hips and then arched her back so he could push the dress up over her breasts, over her shoulders, over her arms, until he let it glide to the floor.

Naomi reached behind Revan's head to pull him down, but he said, "And now we unwrap the presents." His voice was deep and laden with desire.

Watching him while his eyes roamed over her body, over her lace bra and silk panties, her skin prickled wherever his laser-like focus left a trail. Branding her. "Do you know how much I want to kiss every hidden spot of yours? From your head to your toes—and everywhere in between."

"Then just do it. Kiss me, Rev. Do something, *please*."

He gave her the lopsided grin she loved so much and started to lower his mouth to hers, but before their lips met, he turned his head sideways and touched his lips on her neck, right below her ear. His mouth trailed over her collarbone, to the top of her breasts. He cupped one, slid his thumb under the thin fabric of her bra, and started to draw circles around her nipple.

His mouth closed around her other breast and teased it through the lace. She pushed closer into his mouth, threw her arms around his neck, and moaned. His caresses sent fiery signals through her whole body. He switched sides and continued to worship her breasts, one at a time.

He mumbled, "I'm glad to see you're wearing red. But this is in my way right now." He reached behind her and unclasped the bra, letting her breasts spill out of their confinement, then tossed it on the floor.

He filled his hands with her breasts, massaged them, kissed them, his tongue flicking over her taut nipples before he blew short puffs of air on them, only to pull a nipple into his mouth again.

Naomi couldn't lie still. Her breath came in short pants and she sucked in air every time his tongue touched her skin. Her entire body was on fire, and he hadn't even come close to where she needed him most.

Feeling his erection through layers of clothing wasn't enough—it was only a mean teaser. She needed to see him and touch him. If she didn't get her hands on him soon, she'd have to resort to violence. Fingernails-on-bare-skin violence. Naomi reached between them and grabbed his belt buckle again.

"We're far from playing there, sweetheart," he looked up from her breasts. Flick of tongue, puff of air, pulling a nipple into his mouth. Repeat on the other side. And he gave her a predatory smile.

Foreplay involving her breasts had never been as arousing as it was with Revan. "I'll come if you continue that, Rev. Stop it," she panted.

"Why, you don't want to come?" he asked with his mouth hovering over her nipples, and then licked them, both hands filled with her breasts.

"I do, but...ah...no! Stop it."

"Sorry, can't. Busy here. Those beauties and I aren't done getting to know each other."

"There's more to say hello to." She pressed herself against his erection and made grinding moves. He finally shifted and looked at her again. "You're playing unfair."

"Me? Because I remind you there's more to explore? For both of us?"

She was able to push him on his back. "My turn." Her hand slipped inside the front of his pants, where she wrapped her fingers around him and added gentle pressure.

"Nugget...Don't..." His breathing was so labored, she thought she'd have to give him mouth-to-mouth resuscitation. "Or...I won't last."

"Why, you don't want to come? Hmm, sounds familiar." She smiled at him and squeezed harder, touching his moist head. "Take those pants off. Now," she demanded.

"Not...Yet...Not...Like...This..." He tried to pull her hand out of his pants.

She let go of him and in one fluid move undid his belt and unzipped his jeans. Licked her lips at seeing his erection straining against black boxer briefs. She swung a leg over his hips and straddled him. "You don't get to set the rules all by yourself, Shutterbug. Kiss me. Show me what you've got," she said and closed the distance between them.

He ravished her mouth while she hovered over him. Her nipples rubbed over his chest and triggered a carnal sensation that traveled directly to her core. "Make me come, please."

"Hold on a second, sweetheart," he said and put his hands on her shoulders.

What is it now? Naomi couldn't believe it and held her breath.

He lifted her off him and sat up. She resumed breathing when Revan kicked off his jeans, then pushed her on her back and said, "Now, where were we?"

He began kissing her breasts again, then let his tongue trail over her belly and down, holding her hips firmly in place as he began to lick and nibble through the thin, already-soaked silk of her underwear. She put her hand on the back of his head and pushed it toward where she needed him to be. "Rev, please ..."

He stopped and looked up at her from between her legs.

"Why did you stop?" she cried. Every cell in her body was screaming.

"You have to wait," he hiked up his eyebrows and grinned.

"What? I'm so close—pleeaassee, Rev, I'm dying here." Naomi lifted her hips closer to his mouth, to offer him her most needy spot.

"You have to wait," he mumbled, his mouth a scant inch away from her throbbing clit.

"You said you want me to come," she wasn't beyond pouting or begging if it got her what she wanted.

"I changed my mind. Not yet," he slid one finger under the dark red silk. One tiny flick, and she sucked in her breath. "Yes, Rev. Kiss me there." His eyes stayed on hers as he obeyed and kissed her through the silk, then flicked her again. Another tiny flick.

She was so close, could feel the orgasm building up. If he'd only...

"Let's find out what you're hiding here," he grinned and hooked a finger under the top of her panties. He inched them down at what seemed like a micro-millimeter at a time before flinging them in the direction of the other discarded clothes.

"What's that?" he asked, his face hovering over the V between her legs.

"Please, as if you've never seen a hoo-ha." She was about to scream, and not the erotic and passionate kind. This was not the time for playing "I spy."

"The tattoo, Nugget." He touched it.

She had totally forgotten about the tattoo on her lower left abdomen. Not much more than an inch high, and always hidden by her panties.

"Oh. Well... What does it look like to you?"

"A heart and—" he traced it, his touch driving her wild, "—an uppercase R. An intertwined heart and R?" His finger followed the rounded left top of the heart, to the pointy tip at the bottom, then went up the right side of the tattoo, where the rounded right top became the loop of the uppercase R, with the R's leg trailing off.

"Heart R," he repeated, then breathed a small kiss on the tattoo. "What's the R for, Nugget?"

"Does it matter?" She tried to sit up. Not one boyfriend had ever asked about it, not when they were so close to score.

He pushed her back on the bed again and said in a grim voice, "Tell me."

His eyes bored into hers, and she wished she could read his thoughts. His finger didn't leave the tattoo, it slowly followed the fine double lines of the heart. Again, and again. Tormenting her.

It's now or never... Tell him!

"I got it after the college graduation party you and Luca threw for Stella, Jo, and me. You danced with me to 'Heart-breaker.' I got it because of...."

"Yeah?"

"...you," she whispered while her tears spilled over.

Here she was, in Revan's bed, spread out naked in front of him, and the feelings she had hidden for those many years, covering them up by being flippant and funny, were finally spilling out.

"Nugget—" Rev began to say, but she held up her hand. If she didn't tell him now, she'd never tell him.

"I've had a crush on you since I was fifteen or sixteen, but at our graduation party, ten years ago, I fell in love with you. So, I got a tattoo with your initial. And then the years went by. In Paris you told me you loved me like a sister, and it nearly killed me. I tried to accept that I would never have a chance with you. That your T-shirts and this tattoo were all I had of you."

Revan's eyes never left hers when he said in a choked whisper, "Are you saying...the guy who never saw you? The one you've been waiting for..."

"It's you, Revan. Always and only you." Fat tears rolled down her face, ugly but freeing, and she wiped them away with the back of her hand. Her lips trembled when she tried to smile at him.

He stilled her hand, put his hand over hers, and used his thumb to dry her face.

"I've been such an idiot. Don't cry anymore." He lowered his mouth to hers, let his hand roam over her face, then over her whole body. Shimmying out of his boxer briefs, never breaking their kiss, always gazing into Naomi's eyes, Revan spread her legs and positioned himself between them. He reached for a condom, but Naomi pushed it away.

"Nothing between us, please." She knew she was clean and that he got tested frequently because of his hellish trips.

His erection pulsed against her entrance, making her entire body scream with yearning.

"Ready, Nugget?" his voice was barely audible, and she only nodded.

He entered her in one smooth move, never pausing until he was fully embedded. "You okay, baby?"

She nodded again and started to move with him, hooked a leg around his waist to give him more access—and stopped thinking. He thrust into her, giving her what she needed, and when her moaning got more demanding, Revan pulled out one last time and looked at her. Without breaking eye contact, he reached between them, teased her sensitive spot, thrust back inside her, and made her come.

She flew over the top of her climax. Her muscles clenched around him, and when he pulled one of her nipples in his mouth and sucked hard, she came again. Naomi could feel him pulsing deep inside of her, still pushing deeper and deeper. She tightened around him, and he followed her into his own release.

Revan cradled her in his arms and whispered into her hair, "Thank you for not giving up on me."

"How could I? You're all I ever wanted. And how often did I tell you that I always get what I want?"

He laughed softly, "I'll keep it in mind, baby. I love you, Nugget."

"I love you, too, Shutterbug. Always did. Always will."

CHAPTER 37

REVAN—AUGUST 2019

Revan didn't think he'd be able to get any sleep, because all he wanted to do was gaze at the woman in his arms. Somewhere between three and four in the morning they took a break from lovemaking and showered together. Now Naomi was wearing a cute silk bikini bottom and a matching camisole, both covering just enough to drive him crazy. When he heard her slow breathing, he got out of bed and pulled the sheet over her.

Wearing only boxer briefs, he carried the empty wine glasses to the kitchen. Grabbing two bottles of water from the fridge, he noticed the flower arrangement on the counter, plucked out a rose, and went back to his bedroom.

Trying not to wake her, he lay down and pulled her closer until she spooned with him. A memory from their night in Richmond popped up, when she also spooned with him, but wearing that ridiculous bathrobe. He buried his nose in her hair and inhaled the scent of grapefruit, lavender and—her.

He couldn't believe she'd admitted to loving him for all this time. Oh, no, wrong! What he couldn't believe was his own stupidity, his blindness. Images of the past ten, fifteen years flashed through his mind, of Naomi trying to be near him, watching him, coaxing a reaction—anything!—out of him, seeking his touch while pretending it was innocent and accidental.

And her tattoo...her confession almost broke him.

Revan gently pushed her hair out of her face and tucked it behind her ear. "I'll never let you go again, Nugget," he whispered.

And fell asleep with a million tiny images of her playing in front of him like a meteor shower on a clear summer night in the desert.

Revan was painfully aroused when he came awake and was about to pull a sheet over his hips when a hand slipped inside his boxers.

"I didn't get to say hello to you last night. Someone wouldn't let me..." Naomi whispered.

Her head rested on his chest, her hair spread out over his body, and her finger trailed along the side of his boy, who reveled in the attention, standing larger and taller than ever. "But look who's ready to play." Her hand closed around him and she added just enough pressure to make Revan bite down on his lip.

"Sweetheart, be careful there," he croaked and sucked in a deep breath when her fingertip touched his opening. "I don't think he can control himself around you."

"It's okay, I don't mind if he loses control," she looked up to him, then turned her head and breathed a kiss on the side of his swollen head. "Oh, look, he's winking at me. I think he's trying to tell me something."

"I wonder what it could be." He could barely get the words out. And he didn't want to talk. He was thinking along the same lines as his boy.

"We don't need this, I think." Naomi pushed down Revan's underwear. His penis jumped out and fully saluted her.

She kissed his proud, naked boy again, then moved up and followed his line of dark hair until she reached the hollow spot under his throat.

Sliding out of her panties, she gazed into his eyes while she lowered herself on him until he was fully embedded, and then tossed away her camisole, the shift creating just enough pressure to drive him almost to the edge. He began to move when Naomi leaned forward and kissed him.

"Wait a second," he wheezed. "Can we take this off?"

"Take what off? I'm not wearing anything," she asked huskily, guiding one of his hands to her breasts.

"Your pendant, Nugget. It keeps hitting me in my face, and I'd rather enjoy your pretty girls without sporting a bruise on my face when we're done," he held up her gold nugget pendant.

"But I never take it off. I need it. It's my good luck charm," she began moving again, steadily rising, then lowering on him again.

Revan could feel his erection pulsing, warning him to keep up with his lady. "I promise you won't need it." Deeply embedded, he sat up and wrapped her legs around his waist, cupped one breast and pulled her nipple in his mouth. While his tongue played around her nipple, he reached between them and brushed his finger over her clit.

She sucked in a deep breath, then arched into his mouth. Reaching behind her neck, she unclasped the necklace and tossed it on the table.

"Good girl. Now, where were we?" he grinned and leaned back with her. Revan wanted to let her take control of speed and position, but he was so thick and hard, he needed to send her over the top soon and then follow her. He'd go slower next time.

"Come for me, baby. Now," he whispered in her ear. "What do you need from me?"

"Do...whatever...you...want," she panted and rocked back and forth.

He pulled her breast in his mouth, suckled like a hungry baby, while caressing between her legs. She cried out and collapsed on top of him, her contracting muscles massaging his boy with a firm grip.

He flipped them over and looked down at her flushed face. Her eyes were closed, and he felt her still riding the waves of her orgasm while he thrust and retreated until he couldn't withhold his own climax any longer. Like last night, he continued to tease her sensitive spot and buried himself as deep as he could, until he felt her climb over the top again in perfect synchrony with his own release.

He hovered over her and touched his forehead to hers. "Have I told you lately how much I love you?"

"Not in the last hour. But I don't mind repetition," she smiled at him and pulled his face down to kiss him.

"I love you," he kissed her back and rolled them to the side with his arms around her. "Where have you been my whole life?"

"Right under your nose, Shutterbug," she snuggled as close as she could.

"We should probably get up and take a shower. Aren't we meeting the others for brunch at noon?" Rev said after a few more minutes of kissing and holding each other. He felt himself harden again, but knew the timing sucked.

"I don't want to get out of bed," she sighed and rubbed against him, "and I think neither do you."

"Not enough time, Nugget," he grumbled. "I want to go *really* slow next time you're under me."

"What time is it?"

Revan peeked over her shoulder to his side table. "Eleven." He saw the rose and stretched his arm to pick it up. After touching it to his lips, he let it slide over her breasts.

She smiled at him and took it out of his hand, "Are you really sure?"

Revan laughed and squeezed her butt cheeks lightly. "Let's save some fun for later. Do you want to shower together or separately?"

"Together, but I think we'd tempt fate. I'll go shower in my bathroom and meet you in the kitchen in twenty minutes. And I need coffee before we leave the house."

Revan kissed the tip of her nose and rolled over, reached for her necklace, then put it around her neck and touched the little nugget, nestling again between the swell of her breasts. "I think I'm jealous of this little thing," he said with a growl. "And when we come back from brunch, we'll move some of your stuff in here. I'll empty one of the drawers and make room in the closet. Underwear, hygiene stuff, maybe a cute sundress...no, no dress. You won't need a dress in here."

Naomi laughed. "Bossy, bossy... We'll see about it later," she got out of bed, slipped on her panties and picked up the rest of her clothes. Her eyes roamed over Rev's naked body and she winked at him, "See you in a bit, big guy."

Thirty minutes later he watched her coming down her stairs wearing a yellow-and-white dress and swinging white sandals in her hand, her hair still damp from the shower. She grabbed the cup of coffee waiting for her on the counter.

"Thank you, Rev," she looked over the rim of the mug. "In the shower, I was wondering if I have to find a new nickname for you now? You called me 'baby' and 'sweetheart', and of course 'Nugget', but I still like 'Shutterbug' best for you. It's just who you are."

Revan leaned back against the counter and laughed. He crossed his legs at his ankles and drank from his own coffee mug. "I'm sure you'll think of something. Since you've seen all of me now, maybe something a little more, umm, fitting comes to your mind," he grinned and checked the time. "We should go. It's a thirty-minute walk to Positano. Or do you want me to call a taxi?"

"No taxi. And it's not half an hour to get there. Twenty minutes, tops," she slipped on her sandals and dropped her cell phone in her purse.

"Not if we stop for a kiss. Or two. Do you really think we'll get there without making out at least once? I can't keep my hands off you," he wiggled his fingers at her.

"What are we? Sixteen?" she laughed and finished her coffee.

"Let me tell you, Nugget, last night and this morning, I felt like I was sixteen again more than once," Revan said and reached into his pants to adjust himself. "And we'd better go now, or we'll never make it there."

Arriving at the Italian restaurant, he pulled her close and said, "Just letting you know one thing. I'm not answering any nosy questions in there. You okay with that?"

"Absolutely."

The hostess told them where the rest of their group was seated, and Revan and Naomi walked through the restaurant holding hands. They found their friends at a table overlooking City Tavern and the Merchants' Exchange Building, passing their iPhones around, laughing and pointing out things to each other. An ice bucket with an already opened bottle of prosecco and a pitcher of freshly squeezed orange juice stood in the middle of the table.

Stella waved. "I was wondering what kept you."

"Chill, Cinderella, we're only ten minutes late," Revan said. "It's Sunday, and some people like to sleep in." He squeezed Naomi's hand.

Stella gave him a side-eyed look and said, "M-hm..." Her eyes fell to their entwined fingers. With a grin, she repeated, "M-hmmmm..."

Revan wasn't surprised by Stella's pointed look and comment. To avoid any further interrogations, he pulled Naomi in his arms and kissed her soundly.

"Any other questions, guys?" With Naomi in his arms, he looked at each friend individually, starting with Stella, and answered his own question by saying, "I didn't think so."

Before they took their seats, they walked around the table to greet everyone. Revan kissed Stella and Jo on their cheeks, and shoulder-slapped David. Luca pulled him into a man-hug and muttered, "How hard was it?"

"That's between Nugget and me," Revan grinned, then held a chair for Naomi and sat down next to her, his arm on the back of her chair, his fingers caressing her shoulder. He accepted a menu from the waitress and said, "Let's see—I've worked up quite an appetite. And we'll need another bottle of prosecco."

Naomi laughed and reached for the glass David held out to her. "Order eggs, Shutterbug. You'll need the energy."

"Oh, God, what did I do?" Revan smacked his forehead with the menu. He held up the tri-folded plastic card and kissed Naomi behind it.

"Put it down," Luca said, "and don't think we didn't see you guys when you were dancing last night. Or didn't notice the particular song request."

Luca hummed a few notes of "Lady in Red," and David joined him by singing along about someone having been blind. A few other guests looked up and applauded, to which David only waved a hand in the air and called, "Thank you!"

"Do you really want to talk about the dancing?" Rev grinned.

"Let's order," Luca stuck his nose in his menu.

Naomi wiggled her hand to get Stella's attention and stared a question at her. When Stella looked back, Naomi ping-ponged her eyes back and forth between Luca and Jo.

"Nam, got something in your eye?" Jo asked.

"No, it must be a twitch. So, did you guys enjoy the party last night?"

"It was lots of fun. David, any regrets about hanging up your cape after seeing the familiar decorations?" Luca turned the attention to David, who laughed and pulled Stella into his arms.

"No, not one. I've got my girl, I've got a great new career, and working with those kids is surprisingly rewarding. I wonder why I didn't think of doing something like it earlier."

"Look at it this way…your first career paved the way for your second one. But I'm glad your days as a nomad are over, and I can have you to myself," Stella leaned against David's arm.

"True, my love. And guys," David looked at everybody, "let me say this one more time. Thank you for your help. With everything," he smiled at Stella. "I don't think we'd be here without you."

Stella nodded and gave Naomi a long look.

The conversation turned back to the party when Stella asked, "Did anybody else notice Aaron flirting with Mary?"

Jo said, "I did. I'd be so happy for Mom if she falls in love again. She's only fifty-four, and that's too young to be alone for the rest of her life."

"You wouldn't mind if she dated again?" Naomi asked.

"No, I know she loved Dad, and was devastated when we lost him, but he would want her to be happy."

David said, "Aaron is a good guy. He went through a nasty divorce a few years ago. As far as I know, he hasn't been involved with anybody since then."

Jo nodded, "Good to hear. I'll see what I can find out when I see her before Luca and I head back. Isn't he working out of the City?

"He travels a lot, but he has an apartment in Jersey City," David said.

Revan raised his glass and said, "Let's drink to friends and to happiness."

He looked at Naomi, "And to dreams coming true."

CHAPTER 38

⤛∘୧ᔕᔋᖙ୨∘⤜

NAOMI—SEPTEMBER 2019

N aomi closed her suitcase and set it on its wheels. With the twofer party behind them, things finally started to slow down. It was still two more weeks until Stella and David's wedding, and when Revan asked her a few days ago if she wanted to go away over Labor Day weekend, she couldn't think of any reason why they shouldn't go. Just the two of them.

"Couple time. Away from friends and family," as Revan had called it.

She had arranged to have Friday and Saturday off and was now waiting for Revan to come back from picking up his car at the parking garage. Straightening the bedspread, she heard him come into the house and up her stairs. She still thought of this side of the house as "her rooms" and "her stairs," even though she hadn't spent one night in her own bed in the past two weeks.

"Ready to leave, Nugget?" Revan asked and kissed her briefly. "Where's the rest of your luggage?"

"That's it."

"Only one suitcase for three days and nights? How come?" He raised an eyebrow and grinned.

"Maybe I'll stay in our room the whole weekend and won't need any clothes. Only what I'm wearing for the drive," she teased and walked past him, but he stopped her and said, "Be careful what you wish for, sweetheart."

She kissed him and laughed. "As I see it, it would be a win-win situation. Let's hit the road! I can't wait to see where we're going. I don't know why you won't tell me."

"Because then it's not a surprise anymore," he replied with a mischievous grin.

Several hours later, Rev pulled into the parking lot of the hotel in Virginia Beach where they stayed only a few months ago.

"Wow, you managed to get a room here on a holiday weekend. I love this place," she said before she unbuckled her seatbelt.

"Me too, and I want to replace some not-so-great memories with new ones."

"You never cease to amaze me, Shutterbug." Naomi leaned over and kissed his cheek. "More later..."

After checking in, they stopped in front of their room. Naomi said, "Really? You booked my room from last time? We had a big argument after you came barging in here."

"Which is one of the memories to replace. When I saw you on the bed, I was so jealous. You had just told me about your Tinder account, and next thing I knew you were talking to a guy," he tunneled his fingers through his hair.

"And instead of asking me about it, you ran away and out into the garden, where you told me to leave you alone." She stepped closer to him, "Want to know a secret? I've never signed up with Tinder. I only wanted to see your reaction."

"And was it as expected?" He wrapped his arms around her.

"Yes and no. It was one of those confusing moments. Especially when you ran away," she admitted.

"It won't happen again. Do you know why I told you to leave me alone?"

"Well, it was obvious how angry you were."

"Yes, but more at myself than you. Because I didn't know how to fight my feelings any longer. All I wanted to do was crush my lips to yours and make love to you," he played with the zipper on the back of her dress.

"In front of all those people? If I remember correctly, there was a wedding ceremony going on in the gazebo."

"Not in the garden, sweetheart, I needed more privacy for what I had in mind," he pulled down the zipper and pushed the spaghetti straps off her shoulders. "Want to start making new memories?"

"Yes, but I want to start at the pool," she told him and pushed the straps back up on her shoulders again. "I'll let you put sunscreen lotion on my back again." She winked at him.

"You're really sure about this?" Revan stood only a few inches away from her and she could literally feel the sexual tension sizzling between them.

"Yes, so stop tempting me," she turned around and pulled a bathing suit out of her luggage. Then she dropped the dress and her underwear, right in front of him, and slipped into a blue-and-white bikini.

Revan's hands landed on her hips. "Are you wearing this to the pool? Where's the rest?"

She looked in the mirror. "I don't know what your problem is. It's a halter top and a bikini bottom."

"You'll wear one of those cover-up thingies over it, right?" His eyes turned almost black, and Naomi basked in his reaction.

"I'll wear a sarong to the pool, where I'll drop it and sit demurely in a lounge chair. Happy?"

"I'll be watching you, sweetheart. If even one man looks in your direction, we're going back to our room."

"Let them look. You're the one who gets to take me home. And where's your bathing suit? Maybe I'll have to chase off dozens of screaming girls."

"I'm not interested in screaming girls," he pulled swim shorts out of his duffel bag and went to the bathroom. "Give me a second to change."

"Seriously? I changed in front of you."

"And I'm still trying to bring down my boy, so I'd rather change away from you." He closed the door behind him.

"You're no fun," Naomi laughed. Their days were filled with plenty of erotic banter and hints, and every night they showed how much they missed each other during the day.

Everything was still so new, but because they'd been friends for so many years, they didn't have the awkward period where each partner feels the need to tell the other about every little detail of their life before.

She checked her beach bag while she waited. Sunscreen lotion, magazine, water bottle, cell phone.

At the hotel pool, they put their towels on two lounges, pushed them close together so they could hold hands, and adjusted the umbrella before sitting down. When Revan applied sunscreen to her back, she asked, "Remember when you applied it last time?"

"I'll never forget it, Nugget. Remind me later to show you how I'd have liked the moment to end." His fingertips grazed the sides of her breasts.

"Then and now, I was thinking along the same lines."

The next hour went by in companionable silence. He read a book and Naomi flipped through the pages of a fashion magazine.

"Can you believe Stella and David will be a married couple soon?" she asked after a while as she let the magazine slide into her beach bag.

"Hmm?" Revan looked up from his book. "Yeah, I know. By the way, can you get me a pocket square when you pick up your dress? Since you're making the color a royal secret, I can't go and buy one to match it. And, as you've told me repeatedly, their wedding won't happen if the colors clash."

"Already got it, Shutterbug," she patted his arm and left her hand there. "You know, when Stella and I were in France, we talked about dream weddings, probably because we were on a honeymoon-inspired tour. Stella always wanted the fairy tale, starting with the proposal on one knee and a blinding diamond."

"And you?"

She looked at the solitaire on her right hand, a gift from Gram Annie for her graduation. "I told her I'd prefer to pick my own ring and want only a short ceremony without much to-do."

"No walking down the aisle in a big white puffy dress in front of hundreds of people? A shit-eating grin on your face because you caught the big fish?" He put his book away and studied her.

"No. Only me and my man, riding off into the sunset. Like in the movies. Yee-haw!"

"Eloping sounds much better than church bells," Revan mock shivered. He got up and held out his hand. "Come on, Nugget. Let's go for a swim and cool off before this cowboy gets the wrong idea. Later we'll go for drinks. I still want to walk through the garden with you, though."

"We're here until Monday, so we have tons of time."

"No, it has to be today. I want to put all the old stuff behind us, and tomorrow and Sunday will be for new memories," he wiggled his eyebrows at her and showed her his best lopsided smile.

"Have I ever told you how sexy your smile is, Shutterbug?"

"Nope, but when you shimmy, it tells me how it's affecting you, baby."

She swatted at him and they went to the poolside outdoor shower to rinse off before going in the pool. In the water, he held her tight and rested his chin on the top of her head. "Do you know what I want to do right now, Nugget?"

"I have a feeling...but there are people around, so you better behave," she wiggled her butt against his semi-hardness. "Let's swim a few laps. Maybe it'll take care of your current...umm, situation. Or would you like a noodle to float facedown again?"

Revan trailed a finger very low over her belly. Naomi sucked in her breath. "Rev, there are cameras!"

"Guess I'm not the only one having a *situation*," he glanced at her taut nipples, then kissed the side of her neck and reached over her shoulder for two pool noodles on the side of the pool. "To be continued..."

Much later, after sharing a mutually pleasurable shower, they went to the bar and ordered their drinks. Whiskey for him, and a glass of red wine for her.

"Want to sit down, Nugget, or take the drinks to the garden?"

"To the garden, it's so peaceful there. And last time I didn't go down to the pond way in the back."

While they strolled through the labyrinth of low-growing boxwood, he reached for her free hand and rubbed his thumb over it. "When you followed me outside that night, I couldn't think straight. I wasn't just jealous of Marcus, I was spitting mad. Mostly at myself. Because I couldn't get my feelings under control."

"I remember you told me not to touch you. And then, in Charleston, you told me about working through some stuff, trying to figure something out," she said. "Was it us?"

"Yup, and let me tell you, those days were some of the best days of my life, and at the same time some of the worst. I don't think you and I owe each other apologies, because we didn't do anything wrong, unless you consider tiptoeing around each other doing something wrong. I want to tell now how much I regret acting like a child and throwing such a tantrum."

Naomi set her glass on a stone bench and took his face in her hands. "Stop it, Shutterbug. The past is done, and we need to let it go. I want to look forward. Imagine, maybe in many years, when our kids..." she stopped mid-sentence.

His eyes bored into hers, and without looking, he put his tumbler next to her glass and pulled her close. "When our kids what?"

"...ask how or when we fell in love," she swallowed hard, then said, "we can say it was when we had a big argument about nothing."

"It wasn't about nothing, Nugget. It was about everything. It was about you and me," Revan replied. "That argument finally opened my eyes. And it was about trusting our feelings, believing in ourselves," he kissed her nose and her lips. "But there is another reason I wanted us to go away this weekend."

He picked up their beverages and handed her the wine. Then he reached for her hand again and started walking.

"Gram Annie is getting weaker, and we don't know how much more time we have with her."

Naomi nodded and said, "I had similar thoughts. But I won't be able to take many days off in the foreseeable future," she took a sip of her wine. "This one is good. Try it."

Revan put her glass to his nose and inhaled the bouquet of the wine, then took a small sip. "Yeah, you're right. It's a nice dry wine. We'll have to get the name and I'll order a few cases."

"Just like you bought the wine in Charleston. You are the sweetest. And you're spoiling me."

"It's only wine. But you deserve it, sweetheart. And more."

"Gram will never see my wedding or Jo's, so being there on Stella's big day is important to her. It's going to be the placeholder for the ones she'll miss. She'll get to see her girls, as she likes to call us, walking down the aisle together."

Her shoulders shook when she started to laugh. "Like little ducklings, one behind the other, trying not to fall over our own feet. Thank goodness none of us are wearing yellow."

"Just hold off on the falling part till you're close enough for me to catch you, Nugget. When your parents picked Grace as your middle name, they must have had someone else in mind," he teased.

They followed the paths for a while until he said quietly, "So, do you want to have children one day?"

Naomi's heart stopped for a moment. "Yes, I'd like to have a few. I didn't really mind growing up alone because Jo and I were always close. But she's my cousin, and even though our birthdays are only a few days apart, it's not the same as having a sibling. And you?"

"I never gave it much thought, to be honest, but it was one of the first things I should've recognized last year. At our Christmas Eve party, it was bugging me when first Jo, then lover boy, talked about babies."

"Who?"

"Frank, who couldn't keep his hands off you. You've got no idea how much it was bothering me."

"What? I don't remember that," she thought for a second. "Oh, now I do. Shutterbug, did you believe any of their nonsense?"

"It got me thinking. But yes, down the road, I can see a little mini me—or mini you—running around the house."

"Having a tea party with the princess and her dolls?" she teased him, trying to control her raging emotions. *Where's this going?*

Revan looked at her and said, "I'd love it. Or taking our future slugger to T-ball practice."

"Rev, do you really mean it?" she could hardly say the words. Had he just admitted to wanting babies with her? If she had a free hand, she would've pinched herself.

"Every single word, my love." He emphasized every word with a nod of his head. And sealed it with a kiss after calling her "my love."

"Let's go back and get something to eat. Want to stay at the hotel or go someplace else?" Naomi asked.

"I vote for staying here tonight, and on the other days we can eat while we're out. Maybe we can visit Colonial Williamsburg. It's only an hour away," Revan suggested.

"Sounds good to me. I'll go wherever you take me," she agreed and snuggled against his arm.

Three days later, when they were almost back home, Revan asked, "So, what's on the agenda for the next two weeks? Anything you need me for?"

"Let's see. This week is quiet. I told Dinah I'd take her out to lunch, then we'll get a pedi before going to the bridal store to pick up our dresses. And the rehearsal dinner is on Friday of the following week. I'll swing by there a few days earlier to find out if the event planner needs anything from me. But Sandy has been fantastic, and I think everything's under control. We're simply expected to show up."

"So, you won't need me?" he asked again.

"Oh, make no mistake, I need you," she said with a smile. "But not for wedding-related stuff. Why? Do you have to leave town?"

"No, only curious. Has Dinah said anything about the octopus?" Revan kept his eyes on the road. Traffic was heavy because of Labor Day, but Naomi sensed this was much more than a casual question.

"His name's Trevor, as you very well know. And I haven't heard anything new, but he seemed nice when I talked to him at the party. He wants to study Journalism and applied to the University of Maryland."

"How wonderful. Why can't he go to Syracuse or SoCal?"

"Why didn't you go there? You and Luca stayed on the East Coast and went to New York University."

"Nugget, NYU chooses their students, not the other way around. They almost begged us to go there."

"Yeah, well, Shutterbug, get off your high horse. I think it's wonderful for Trevor, and you better be nice to him. He told me he'd like to talk to you about photography and that he might be interested in filmmaking."

"Which isn't my field of expertise. SoCal sounds better and better for him."

"Don't act like a grumpy old man. And please behave around Trevor. Even if only for Dinah's sake." She put her hand on Revan's thigh.

"Nugget, hands away. Don't distract this grumpy old man from driving." He picked up her hand and kissed the palm, then put it back on her own leg.

Naomi laughed. It had been a wonderful weekend and she felt relaxed—and happy.

She only hoped the happiness would last.

CHAPTER 39

Naomi—September 2019

Finally! Stella's wedding weekend had arrived.

Naomi walked from her old bedroom into her bathroom and added a dab of her new favorite scent to her wrists and on her neck, then brushed her hair behind her ears. After finding a sample of the perfume in a magazine, she liked it immediately and bought a small bottle. When she read the product description and sales pitch, she identified even more with it. *A fragrance for joyful and carefree women, inspired by an Italian island in the Mediterranean Sea*, and—her favorite—*the essence of pleasure!* Which she could attest to, because Revan seemed to like it immensely and often tucked his nose in and inhaled deeply in the spots where she applied it.

Music drifted through the house and she hummed along to "Take my Breath Away."

Revan had asked her why she didn't get ready in his room, but she wanted to see his reaction to her dress. And she highly doubted she'd be ready in time if he was "helping." He tended to sneak up on her and distract her with kisses and a bunch of irresistibly sexy moves. Which she usually didn't mind...

She gave herself a last full once-over in the mirror.

For the rehearsal dinner today, she opted for a full-length wrap-style dress with elbow-length kimono sleeves. It had a fitted waist with ties, a thigh-high side slit and low V-neck, and the sapphire-blue color complimented her eyes. She planned to pair it with blue two-inch strap-sandals and minimal jewelry. Only her grandmother's diamond ring, her gold nugget pendant, and simple diamond stud earrings.

"Nugget, how much longer are you going to be up there?" Revan's voice called through the house. "We have to leave now unless you want to be the last one to get there. And you know what everybody will assume then."

"As if you care what anybody else thinks," she called back and turned off the light in her bathroom. "Ready or not, here I come."

Carefully making her way down the stairs, she took her time and held on to the handrail. She was barefoot, not wearing her heels yet, but knew her penchant for unfortunate missteps. Halfway down she stopped when she saw Revan waiting for her at the bottom of the stairs.

She licked her lips and said, "Wow."

He wore a pair of dark blue jeans, a white button-down dress shirt with a blue tie, and a dark gray blazer. David had *begged* the men to dress casually, and she suspected it had a lot to do with him not wanting to dress up either. Stella hadn't given out similar instructions, but Naomi didn't mind. Didn't most women enjoy dressing up for an occasion? She was no exception.

"Nugget, I'll have to hire bodyguards for you. You look blazing hot," she saw him swallow before finding his voice again. "Forget the bodyguards. I don't trust anybody with you. You look... I won't be able to take my eyes off you."

"We'll have a staring contest then. Because you don't look too shabby, either. Not at all."

He held out his hand, and she took it as soon as she reached the bottom of the stairs. Revan raised the inside of her wrist to his nose and inhaled the perfume. Then he kissed the same spot and said, "And already I can't wait to come back home," which made her laugh and playfully smack his arm. But hearing him say those words made all her pleasure points tingle in anticipation of him paying a thorough visit later.

"Do you think there's dancing tonight?" she asked.

"If there is, you're only dancing with me."

Naomi rolled her eyes and patted his cheek, "We'll see."

Throughout the evening, Naomi could feel Revan watching her. He eventually relented and didn't object to her dancing with David, Luca, and a few other men. She didn't need his permission, but it was sweet knowing he could be so possessive. And it might also have had to do with her threat to sleep in her old bedroom if he didn't stop his territorial behavior.

Hours later she sat in a corner of the room and slipped out of her shoes while she searched for Revan. She spotted him with her grandmother, their heads together, him holding Gram's hands and nodding about something she was telling him.

Naomi debated whether she should go and join them, but then she saw Rev and Gram looking up and directly at her. She waved, then kissed the tips of her fingers on one hand and sent those kisses through the air. Both started laughing and returned the air-kisses. Gram patted Revan's face before he got up and walked over to her.

"What did you two do over there? Wait..." she held up a hand, "...the question should be, do I even want to know what you plotted, especially because my meddling grand-mother was involved. I still haven't forgotten her little scheme with the hotel rooms."

"Nugget, don't be so nosy." Revan pulled her out of the comfortable leather chair, sat down and pulled her into his lap. She nestled her head on his shoulder.

"Gram Annie made me promise to always take good care of you," his mouth was close to her ear.

"*What* did she do? Did she lose her mind?" Naomi tried to sit up, but he held her firmly in his arms.

"I told her I want to marry you," his lips touched her ear as he said the words, and his arms held her even tighter than before.

"Why?" she whispered.

"Because it's the truth."

"You didn't think you should've asked me first?" She hadn't moved, still had her head on his shoulder.

"No, because a) I didn't ask her for your hand, and b) neither is this a marriage proposal. But I wanted her to know what my intentions are." He started nibbling on her earlobe. "But I have another confession to make, Nugget."

"Shouldn't you tell Gram first?" she couldn't help teasing him. "Okay, what is it?"

"I would marry you tomorrow if I could."

She raised her head and looked at him. "I don't know what to say, Rev."

"You don't have to say anything, Nugget. Just relax in my arms for now. Oh, I almost forgot to tell you..." he lowered his voice, "I love you."

"I love you, too," she took his face in her hands and kissed him. "Do you think we can go home? Or would it be rude?"

"Nugget, everybody knows what we have to do tomorrow. I think we can leave without causing a scene. And I have plans for us tonight." He picked up her pendant and twisted it between his fingers.

The next morning Naomi stretched her arms over her head, then reached for Revan. Her hand hit the empty space next to her. When she checked the time on her cell phone, her eyes flew open. It was 8 am, and she was supposed to meet Stella and the other bridesmaids at nine.

Shit! She barely had time for coffee, a bite to eat, and a shower.

Good thing hair, makeup, mani-pedi, etcetera were all part of their getting-ready routine in Stella's bridal suite at the hotel.

She smelled the coffee before she saw Revan. He walked into the bedroom, wearing only his boxer briefs, and handed her a cup of coffee. "Glad you're up, Nugget. You have an hour until you meet the other ladies."

She accepted the coffee mug with a smile and used her free hand to cover her chest. "Stop staring at them." Normally, she wore panties or sleep shorts and a tank top at night, but last night—*make it this morning*—they didn't go to sleep until the early morning hours, and all she had on right now were her bikini panties.

"Then you should wear something. But I like it better this way," he kissed her briefly and cupped one of her breasts, his thumb teasing a nipple. "I can't wait to see you in a few hours. Let's get those two hitched, Nugget, and then go home as soon as we can."

"Shutterbug, sometimes you knock me over with your romantic side." She got out of bed, picked up her dress from last night and put it on a hanger in Revan's built-in closet. She'd been leaving more and more of her clothes in his bedroom.

Naomi arrived at Stella's suite at the same time as Dinah. The teenager was already giddy and babbling. "This is so exciting, Naomi. And before we go in there, I want to say thank you for convincing Rev to talk to Trevor yesterday. It meant a lot to him, because he's a big fan of Revan's work."

"I'm happy Trevor is what you had hoped for. He seems very nice. But never forget that Rev means well. Give him time. He'll come around. Now let's go in and get ready."

Stella, Jo, and Sabrina, as well as Stella's and David's mothers, were already there, together with the official wedding photographer. The mothers brought up old memories of Stella and David as children while they nibbled on finger sandwiches and had champagne and orange juice. Naomi was happy to see Stella in a dreamlike state.

They laughed when the event planner let it slip about how the groom was getting visibly nervous. "He keeps checking the time and using his handkerchief to blot his forehead, and if he paces much longer, he'll end up with holes in the bottom of his shoes."

"You'd think he'd be used to being in front of an audience," Lucy, David's mom, said, "but I guess this is different." She gave Stella a hug. "Welcome to our family, honey."

Sabrina said, "Imagine when you're giving birth to your first child! Can you imagine him at the hospital? If he can't be patient today, he's going to need a sedative when you're in labor for twenty hours or so. They'll have to knock him out before they take care of you."

Stella fluttered her hand and said, "If I think about that now, my makeup will be ruined." She raised her champagne flute and looked at the women in the room, then said,

"Thank you for sharing this moment with me. You're the best."

The women raised their glasses and clinked them before taking a sip. Stella winked at Dinah, who also had a small amount of champagne in her glass, heavily diluted with orange juice.

Naomi said, "Let's go, soon-to-be Mrs. Danvers. Before the *Troub* sends out the *troops*."

"You think you're so funny, Nam," Jo laughed. "Wait until it's your big day."

"Maybe you'll get married before I do," Naomi countered. "I'll be there when you're dragging Luca down the aisle…"

Jo let the bait whiz by while simply hugging her. "Yeah, yeah, cousin dear."

Nicole, Stella's mom, tried to hide a laugh behind a cough. "I'm not giving up hope for my son yet. His father wasn't in a hurry either, until Luca announced his pending arrival. Then Kevin couldn't get the marriage license fast enough. All it takes is some motivation," she hugged Jo.

"Are you telling me to get knocked up by him? You're forgetting we're friends. We're not dating," Jo said, not quite able to hide the undertone of sadness in her voice.

"I haven't forgotten, but don't give up hope," Nicole said.

Sandy knocked on the door and called, "Showtime!"

Naomi arranged the lace train of Stella's dress, and they opened the door to reveal her father awaiting her. Kevin held out his arm and kissed his daughter's cheek.

"My baby is getting married. You look wonderful, honey."

"Thank you, Daddy."

Kevin gave his wife a kiss and said, "Nicole, you look just as beautiful as you did thirty-six years ago, darling."

CHAPTER 40

Revan—September 2019

A pianist played soft classical music while Revan waited with David, Luca, and two of David's cousins in front of the arbor in the hotel's sheltered backyard. Together they watched while the guests arrived and took their seats.

The mid-September afternoon was sunny and warm, but mercifully without being muggy. A mild breeze rustled the leaves which had yet to turn their colors.

Revan secretly had to admit that it was the perfect setting for Stella and David's wedding ceremony. The historic hotel and inn in the middle of Philadelphia had a beautiful four-season room resembling an enormous greenhouse with removable glass doors. Old trees provided shade and privacy, and low-growing rose bushes, artfully arranged pots and perennials filled the air with fragrance. Above them birds sang out love songs to their mates.

Revan loved this city. As much as he had enjoyed the thrill of traveling to bleak and war-torn countries, he was grateful for the beauty of his birthplace. The combination of historical buildings and modern architecture and the lushness of parks and gardens never ceased to amaze him. It was the perfect place for him to settle down with the woman he wanted by his side for the rest of his life. And the only woman he could imagine as the mother of his future children.

A movement next to him brought Revan out of his daydream.

"David, man, stop walking in circles. You're making me dizzy," he said.

"I can't stand this waiting. This is ten times worse than any jitters before the premiere of a new show," David said and checked his watch for the umpteenth time. "Still five minutes to go. I wish they'd just come downstairs so we can get started."

"What's the rush? You'll have my sister around for the rest of your life," Luca laughed.

"I need to see her. What if she's changed her mind?"

"I highly doubt it. You're stuck with her, buddy," Luca said. "And you're sure about what you're going to do?"

"Yes, it's the only way I can avoid bawling like a baby. I need to focus on something else," David said and cleared his throat.

Luca held up his hand and announced, "Then brace yourself. I see Dinah crossing the foyer."

The music stopped playing, then the pianist pointed his finger toward David, nodded at him, and hit the keys again.

David stepped away from Revan and Luca, stood in front of the arbor, adjusted his dark gray tie, and began to sing in his world-famous tenor voice about a beautiful, sweet girl, about a love to dive into, about sharing dreams and dancing in the dark.

Revan's hands were sweating. He focused on his friend, the man whose wedding rings he guarded in the pocket of his tuxedo jacket. The man who had found the love of his life, and who poured his heart and feelings into a song about his perfect woman.

He watched while David gazed down the aisle while he sang, probably not even seeing Dinah walking toward them, followed by Jo and Sabrina.

He didn't think David took in the burgundy-red bridesmaid dresses and the smiles on the women's faces.

He saw the moment when David's eyes latched on to the last person stepping through the doors into the garden, smiling on her father's arm, wearing a sleek ivory wedding dress that accentuated her slim figure and made her look like a fragile porcelain doll.

Dinah, Sabrina, and Jo arrived at the arbor and took their assigned positions on their side of the bridal arch, which was decorated in green ivy and roses in different shades of red.

But the woman who walked in front of the bride made Revan's heart race. He had a hard time breathing, broke out in a full-fledged sweat, and needed to loosen his tie and dress shirt. But managed to resist.

Naomi wore a floor-length champagne-colored, one-shoulder dress with a burgundy satin waist sash trailing down her left side. Like the other women, she carried a small bouquet of yellow, salmon, and blood-red roses. She smiled at a few guests on both sides of the aisle.

To Revan, she looked like a goddess, a mystical object—a Fata Morgana, a mirage. Their eyes met, and he lifted his foot to take a step forward.

To her.

A tug on the back of his tuxedo jacket pulled him back. Revan rolled his shoulders to free himself from the grip. He took another step, only to be held firmly in place.

Naomi arrived at the front of the aisle, winked at him, and smiled at David. She took her spot in front of the arch, where she prepared to receive Stella's bouquet.

David finished his love song just as his bride reached him. Her father hugged him, then put Stella's hand in David's after kissing his daughter's cheek.

Invisible ties pulled Revan toward Naomi. Another strong tug forced him to take a step backward. Over his shoulder, he saw Luca grinning, "Not your turn."

Revan didn't hear one word of the ceremony. His eyes were glued to Naomi, and he only woke up from his trance-like state when her eyebrows went up and David said to him out of the corner of his mouth, "The rings, please, whenever you're ready."

He pulled them out of his pocket, handed them over, and went back to gazing at Naomi, who never stopped watching him.

The officiant said, "Do you, David..." and Revan shut out of the world around them.

He mouthed to the only person who existed in his universe, "Marry me."

And when she mouthed back, with tears in her eyes, "Yes," he knew there was no luckier man in the world.

The seconds until Naomi was on his arm felt like eternity. Following the bride and groom, they passed Gram Annie, sitting frail and tiny in a wheelchair, giving them a shaky thumbs-up. Revan grinned. She hadn't missed his proposal to her granddaughter—and she approved.

The reception was a lively and entertaining mix of speeches, jokes, toasts, and excellent food. But the time seemed to drag like molasses for Revan. He didn't get a chance to talk to Naomi in private, he couldn't kiss her like he wanted to, and the one time when he pulled her out of the room for a passionate lip-lock didn't last more than a few moments.

Stella and David left the reception an hour after the dancing started, sent off by much laughter, well-wishes, and not-so-subtle hints about how they should spend their wedding night and honeymoon.

Revan pulled Naomi onto the dance floor and into his arms. He whispered close to her ear, "I wasn't prepared today, Nugget. Mine had to be the lousiest proposal in history. I'm afraid I butchered it badly, I didn't even have a ring."

"I thought it was sweet. But did you mean it?"

He lifted her chin and said in a deep, no-nonsense voice, "Baby, do I look as if I'm joking?"

"What makes you think it wasn't perfect?" she asked him and clung to him while they danced slowly in one place.

"You didn't hear me. I don't have a ring," he said through his teeth and looked deep into her eyes. "I briefly considered borrowing Stella's wedding band, but I didn't think David would appreciate it."

Naomi couldn't help but laugh out loud. A few people around them turned and looked at them. Revan distracted them by kissing her soundly, then put his mouth near her ear again. "We'll fix this very soon, Nugget."

"Relax, Shutterbug. We'll talk about it later. Let this weekend be all about Stella and David. I'm not going to disappear into thin air at the stroke of midnight, I promise."

"I know, baby, because I know exactly where you'll be and what I'll be stroking at midnight," he pressed her as close to his body as possible to emphasize his words.

Naomi pressed the tip of her finger to Revan's lips. "You're bad, Mr. Forrester. To let you cool off, I'll go dance with Luca now," she looked around but didn't see him. "Where is he?"

"Good luck. He just walked into the garden with Jo."

"Let's follow them. What do you think they're doing out there?"

"I don't care what they do, Nugget," he stroked the side of her face with the backs of his fingers.

"Something's going on between them. Why does nobody believe me?" Naomi pouted.

"Because we'll find out in due time, sweetheart. And I only care about us right now." He lowered his mouth to hers and said, "You know what I really want to know?"

"No, what?"

"What color you're wearing," he whispered.

"Who knows if I'm wearing..." she left her sentence unfinished, kissed him back and lifted an eyebrow.

"Are you saying..." he grabbed her hand and strode toward their table. "We're leaving right now."

"We can't leave before Stella and David."

"Nugget, they've left already. You waved them goodbye. But I do appreciate you only having eyes for me."

"Don't get too cocky, there. It slipped my mind for a moment, okay?"

"Bad phrasing, baby. Let's go."

They arrived at home thirty minutes later. Thirty minutes during which Revan had an exceedingly difficult time behaving like a gentleman and not giving their taxi driver a free peep show. The moment they walked through their front door, he dropped his jacket on a chair and put his hands around Naomi's waist to pull her toward him. "This waiting is killing me, baby!"

He let his hands slide to her butt and gave it a squeeze, then he slowly grabbed the satiny fabric of her dress and bunched it in his hands, pushing it up over her thighs, to her hips.

"Stop right there, Shutterbug. You're wearing much more than I am, so it's only fair to get rid of this," she started to pull off his tie, then unbuttoned his shirt, "...and this," she reached for his belt.

"Upstairs. Now," he started walking toward the stairs, never letting go of her hand. In his bedroom, he tossed his shirt on the floor and stepped out of his socks and pants. Only wearing his boxer briefs, he looked at her and said, "I think now we're even."

Revan reached around Naomi, found the zipper, and lowered it while at the same time he guided her to the bed. He pushed the dress over her shoulders, down her hips, and let it slide to the floor.

"No bra?" he traced the outside of her breasts.

"It's called built-in," she whispered.

"You are magnificent." He felt lightheaded. All his blood had collected in one body part. Which was hard as iron. Thinking, breathing, talking were almost impossible.

"And this has to be the tiniest pair of panties I've ever seen." He stroked the cream-colored lace thong with a fingertip, then pulled it down her thighs. "Cute, but in my way."

He pushed her back against the pillows, spread her legs wide, and settled between them. His tongue touched her, making her flinch and suck in a breath. He flicked his tongue over her again, and she moaned. He left a tiny kiss on her needy spot, before raising himself up. His erection pressed against her, seeking entrance.

"Don't wait, Rev," she lifted her hips.

Kissing her tenderly, he guided his already well-lubricated head a few times over her folds, then filled her with one deep thrust.

She moaned again and started to move against him, "Now!"

"Aren't you the impatient one, my love?" he pulled out, took one of her erect nipples in his mouth and sucked on it. Then entered her again, hard and fast.

Naomi gasped.

Her moaning turned to begging, her begging turned to demanding, but he was determined to make her wait until they reached the highest possible point together. To let them experience their free fall in unison.

He wanted to tell her, "With this, I take you…" but remained silent and made his vow to always be hers through body language.

When he finally couldn't hold himself back any longer, he reached between them. Naomi cried out his name and tightened her core muscles around him with her climax. Together, they rode out their highs, coming again and again before collapsing and falling asleep in each other's arms.

CHAPTER 41

REVAN—NOVEMBER 2019

They spent the first weekend of November in New York City. Revan had been invited to showcase some of his work at a new photography museum's upcoming exhibition. The museum wouldn't open their doors until December, but Revan met with their representatives to discuss details and asked Naomi to join him on the trip.

It was a mild day for the season, and by midafternoon Revan and Naomi strolled through the Diamond District to Bryant Park, past the New York Public Library and toward Grand Central Station. Halloween decorations, both fake and real jack-o-lanterns and colorful cornucopias in all sizes, filled store windows and window boxes, but here and there first Christmas decorations began to pop up.

He didn't bring a camera with him, but paused frequently to take photos with his iPhone, mostly of Naomi. Sitting down on a bench, she reached inside her purse and pulled out a snack-size package of crackers.

"Nugget, what's up with the crackers? We can buy a sandwich if you're hungry."

"No, my stomach's been queasy. It helps if I'm eating a few crackers." After munching a few, she got up and yawned. "Maybe we should have dinner early and call it a day. I'm tired."

Holding hands, they kept walking. "It's not even four o'clock. Since when are you tired in the afternoon?"

"For the past week or so. It'll help if I can sleep in this weekend."

"Let's grab a cup of coffee. The caffeine will keep you awake," Revan said and led her toward the nearest coffee shop.

"No, thanks. The stench in there is disgusting. It stinks as if the coffee's been sitting in the carafe all day. I can smell it even here." She pinched her nose. "But go ahead. I don't mind if you get some."

He gave her a questioning look. "Are you sure everything's okay? Since when don't you like coffee?"

Naomi shrugged, "Go, get your coffee."

He pulled her into his arms. With a strange expression he said, "When was your last period, baby?"

"What does it have to do with coffee?"

"Nugget, you're nauseous, you're tired, and you can't stand the smell of coffee. It sounds a lot like what happened when my mom got pregnant with Dinah. She thought she was going through menopause early when she didn't get her period, even though she was only forty. But you, sweetheart, are a little too young for that."

"Oh, stop it. It's just a twenty-four-hour bug."

"You said you've had those symptoms for close to a week. And, come to think of it, those two lovely girls..." he let his eyes drop to her chest, "...have filled out a little bit lately, too. I'm not complaining..." Revan moved his hands over her shoulders and back and asked again, "So, when was your last period?"

"Hm, let me think... I remember I had it shortly after Stella's wedding, which was in the middle of September."

"And since then?"

She opened the calendar app on her phone. "That was the... oh no, the last time." She counted weeks. "Holy cow; I'm ten days late. But it's not possible. I'm on the pill."

Naomi rubbed her arms. "Rev, what are we going to do?"

He pointed to a pharmacy and said, "What every couple is doing in the same situation. We're buying a test."

"Don't you want some coffee first?"

"No, sweetheart. This is more exciting." He put his arm around her shoulders and crossed the street with her. Ten minutes later Naomi still stood in front of the shelf and painstakingly read the instructions on every package until Revan picked three and said, "These should do."

Back in their hotel room, she asked, "Which one should I use?"

"Nugget, we're not going to play eeny, meeny, miny, moe. Go pee on those thingies, all three of them." He pushed a bottle of water into her hand and said, "Here, drink this first so you have enough to squirt on them."

When she came out of the bathroom, less than five minutes later, Naomi held the three plastic sticks in her hand. Her hands shook and her lips trembled.

"What do they say?" Revan stopped his pacing between the bed and the window, raking a hand over his already disheveled hair.

"They say...they..." she stammered and looked at her hand.

"Out with it," he strode over to stand in front of her.

"We're having a baby next summer," she whispered and looked up.

He grabbed her around the waist and swung her around the room. "Wow—a baby!"

Kissing her tenderly, he sat down on the bed with Naomi still in his arms and leaned down to pat her flat abdomen. "Hi, there. Can you hear me? I'm your daddy."

She pulled his head up. "You're so happy."

"What's wrong, Nugget? You're not?"

When she shivered, he immediately reached for her sweater and put it over her shoulders. "It's just so unreal. We didn't plan this."

"No, we didn't, at least not so soon. But here's the important part. I love you, and I can't wait to meet our little one," he touched her belly again. Gentle and caring.

"But I'm on the pill," Naomi said lamely.

"You've said it, and I know it, but nothing is foolproof." He kissed her lightly and said, "We certainly haven't been celibate, Nugget."

"No, I know," she put her hand over his. "Rev, this is my fault. There might've been a day or two when I forgot to take the pill."

"It's nobody's fault, and we're in this together. Please don't tell me you're having second thoughts," Revan asked. "You don't seem happy."

"I *am* happy, of course I want our baby," she said. "I'm just surprised, and don't know what to say."

"Naomi, it'll pass, believe me. You being speechless won't last long," he said with a grin.

"Getting knocked up after a few weeks of dating—go figure." She rolled her eyes. "What are we going to do now?"

"Now I'm taking you ring shopping. I know you want to wear Gram Annie's diamond ring, and I'm fine with that. I know how important it is to you. But," he picked up her left hand and drew circles around her ring finger, "I would like to pick out a set of wedding rings. Maybe you can find something with diamonds in your band, and wear my ring with Gram Annie's ring?"

Naomi nodded, "I'd love to, Rev."

Revan kissed her before saying gently, "Let's go, baby." He whispered to the tiny seed inside her belly, "You, too, little munchkin. Let's help your mommy choose something special."

Two hours later they left Tiffany's with Naomi carrying a signature blue shopping bag. After she settled on a white gold eternity band with diamonds on three sides and milgrain beading which matched the one in her grandmother's solitaire, Rev picked out his own ring, a simple white gold band with a little bit of milgrain beading as well.

When they met Luca and Jo for brunch the following day, and two sets of eyes were on her after she declined a mimosa, Revan reached for her hand and told them their news.

"Are you planning to get married?" Jo asked Naomi. "What did your parents say?"

"Well, nobody knows yet. We didn't even tell anybody about Rev proposing to me at Stella's wedding. And we thought…" she looked at Revan. They had discussed this detail last night, so he finished, "we're planning to get married by a Justice of the Peace. Only us and our witnesses, which we hoped would be you two."

"Man, you don't have to ask me twice," Luca said and held out his fist for Revan to bump.

"Me neither," Jo said, and got up to hug them.

"But we don't want to tell anybody until after the fact," Naomi said. "We want to marry here in New York at the City Clerk's office, and then we'll have a big party at our house on Thanksgiving. We'll tell everybody then."

"I like the idea," Luca said.

"Good thing it's only a few weeks until Thanksgiving. This would be hard to keep a secret for long," Jo said.

"I know," Naomi said. "I can't even tell Stella."

"We'll come back next week to apply for the license, and if it works for you, we'll say our 'I Do's' the Monday before Thanksgiving," Revan said.

"I'll make sure to take the whole week off," Luca said and shook his head at Revan. "I knew something was up when I had to pull you back at the wedding. You were ready to sprint down the aisle, man. I'm happy for you."

"I'll figure out a way to take the week off, too. A few of my clients at the gym already told me they'll be away," Jo said. "This is so exciting. Two weddings in one year, wow!"

"Funny how things work out sometimes, don't they, Rev?" Luca said. "Who would've thought you'd be the first of us to become a parent? Stella beat you in the marriage category, but you take first place in the baby department."

"Excuse me, but he's going to share that particular reward with me. Fifty/fifty. Including diaper duty," Naomi laughed.

"I know this is all brand new, but have you thought about how much traveling you'll do once the baby arrives?" Luca asked.

Revan leaned back in his chair and played with his coffee cup. "I think I told you about my colleague, Ahmad."

"Yeah, how's he doing?"

"He recovered, and the shrapnel didn't cause any lasting damage, but he will always have the scars. He's grateful to be alive and with his family. And he gave up traveling to war zones. After what happened to him, I started thinking about our suicide missions. Because, quite frankly, that's literally what they are. None of us know when our time will run out, but I'm not about to risk leaving Naomi—and now the baby—alone. There's plenty of dirty laundry to air in the Western world, more than enough to keep me busy," he squeezed Naomi's hand.

"Scotty losing Marnie so tragically was another eye-opener for me. Naomi saw me after you emailed me, and she can attest to what a terrible place I was in. That's when I realized I needed to fight for Naomi—and for us." He raised a hand and pushed a strand of hair behind her ear. "I'm successful, I've won awards. Hell, I'm going to have an exhibition here in New York by the end of the year. It's all coming together for me. And I'll do everything in my power not to threaten any of it."

Before they said goodbye later, Revan pulled Luca aside. "Listen, we have to talk about the house. Not today, but I want to buy you out. Once the baby arrives, we'll need more space, and the house is big enough for a family if I do some modifications. But I'd say its days of being a bachelor cave are over."

Luca nodded and said, "Works for me. We'll figure it out. In fact, it comes at a convenient time for me. It hasn't been made official yet, but I'll be the News Bureau Chief at our Washington office as of early next year. A chunk of my share of the mortgage was covered by Stella's, then Naomi's, rent payments, but not all. And not having a mortgage in Philly will make it easier for me to buy something in DC. But there's no rush. We'll sit down together and look at the numbers. Maybe during the Thanksgiving break. Jo and I were planning to visit for a few days anyway."

"Congrats on the promotion. You deserve it," Revan and Luca shared a secret handshake. Then he added, "Anything between you and Jo going on I should know?"

"Not you, too. I've got nothing to tell you, buddy," Luca laughed. "Why's everybody so interested in what we're doing or not doing?"

"I don't think I need to answer your question," Revan replied. "One more thing. We need to see each other more often. Playing phone tag and texting don't replace talking in person. Some of our conversations this past summer were very eye-opening, as you can imagine. Friends for life, buddy!"

"Friends for life—our old motto," Luca confirmed with a nod and another one of their secret fist-bump-hand-clasp combinations.

CHAPTER 42

NAOMI—THANKSGIVING 2019

Naomi retrieved the last platters of appetizers from the refrigerator and set them on the counter, since their guests were scheduled to arrive any minute. Revan came into the kitchen carrying a cardboard box full of prosecco and other wines.

"I'm glad for the extra fridge in the basement. No idea how we could've fit everything in the wine fridge up here. And since we're adding to the family," he paused to rub her still-flat belly, "two refrigerators won't be excessive. By the way, the food looks delicious."

"Don't touch it," Naomi said. "You can thank the deli for it. I wouldn't have been able to prepare all this."

He leaned in and kissed her briefly. "How are you feeling, baby?"

"Are you asking me, or whoever's snoozing in there?" she laughed.

He grinned. "For now, you're the only one who can answer me."

The doorbell rang, and within minutes their house was bursting with laughter and a cacophony of voices. Gram Annie sat in a wheelchair, wrapped in a warm blanket despite being close to the fireplace. She smiled at Naomi and held her hand. "I'm so glad I'm able to be here today, my dear. And to see you so happy."

"Me, too, Gram," Naomi fought with the tears burning her eyes. Imagining her grandmother not being around much longer was almost impossible, and she cherished every moment she could spend with her.

"Who wants a glass of wine?" Revan called. "We've also got whiskey or beer. Peanut, Trevor, sodas are over there for you guys."

Naomi heard Dinah say, "I really wish he'd stop calling me Peanut." To which Trevor replied, "I think it's cute, Peanut."

Naomi snickered and headed for the kitchen to get ice for those who needed some, when the doorbell rang again. She looked around. Everybody was here. Who could it be?

Her father called, "I'm closest to the door, I'll get it."

"Thanks, Dad," she called back.

"I have a delivery for Mrs. Forrester."

The young delivery man tried to look around the enormous arrangement in his hands. There had to be at least two dozen light pink and almost purple roses, some white baby's-breath, grayish-green eucalyptus twigs and dark green fern leaves.

Revan's mom said, "That's me, but there has to be a mistake."

"I'll take it, thank you," Revan said and tipped the man. He carried the arrangement past his mother to an empty side table and plucked an envelope from its plastic holder. "This is for Mrs. Naomi Forrester."

Naomi covered her mouth to stifle a loud gasp. Before she could say anything, Revan's mom said, "Excuse me, but can you read the name again? We'd all like to hear it." Alicia gave her son a pointed look, telling him, *And don't play dumb with me, I wasn't born yesterday.*

Revan ignored his mother and gave Naomi the envelope. "I hope you like the flowers."

"I do, thank you!" She took two photos from the envelope. In the first, they sat on the steps of the manor house at Magnolia Plantation, with Rev's arms around her shoulders. In the second, they stood in front of the New York City Marriage Bureau, holding hands. Naomi grinned at him, "Aww, you can be such a romantic."

Revan cleared his throat, "The things one does for love..."

Then he pulled Naomi against him, her back to his front, folded his hands over her belly and said, "Okay, folks, listen, I'm only saying this once."

Naomi put her hands over his.

"What is on your left hands?" Dinah blurted out.

"Rings, Peanut," he said with a grin.

Stella squealed and clapped her hands. She looked from Naomi to Revan, from their faces to their joined hands. Then she poked David, who tried to pull her into his arms, and pointed to the rings.

Naomi held up her left hand, with Gram's diamond ring and the brand-new dazzling eternity ring on her ring finger and beamed. "Surprise!!"

"When?"

"What?"

"Wow."

"How?"

"Congratulations!"

"Umm—details??"

Everybody gathered around Naomi and Revan, crowding closer and closer.

"Stop!" Revan called out and held up a hand. "We know this is unexpected, and we hope you'll forgive us for the secrecy, but yes, we got married on Monday in New York."

"New York?" Revan's mother put her hands on her hips.

"Without us?" Naomi's mother asked, her voice wobbling.

"Stop—and please give us room to breathe," he called again, but grinned like the Cheshire Cat. "We'll answer—most—of your questions. But this is what was right for us. And believe me, you didn't miss much."

Naomi said, "The whole ceremony lasted less than five minutes. I was still shrugging out of my jacket while the officiant droned on about something and suddenly barked at Rev, 'Do you want to marry her?' I think we interrupted his lunch break"—she giggled and turned to Rev—"did you notice the smudge of mustard at the corner of his mouth?"

He smiled and added, "We asked Jo and Luca to be our wedding witnesses, because they were with us at the beginning of November when we made this decision."

All eyes went to Luca and Jo, who were sitting with Gram Annie and watching from the sidelines with smiles on their faces.

"Beginning of November?" Naomi's mom narrowed her eyes.

"Why the rush?" Revan's mom asked and tilted her head.

Naomi asked Revan, "Want me to answer?"

He touched his lips to hers briefly, then said, "Go ahead, Nugget."

"Well, we seem to be doing things in a somewhat different order than other people. Revan asked me in September to marry him, but it was more...let's say, informal. We agreed to take our time. But these two..." Naomi reached for Rev's hand and together they touched her belly, "had other plans."

"Wait a minute! These...*two*?" Revan's mom interrupted her. Her eyes went to their clasped hands.

Naomi nodded and said, "Yes, we found out three weeks ago that I'm pregnant. And last week, at the doctor's office, we were told we're having twins."

She snuggled deeper into Revan's arms. He looked at his mother and said without moving a muscle, "Mom, you can officially add another place setting now at family dinners. And soon, two high chairs."

The women in the room started hugging each other while the men seemed content with shoulder-slapping until Revan's dad called, "Son, where are you hiding the bubbly?"

Naomi laughed, "Open the bottles before they take the house apart."

Gram Annie waved her over and said, "Finally! I'm so happy for you and wish I could be around to meet your darlings, but I'll be watching from up there." Naomi didn't know what to say, and could only hug her precious grand-mother.

When Revan brought a glass of prosecco for Gram Annie, she said, "Two things, my dear boy. There's a set of car keys and the deed for my Porsche in the bank deposit box for you. I told you it had to stay in the family. But, most important, take good care of my little girl." She weakly squeezed Revan and Naomi's hands.

"I will, Gram Annie, always. I promised you, remember?" Rev's voice was raspy. But when she winked at him and said, "Well done, sweet boy, even though it took you long enough," he couldn't help laughing, and she joined him.

Much later, long after their guests had left, when Naomi lay in Revan's arms, sated, content, and bursting with love, she wiped away a tear and made a silent promise. If one of the babies was a girl, she'd name her after her beloved grandmother.

Who peacefully slipped away as the new morning broke.

THE END

AUTHOR NOTES

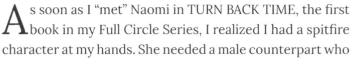

As soon as I "met" Naomi in TURN BACK TIME, the first book in my Full Circle Series, I realized I had a spitfire character at my hands. She needed a male counterpart who wouldn't let her steamroll over him, and that was Revan. They were perfect for each other.

I don't know how often those two brought me to tears while writing their story. Mostly happy tears—because they're both such ridiculously fun, and complex personalities. The underlying tension between them tugged at my heartstrings—while their cat-and-mouse game got on my nerves at times. Couldn't they just make up their minds? Clearly not, or this book wouldn't have been written.

In October 2019, I had the pleasure of spending a few days in Charleston, SC—and fell in love with the combination of charm, history, and architecture of this diverse city. From visiting Magnolia Plantation to going on a guided tour of Charleston's oldest cemeteries, eating more than one fantastic meal at East Bay Meeting House or enjoying a glass of wine overlooking the rooftops and the harbor of The Holy City, I was mesmerized.

When I needed to get Naomi and Revan out of Philadelphia for some alone-time, a trip to Charleston, including two memorable stops on the way there and back, seemed like the logic solution.

Another city that played a huge part in Naomi and Revan's story is New York City. Almost three decades ago—we still lived in Germany—my husband and I eloped and got married there. Not even our parents knew, only a dear friend who flew in to be our wedding witness. I enjoyed including this brief, but special, moment of our lives and making it part of this book—and yes, we *did* interrupt the officiants lunch break, and yes, he barked at Axel when he didn't say "I do" fast enough.

This book could not have been created and published without the endless support of my husband and son—Axel and Mika, thank you for everything!

Furthermore, thank you to Kristy Murphy, Nancy Porter, Joyce Greenfield, Kendra Wallace, Kathleen Weekes, and Susan Blair for valuable feedback during different stages in the creation of this book.

I hope you enjoyed reading Naomi and Revan's story as much as I loved writing it. If you did, please take a moment to leave a short review on Amazon, Goodreads or BookBub.

Thank you for reading this book!

Annette G. Anders

REFERENCES AND ACKNOWLEDGMENTS

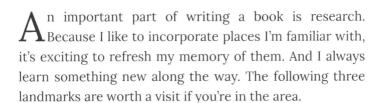

An important part of writing a book is research. Because I like to incorporate places I'm familiar with, it's exciting to refresh my memory of them. And I always learn something new along the way. The following three landmarks are worth a visit if you're in the area.

- Magnolia Plantation, Charleston, SC: Founded in 1676 by the Drayton family on the banks of the Ashley River, it opened its gardens to visitors in 1870 and is the oldest public garden in United States. www.magnoliaplantation.com

- Empty Sky Memorial and Central Railroad of New Jersey Terminal, Liberty State Park, Jersey City, NJ

Producing and publishing a book involves much more than bringing the story to paper. Thank you to the following for helping me make this book shine:

- Editor: Faith Freewoman, www.demonfordetails.com

- Book cover design: Brandi McCann, www.ebook-coverdesigns.com

- Interior design layout/formatting: Nanette Littlestone, www.wordsofpassion.com

- Author photograph: Teresa Johnson, www.teresajohnson.com

If you like to listen to the songs mentioned in this book, check out my Spotify playlist for IN DUE TIME—and maybe dance along.
pen.spotify.com/playlist/34sCxyJEO5lKwoUyg8xBRN

ABOUT THE AUTHOR

$\infty\!\frown\!\sim\!\!\circ\!\!\sim\!\!\sim$

A nnette G. Anders grew up in Germany with a love for books, music, and traveling. She always liked the idyllic world created by Astrid Lindgren and the heroines of Jane Austen, doesn't tire listening to ABBA, but also enjoys classical music. When she can't travel, Annette explores the world through the eyes of her favorite writers.

Annette has worked for many years as an Executive Assistant in international research and business consulting institutions in Germany and Switzerland. In 1998, she and her husband moved to the United States, where they raised their son. In 2018, she turned her love for books into a freelance editing career—and found the courage to write her first book in 2019.

Her favorite pastimes include reading, photography, and spending time with family and friends.

Annette looks forward to hearing from readers. Follow her on social media or join the mailing list through her website.

Website: www.AnnetteGAnders.com
Email: author@AnnetteGAnders.com
Facebook: www.facebook.com/AnnetteG.Anders

THE FULL CIRCLE SERIES

TURN BACK TIME:
Stella and David's story

IN DUE TIME:
Naomi and Revan's story

TIME IS ETERNITY (coming fall 2021):
Jo and Luca's story

Made in the USA
Monee, IL
19 March 2021